Dressed up
in Armour

Book no. 2 in the Dressed up series

BY LOLO STUBBS

LOLO STUBBS

IN SUPPORT OF

women's aid
until women & children are safe

CHARITY REGISTERED IN ENGLAND AND WALES 1054154

Bronzite Books Publishing
Colony
5 Piccadilly Place
Manchester
M1 3BR

www.bronzitebooks.co.uk/
info@bronzitebooks.co.uk

"

It means the world to be able **support Women's Aid** through my books. I hope that Dressed up as Love will help people understand that **it's not as easy as people may think to 'just leave'**. I drew on my own experiences and those of my friends and family, to create something that so many **women can relate to**.

Lolo Stubbs
Writer & Expect Respect ambassador

women's aid
until women & children are safe

CONTENTS

CHAPTER 1.

STEP BY STEP

She was relieved to turn off the hectic main-road onto a calmer one and escape the crazy London traffic. Then it suddenly dawned on her that she was here... on the road of her new home - her new life; her stomach churned slightly. The long, wide, tree-lined road was filled with cars parked on either side. She slowed down as she drove past the houses, squinting to see the numbers. She must have missed number 8 but she could see number 12, so she decided to pull over. There was nowhere to park so she had to drive a little further up to find a space.

She couldn't believe she had actually made it there. It had been a long and emotional journey and she had used all of her strength to stop herself from turning around and retreating back to Manchester.

It was just beginning to go dark, the streetlights were still warming up and she felt a little apprehensive as she opened her car door to get out. She looked around, she could hear distant sounds from the bustling city, muffled by the gentle breeze that was rustling the leaves on the trees above. As she lugged her suitcase from the boot of her car, she felt completely drained and zapped of all of her energy. She locked her car, checking it twice, and glanced down at the piece of paper that she had written the address on. She took a deep breath, willing her feet to start moving. "Just take the first step!" She said to herself. She cautiously approached the house dragging her only suitcase behind her and struggling to keep hold of her bulging night bag that was balancing precariously on her shoulder. She carefully counted down the numbers on the houses to make sure she would knock on the correct door. The last thing she needed right now was to knock on the door of the wrong house. Her stomach was in knots and the hand that she was holding the piece of paper in began to shake uncontrollably. She immediately began to feel very nauseous as the enormity of the situation hit her.

'So, you're just going to walk up to this door, then walk in and start living there - with a bunch of strangers? Yeah, great plan Melissa!'

There it was. She looked up at the imposing Victorian home, she was in awe of its beauty and its impressive bay windows. She was comforted instantly by its beautiful exterior. The front door was a dark burgundy colour that notably needed a lick of paint, yet it was inviting enough that she moved further up the path to the bottom of the stone staircase that led up to the front door. She hoisted her suitcase up the six worn steps that were leading her into a new world, a world she wasn't sure she was ready for just yet but she was heading towards it nonetheless. Her overnight bag frustratingly swung in front of her with each step and she was becoming increasingly stressed and flustered as she got nearer to the door. As she went to raise her hand to press the doorbell, she became frozen with nerves. She contemplated turning around and getting straight back in her car.

'I can't do this!' The voices of courage and fear started battling in her head, 'You CAN do this Melissa - just knock on the door', 'No way! I can't! God only knows who's in there and I'm going to live with them!,' 'Just knock on the door for goodness' sake!' She feared that if they had already noticed a glimpse of her hovering on the top doorstep, talking to herself then they may think she was completely crazy and not let her in any way!

She decided to take the plunge and before she could talk herself out of it, she rang the brass doorbell. She took one long breath and exhaled loudly, there was no turning back now. She suddenly remembered that she had just endured a long, emotional and stressful journey and so she probably needed to tidy herself up a bit. She hadn't given her appearance a second thought, now she was worried what kind of first impression she would make on her new housemates. She frantically brushed her hair with her fingers and smoothed the stray strands off her face. The last thing she wanted was to walk into her new life looking broken by her past. She wanted this to be a fresh start. 'Why didn't I sort myself out before I got out of the car?', angrily questioning herself for not thinking about how she looked sooner. But it was too late as she heard footsteps from inside heading towards the door, a light went on inside the house and a large shadowy figure appeared behind the stained-glass panels within the door. The door was flung open, and a rather fabulous character stood there greeting her with a wonderful warm smile. "Hey babe! I take it you're Melissa?"

He was tall, medium build and he was wearing a bedazzling white blazer that was decorated with diamantes, blue ripped jeans, and a pink t-shirt. His hot pink eyeshadow matched his t-shirt perfectly and she had never seen such impressive eye makeup. His eyes were almost caramel coloured with a dark brown line enhancing his pupils. He had bleach blonde hair that was styled in an oversized quiff and was as suitably flamboyant as the rest of him.

"Yes, yes I am" she smiled back, and a little of her fear drained away.

"Amazing! Come on into the party pad!"

'The party pad' she thought happily. 'This is exactly what I need right now'.

"So, I'm Giorgio, this is my house - well it's my mum and dads but they're back in Italy now, so I'm the king of the castle at the minute." He paused and turned back towards Melissa. He could see she was struggling to carry everything. "Give me that bag before you fall over babe!"

"Oh no. I'm fine, don't worry!" She was mortified, she felt like she was unravelling in front of him.

"It's no trouble, give it here!" Giorgio, reached out and lifted the holdall off her shoulder. She flinched slightly. Her hands were still trembling and she was sure that Giorgio would have been able to hear her heart thumping. Melissa was immediately enchanted by Giorgio, so she couldn't understand why she felt so jittery. He was bold, his aura oozed confidence, but not an ounce of arrogance and there was an overwhelming kindness that spilled out of him. He threw her bag over his shoulder and gestured for her suitcase too, she reluctantly handed it over and then they started walking – or rather strutting in Giorgio's case - down the

7

hallway and the few wooden stairs that lead them down to another floor.

"So, before I show you to your room, which is upstairs, you need to come and meet the gang babe! We're all in the kitchen, we need to toast your arrival with a drink!"

"Oh, I'm so sorry, I haven't brought any drink with me" her face was fraught with worry, "Is there a shop nearby? I can nip out and get some now?"

She could not believe she had arrived empty handed, all she had been thinking about was getting here in one piece and the enormity of the whole situation, the last thing that she envisioned was welcome drinks in the kitchen.

"Oh don't worry, honestly we're never short of drinks in this house." Giorgio kept walking so she continued to follow him. They passed a mirror in the hallway as they got nearer to the kitchen and she caught a glimpse of herself - her eyes were puffy from the amount of times she had burst out crying on her way down there and her hair looked worse than she had imagined, although when she recalled how many times she had pulled at it throughout the journey she wasn't surprised. 'I can't meet everyone like this!' she panicked.

"Oh Giorgio, sorry can I just use the toilet first please, before I meet everyone? I'm bursting for a wee after that long journey." That did not come out in the way she had wanted it to. She really wanted to seem at least a little sophisticated and telling him she needed a wee wasn't probably the best start.

"No you can't! "Giorgio quibbed back.

"Oh, I'm sorry, I…" Melissa was taken aback and felt really embarrassed.

Giorgio laughed, "Of course you can babe, I was only kidding, you don't have to ask! There is one just here" he pointed in the direction of two doors to his left. She went to reach for the handle. "Not that one hun, that's the utility room, this one is the bathroom." He turned on the light and opened the door to a fully tiled room with a little shower, sink and toilet. A wave of laughter echoed down the hall from the kitchen and her stomach flipped.

"I won't be a minute. Could I just have my holdall please? I might as well freshen up quickly too, if you don't mind."

"Of course!" he passed her, her bag. "That's the kitchen where the party is at when you're done!"

"Oh, should I get changed if it's a party?"

Once again Giorgio laughed, "I like you already!" he said warmly. "Don't be daft, you've just driven for four and half hours, it's only everyone that lives here so it's chill babe. Ash will be in her pyjamas as soon as she gets home, so don't worry, you're absolutely fine as you are." He smiled. "I'll leave you to it hun! I'll get you a drink ready." He spun theatrically down the hallway towards the kitchen.

She quickly shut the door before the tears that were welling up in her eyes ran down her cheeks. She leant back against the tiled wall behind the door and closed her eyes. She had no idea why she was crying, or why she felt so scared of walking into the kitchen. She began to breathe heavily, and she opened her eyes looking up towards the ceiling, trying to ward off the second wave of tears that was building up.

"Come on, you can do this! Pull yourself together!" She whispered to herself and took some deep breaths, before putting her head back down to look forward. She was thankful and relieved that there was a large mirror above the sink, and that she hadn't walked into the kitchen looking like she did. She quickly snapped herself out of her frenzied state and started rummaging round her bag. She was looking for anything that she could use to try to make herself look and feel more presentable. There was no order to the contents of the bag, everything was just bundled together in a big mess - just like her. 'Thank god the hall had been so dark, that Giorgio hadn't really been able to see me properly yet!' she thought. She looked dishevelled and lost. 'Here I am moving into a house with a stylist, a make-up artist and god only knows who else and I turn up with wild stress hair, swollen eyelids and stains down my top. I knew I shouldn't have tried to drink that coke whilst I was driving.' She was getting increasingly angry at herself and becoming more and more terrified at the thought of walking into 'the party', her bladder

11

started to hurt slightly and she rushed over to the loo. She hadn't stopped the whole way down here. She had switched from flight or fight mode like a pendulum the whole way and she worried that if she veered off course, even for a minute then her strength would have disappeared, and she would have talked herself out of it and turned around. It wasn't that she wanted to go back to Chris and that house, not for a minute, but somehow at times, as strange as it may seem, this new life seemed scarier. At least she knew what to expect in her old life.

She flushed the toilet and returned to the sink to wash her hands. After she dried her hands, she quickly threw on another top, it was full of creases, but she thought that it looked better than being full of coke stains. She gathered up her hair, then tied it up into a large loose curly bun and pulled a single curl down onto her face from each side; she hated having all of her hair off her face, she always felt too exposed.

She had managed to locate an old mascara on the inside pocket of her bag. It was a little crumbly, but she managed to apply enough to make her look better than she did when she arrived. The only other thing that she could find was a small tin of lip balm, so she applied it liberally to her lips. She paused, taking stock of her day. She had done it. She still couldn't believe it. She had finally done it. She had left Chris. She had left behind everything that she knew and now she was here - in London! She glanced back up at the mirror. The girl looking back at her may have looked distressed and exhausted, she may have felt weak and drained, but inside her there was an undeniable strength and resilience that she had dug deep to find over these last few weeks and she wanted to cling on to that for dear life. As she thought back over everything she had been through and everything that she had overcome, she smiled proudly at herself 'I can do this'. She had already faced her biggest fear, and escaped Chris's clutches; he had tried to squeeze the life out of her and strip her of strength but he had not succeeded. She continued to smile, if she could do that she could do anything, 'It's time for a new start.' She felt hopeful and terrified all at the same time. She decided it was time to stop hiding in the bathroom, dive out of the bundle of emotions she was caught up in and into her future.

She walked into the kitchen shyly and instantly felt very drab compared to everyone else there - who all seemed stylish and chic. It was a large, long kitchen with wooden patio doors at the end of it that looked straight onto the back garden. Everyone was sitting around the pine wooden table, in the middle of the room and each one of them turned around to say hello and welcome her. Giorgio whizzed through the introductions and she couldn't remember a single name, she was too busy trying to analyse what they were thinking about her. She watched quietly as the seemingly big personalities that lived at the house each took centre stage; she felt very overwhelmed and out of place. She took a deep breath discreetly and echoed a fake laugh in response to their combined laughter - when in fact she had no real clue why they were all laughing or even what they were talking about. Aside from Giorgio, there were two men and a young woman. One of the men was wearing a suit, like he had just finished work and he had dark slicked back hair. He had his arm around the young woman who was wearing a red shift dress and she had a poker straight platinum blonde bob. The other man was the most casual of the bunch with an effortless funky style. She took a large gulp of the drink that Giorgio had kindly plonked in front of her…as she swallowed it she realised it was Vodka and Coke, she shuddered and grimaced as it went down - she hated Vodka and Coke. She hadn't drunk it since it made her really sick as a teenager, but she was too polite to say that, so she would have to try and drink it. She couldn't turn up with no drink and then waste one they had kindly given to her. She had been sitting there for around fifteen minutes, desperately trying to take everything in, but she almost felt like she was dreaming, it just didn't feel real. She was still trying to analyse the different characters in front of her and trying to figure out who she felt like she would be able to relate to, when her eyes were drawn to the kitchen door by the sound of heels approaching. She was keen to see who would be joining the kitchen party and this overwhelming new life that she had thrown herself into. In walked a young woman, she seemed slightly older than Melissa. She was talking on the phone and her

15

long layered, brown-copper hair coverered her face slightly as she looked down as she came through the kitchen door. She didn't acknowledge anyone and headed straight over to the fridge. She was wearing black combat trousers with court shoes, a black top, and a leather jacket. Melissa watched as she opened the fridge door, she ended the phone call without saying a word. She slammed the fridge door and let out a frustrated sigh, before she swiftly turned round with a bottle of white wine in her hand, taking a swig straight from the bottle. Giorgio shouted over the music that was blaring loudly from the stereo. "Ash, Melissa's here and she's a beauty just like you!" Ashlyn swept the hair off her face and looked around the dining table, scanning for a new face.

"Oh hey, how are ya?" she asked with a strong Irish accent. As her eyes met with her's, Melissa was blown over by her beauty and her unusual bottle green eyes.

'Giorgio was right, this girl was beautiful - way more beautiful than me!' she thought. In fact, she was almost mystical looking, not to mention one of the most stylish people she had ever seen in real life.

She pulled out one of the rustic wooden chairs next to her and sat down.

"So how are you doing? How was your journey down here?"

"Oh, it was ok. I'm a bit shattered now, I wasn't prepared for the crazy traffic and the other drivers once I hit London. I was screaming out loud at a few points!"

A few of the group chuckled. "London drivers are nuts, so is the traffic, that's why none of us bother having a car now. The trains and the underground are great, you can get anywhere in the city really and the bonus is you can drink whenever you want then!"

Melissa laughed, "Well, I'm definitely ready for a drink after that journey!"

"Well, you could have fooled me, you've been nursing that for 15 minutes, get it down your neck babe and I'll get you another one - you don't have to be shy here hun!" Giorgio reassured her.

"Thank you, I know." She proceeded to take a sip trying not to wince. She knew he had just told her not to be shy, but she didn't want to seem ungrateful. She was still embarrassed that she hadn't brought a bottle, the last thing she wanted was for everyone to think that she was a sponger.

"You don't like that do you?" Ashlynn questioned.

"Yes...it's ok, thank you."

"Don't drink it if you don't like it. Giorgio thinks everyone should love Vodka and Coke, but give me wine any day of the week!"

"Hey! I was just making her feel at home!" Giorgio protested.

"You did, thanks Giorgio - this is fine, honestly!" She didn't know why wasn't taking the opportunity to get out of drinking the vodka and coke, "I would normally drink wine myself, but I forgot to stop at the shops before I got here, so I've not got anything with me."

"Give over, we've got plenty of wine here, you can get some tomorrow. Is white, ok?" Ashlynn asked as she got up from her seat and removed the drink from in front of Melissa. "Here" she handed it to Giorgio, before reaching for a wine glass out of the cupboard and then heading to the fridge to grab a second bottle for Melissa. She headed back to the table and placed the bottle and the glass in front of her.

"There you go!" she poured Melissa's first glass for her, "Cheers!" she clinked her glass towards Melissa's. "Oh, thank you! That's so very kind of you – cheers!"

Melissa was so relieved, she was in desperate need of a drink after the day she had, but no amount of stress was going to make that Vodka and Coke go down any quicker than it was. Ashlyn didn't seem obviously warm in her expression and tone, but Melissa felt warmth from her.

"Cheers to our new housemate Melissa everyone!" Giorgio raised his glass in the air and the others raised theirs to join in the toast too.

One of the guys at the table got up - the casual one. He was quite tall and slim. His dark black hair was stylishly unkempt and was past his ears in length. "I'm having a joint, does anyone want one?"

Melissa was a little taken aback by his openness and scanned the room to see what everyone's response was. No-one flinched so she presumed this was common practise.

"No thanks, Kieran, not tonight."

'Kieran, that's it!' She was glad his name had been mentioned again.

"Yeah, me neither I'm just sticking with the alcohol tonight!"

Melissa felt like she better respond too, "Erm, no thanks, I'm ok thanks."

"Cool!" Kieran turned and headed to the back doors.

As the drinks continued to flow, and the more rowdy everyone became, the more comfortable Melissa felt, as their world became more blurry, she felt less visible, less exposed. She felt very comfortable being surrounded by people who were drunk, as there wasn't much focus on her, they were all in their own little worlds laughing at their own jokes. The more she drank the happier she felt, the cold wine was going down with ease, and she began to feel a million miles away from her 'real life'. It was already so much easier to put on a front here because no one knew her, no one knew what had just happened to her, so there was no interrogation and no questions of concern. She could just pretend that nothing had ever happened and enjoy herself.

"Right guys, we're off to bed now!" The guy in the suit stood up from his chair holding the blonde girl's hand.

"So this is probably the most you'll see of Charlie and Maddy, Melissa. They have the basement and they're in a little love bubble so you're very honoured that they made an appearance tonight!" Giorgio explained.

'Suit guy - Charlie, Blonde girl - Maddy!' Melissa took a mental note of their names, although it sounded like she wouldn't see them much anyway.

"Let's all have a joint now the sensible ones have gone to bed! Come on, it will be funny! Roll a couple for us, Kieran. We'll raise a joint for Melissa!" Giorgio laughed.

Melissa glanced around with an awkward smile, the others were laughing and moving from their seats heading towards the back doors. As they stepped out into the garden Melissa couldn't believe how big it was, she hadn't really envisioned it having a garden at all with being in the city, never mind one that was so big. There was a large paved patio as soon as you stepped out of the back doors, with a long lawn that led down to some high fencing that was framing some rather large and tall trees. The house was much more homely than she had imagined it to be.

Kieran lit one of the two joints that he had rolled and handed the other one to Ash. Melissa was standing between Ash and Giorgio when Giorgio put his arm around her.

"You look freezing cold babe! Go get your coat on!"

He was right she was freezing, and she felt both awkward and comforted by Giorgio cuddling her. She thought it was kind of him to think of her, but she kept flitting back to realising she had only just met these people and she should not be so trusting of them just yet. She had always trusted people too quickly and she didn't want to make the same mistakes again. Despite parts of her feeling like she needed to keep her guard up, another part of her just wanted to get out of her own head and feel relaxed, so she took the spliff that Ash handed her and took a long deep drag. She inhaled it as long and hard as she did with cigarettes, but she wasn't used to smoking weed and it cut sharp at the back of throat, her lungs felt like they were burning and she set off coughing. She felt a little embarrassed at being an obvious amateur, but it was not long before the high began to kick in and she felt instantly lighter. A whole weight lifted right off her shoulders and she started giggling. She laughed so much she thought she was going to cry, although she had absolutely no idea why she was laughing. The way she was chuckling made everyone else laugh too. She looked up at the black marble sky, it was a vastness of magic and endless possibilities, just like her life now. She felt so liberated and she soaked it up. As they continued to pass the joint back and forth, she felt so high and after a few more drags she suddenly felt very dizzy.

"I'm going to go to bed, if I can, please." Melissa pointed to the door. The drinks, the tiredness and the joint had made her reach the point of enough is enough, she needed to lie down. The day had kicked the shit out of her and she had nothing left to give.

"Aww, you're going to bed?" Giorgio looked sad to see her leaving, then he strutted over and linked her arm to lead the way. "We'll let you off tonight babe, but only because it's your first night and you'd have had a long day. Tomorrow we will party until the sun comes up, ok?"

"Ok." Melissa agreed, her eyes half closing as she walked propping herself up slightly on Giorgio.

As they climbed what felt like a mountain of stairs, Melissa swayed and stumbled, requiring Giorgio to prop her up on one side and the sweeping traditional banister to aid her on the other side.

"You're on the top floor, Ash is next door to you and the loo is on the floor below you, here he pointed to a door to his right as they then continued up even stairs. As they reached the end of the last flight of stairs, Giorgio realised he hadn't brought Melissa's bags with them.

"Oh shit, I've left your bags downstairs."

"It doesn't matter!" Melissa slurred, as she continued into her room without even looking at it, before collapsing straight on to the unmade bed.

"Night babe!" Giorgio shouted from the door, with a slight chuckle, before closing it, and the light went out along with him. Melissa closed her eyes and went straight to sleep.

CHAPTER 2.

LEARNING TO BE FREE

Melissa had woken up around an hour ago, but it was only now that the light was bright enough for her to see the room clearly. She had lay there in darkness for the last hour, alone with her thoughts. She felt completely numb. She looked around the room, studying her new surroundings. She hadn't even glanced at it last night before passing out on the bed. It was nice, it was clean, it was a blank canvas.

She reflected on the situation she had found herself in. She had gone from being a homeowner, to renting a small room in a house full of strangers and she had spent last night sleeping face down, fully dressed on an unmade bed.

Everything suddenly began to feel so real and frightening. She had escaped her old life so why did she feel so scared? She was consumed with pain, even though she knew she had made it to exactly where she needed to be. But what now? What was she going to do with her life? She had no job, no family nearby, she didn't know if she would properly fit in here. She didn't even know what today would bring? Last night had been fun, but the uncertainty of everything in the cold light of day was agonising. She took a couple of deep breaths, and she talked herself round. When she thought about it rationally, no one ever really knew what was around the corner, so in that respect she wasn't really on her own. She realised right there and then that this wasn't the end of her journey as she had first thought, but it was just the beginning of it. She had so many emotional wounds that were still wide open and they were in desperate need of stitching and bandaging up. As she lay there she felt she was bleeding inside, she breathed through the pain and reassured herself that she was going to be ok. She hadn't come this far to only come this far. She slowly hoisted up her body, willing it to trust her judgement.

The first step she was going to take was to go and get her bags, if she unpacked a bit then it would make it feel more real and make her feel more at home. The problem was that she had no idea where they were, or even what time it was. The fear started to take hold of her again as she became wary of leaving her room in case she couldn't find her way back; she seemed to go up an endless number of stairs and pass several doors last night. She felt intimidated by her unfamiliar surroundings. She couldn't believe that she had been in the same clothes (bar her top) for over 24 hours, all of which now stunk of spilt alcohol and cigarette smoke. She hadn't showered since yesterday morning and she just felt grubby.

Her thoughts went back to the last six weeks when she was in between homes and she had to kept nipping back to the house to take a shower, making sure she only went when Chris was out. Each time she was there she was crippled with fear throughout. Officially it was still her home. She had every right to use it, but it made her skin crawl to think that he could have come in at any moment and seen her naked. He had removed the lock on the bathroom door towards the end of their relationship and she kept waiting for him to burst through the door. Her eyes flooded with water as she recalled how vulnerable she was. She shook her head to shake out those thoughts and gave herself a pep talk.

"You're not there anymore Melissa, come on. You can do this, just put one foot in front of the other."

She decided that regardless of her fear she needed to go and find the bathroom, locate her bags and somehow attempt to scrub away all of the trauma of the last 24 hours, or ideally the last six weeks. If only it would be possible to wash away the last five years. She managed to make it to the bedroom door without talking herself out of it and slowly opened the round black door knob, cringing everytime it made a slight noise. She was certain it was only really early, as it had only just become light. She tiptoed onto the landing, trying extremely hard not to make a sound as she went past the first door that was immediately to her left. She remembered Giorgio had said it was Ashlyn's room, her memories of the end of the night were quite blurry though. Just as she carefully took another step, she landed on a loose floorboard that was hiding under the cream carpet beneath her feet and it let out a large creak.

"Oh, shit!" she whispered to herself as she started to tremble a little.

She felt like she was an intruder in someone's home. She was sure that she embarrassed herself last night and that everyone is probably wondering what on earth they have let themselves in for letting her live with them. For a second she thought about leaving, maybe she wasn't where she was supposed to be if everything felt so scary and uncertain.

It wasn't too late, she could just get in her car and drive back to Manchester, she wouldn't need to explain, she could just grab her bags and go. But a voice inside her told her to stay.

She continued to creep along the landing and started making her way down the first flight of stairs. As the stairs finished, she was facing two pine doors which were both closed and the bannister that wrapped around the landing led her round to the top of another set of stairs She had no idea whose rooms she was passing, and she still could not see her suitcase or bag anywhere, so she continued along the long landing. She noticed the bathroom, as the door was wide open and there was another door at the far end of the landing that was also shut. The further set of stairs led down towards the front door. It's beautiful stained glass panels were transforming the sunlight into a rainbow of colours that beamed up the walls and across the original tiled floor beneath it. She felt a little more at ease and her shaking subsided slightly as she replayed her warm welcome last night. She wondered what time they had partied until. It was obvious that she was the only one in the house that was awake, you could have heard a pin drop. It was so quiet.

As she reached the bottom of the stairs she noticed her bag wasn't there, but she did spot a tall grandfather clock and saw that it was only 6.30am. She hadn't realised that it was so early and she started to worry again that she may wake someone up trying to locate her belongings.

She remembered that Giorgio had taken her bags into the kitchen so she was hoping that they would still be there. The wooden floorboards creaked slightly as she made her way towards the kitchen door. She opened the door and began to scan the room. Every surface in the room was filled with empty cans, bottles, and glasses, and the light that shone brightly through the patio doors was reflecting off them. The chairs were strewn about all over the room, just as everyone had left them the night before.

"There it is!" She spotted her bag to the side of the small dark brown leather sofa in the corner of the room and as she got closer, she saw that her suitcase was propped up neatly behind it. She picked them up, not wanting to use the wheels on her case as it would be too noisy and she quickly remembered how heavy they were. She wondered how on earth she was going to get them all up the stairs. She didn't feel strong enough to carry them both, especially without making any noise. She thought she should tidy up, they may think badly of her if they knew she had been in here and not bothered to do it, but she just wasn't sure if the rest of the house would be able to hear her clearing everything away, If they could, then they would be angry at her for waking them, so she thought it was best to leave it and she come do it later.

She remembered that the second bathroom next to the kitchen had a shower in it and she went to walk in, but then she questioned whether she would seem cheeky just getting in the shower without asking. She thought it was best to wait and ask if it was ok if she used the bathroom first...but she felt so disgusting she didn't want to sit in her unwashed skin any longer. She decided she could probably manage to have a quick shower without anyone noticing. She had a towel in her bag and she could dry the shower afterwards and no one would be any the wiser. She was used to hiding her actions and making sure any evidence was removed.

She stepped into the shower and felt a slight sense of relieve as the warm water blasted onto her body. Then it suddenly dawned on her that she hadn't packed any toiletries. She desperately needed some shower gel to freshen up and she noticed a few different ones on the rack, she was sure no one would notice if she used just a small amount, she just had to remember to dry the bottle. They would however notice the stale smell of sweat that was surrounding her if she didn't use some. She nervously squoze out the tiniest amount and lathered it up to make the most of it. It felt so nice to shower without worrying that it would become freezing cold at any point. Turning the hot water off would be a regular 'joke' that Chris would play. She dried herself before stepping out of the shower and then used the towel to dry the shower cubicle down. She quickly got changed into a fresh tracksuit and wrapped the sodden towel up in her dirty clothes. The smell of the towel and her clean clothes reminded her of the life she had just fled, so she decided right there and then it was time to change her washing powder. She was thankful that she remembered her toothpaste, so that she didn't have to take anyone else's, and she started to brush her teeth vigorously. As she looked at herself in the bathroom mirror, she felt a surreal feeling of dread again and her mind quickly wondered. It was as if she was there in person going through the motions that were expected of her, but her mind and soul had drifted off somewhere to watch her.

She wiped around the bathroom again, to ensure that it was exactly the same as it was when she had walked in. She gathered up her things, finding it harder than before as she now had a wet towel and her old clothes bundled under her arm.

As she came out of the bathroom she noticed a sideboard filled with photo frames, in fact the hall and stairs were still adorned with an array of family photos. Photos that span generations. Many of which featured numerous family members and friends all sat around the table that still stood strong in the kitchen now. Each face beaming with huge smiles, young children, including Giorgio, with faces full of pasta sauce and napkins tucked into their necks to protect the handmade knitted jumpers.

The more she looked around there were signs everywhere that this was once a 'grown-up's' house, one that had been lived in and made a lovely home for a loving and vibrant family.

She finally got back to her room, her knuckles were white and her arms were shaking, her legs almost buckled from underneath her and she dropped her stuff to the floor.

After having a moment to regain her strength she started to unpack her things. It then dawned on her that she hadn't even looked at her phone today. 'I could have checked the time on that!' she thought.

She picked it up to see that she had 10 missed calls and 6 messages. The messages were from her dad, one from each of her sisters, one from Colette, one from Vicki and of course one from Chris.

Apart from Chris, they were all checking to see if she had got to London ok and if she had settled in well. She felt bad that she hadn't responded yet. She sent everyone a message reassuring them that she was fine and having a fantastic time so far, everyone except Vicki, who she decided to call as she was one of the missed calls. (The other 9 were from Chris.) She didn't open the message from Chris, she was getting used to it in some ways as he hadn't stopped trying to contact since she left him, but she just tried to push it to the back of her mind. She was reassured however by the fact she was miles away and he couldn't do anything more than ring her. It was only 7.30am so she decided to wait a while until she called Vicki, as she imagined that she wouldn't be awake at this time on a Saturday. She continued to unpack, to keep herself busy and stop herself from looking at the message from Chris. She didn't know why she was ever intrigued by any of his messages. She wasn't even sure it was that she was curious, it was more something that she couldn't stop. She knew after her not replying to so many messages he would start to turn nasty, so she tried to reply to at least a couple to stop him turning.

Her bedroom was all magnolia and the wrought iron doble-bed took centre stage. The mattress looked new, but she couldn't be sure - she certainly hoped it was, seen as though she had spent last night face down on it! There was a traditional sash window on the wall opposite the bedroom door, with a pine dressing table just to the side of it. She folded her clothes and placed them inside the wardrobe that was built into the alcove. It was right next to the original fireplace which had quickly become her favorite feature in the room. There were two pine bedside tables either side of the bed and apart from that the room was completely bare. It was a blank canvas, just like London, it was an opportunity to make this space and her life exactly as she wanted it to be. That feeling of hopefulness that she had when she accepted the offer of moving here washed over her once again and she smiled at the prospect of being happy.

It was now 8.45am and she couldn't wait to call Vicki any longer. She was so desperate to arrange a catch up with her. She'd hoped that by seeing a familiar face and getting out somewhere in London would help to make all of this feel a bit easier, more real.

"Hey, you, so I'm here, I made it! Sorry I didn't text you yesterday, I ended up a bit worse for wear… I had a few drinks with everyone, and I don't really remember going to bed to be honest! Everyone seems so nice!" Melissa proclaimed.

"Oh, I'm so pleased you made it! You had me a bit worried last night when you didn't get back to me, but I'll let you off if you were busy getting to know everyone! They're all great aren't they! I knew that you would fit in!"

"Yeah they're lovely, they made me feel so welcome. Thanks again for sorting the room for me Vic. So do you want to meet up one night for a drink or something now I'm here? I can't wait to see you!"

"Well, the thing is I'm not actually in London anymore."

Melissa was stunned into silence, it took her a minute to compute what Vicki had just said to her, "What do you mean? Oh, you mean you're visiting your parents?"

"No, well, we're actually at Lewis's parents. It was Lewis' room that you're in, that's why I know them all so well and how I knew it would be the perfect fit for you. Please don't be mad, I just knew you wouldn't have done it if I would have told you before you came."

"Why, where do Lewis's parents live? Why would I be mad hun, I wouldn't get mad at you, you know me!"

"I know hun, well it's just we're not staying at Lewis's parents for long, it's just until our flight this week. We're moving to Australia you see."

"What! Australia?"

"Yes, that's why Lewis left the house and why I didn't ask you to come and live with me. Listen Liss, you don't need me, you'll be just fine, but if I'd have told you, I knew you wouldn't have come."

Melissa felt confused and a little hurt, but being the non-confrontational type that she was she didn't say anything about how she truly felt.

"OK...so, what's taking you to Australia? Do you mean you are going travelling for a bit...or are you moving there for good?"

"Well, Lewis has got a 12-month contract over there and there looks to be lots of opportunities, work wise, for me too, so hopefully it will be a permanent move. You'll have to come and visit us! We'd love to have you come and stay!"

"Well, I will, but only if you'll actually be there once I get there!" That was about as confrontational as Melissa was going to get.

"Aw Liss, honestly I'm sorry if you feel like I tricked you... well, I know, I kind of did, but it was with the best of intentions honestly. Look, I know I don't know exactly what's been happening between you and Chris, but I do know you've not been yourself for years now and I know that those guys, that house and London will be the best thing you've ever done for yourself. Promise me you will stay and give it a real chance? I didn't know anyone when I went to uni and look at me now! You deserve to be happy, Liss and I know you will be there."

"Well, I'm not going to lie, I did not expect you to drop that bombshell, and I was really looking forward to you being around, but I want you to be happy. You deserve it and I promise I will give it my best shot!"

"Amazing! I knew you would understand!"

"So, am I going to see you before you go?"

"Well, I would have loved to but we leave tomorrow night and I've still got so much to do! But you know I love you don't you!"

"Tomorrow! Bloody hell Vicki, well at least you've told me over the phone and not over a text! Right, go, get done what you need to do and I will hold you to that trip to Oz by way of an apology for making me move all the way down here and then abandoning me!"

They both giggled, sarcasm was Melissa's defence mechanism. She did understand what Vicki was saying though. She wouldn't have ever moved down there if she knew that Vicki wouldn't have been there. But equally she didn't like to feel as though she had been tricked and deceived - she'd had enough of that. She also couldn't help but feel a little rejected, not to mention that London now seemed even more daunting than ever before.

"Ok, I'll get going then, you have fun. Giorgio and Ash are amazing and totally your kind of people by the way, and everyone else is fab too. Honestly hun, you'll thank me one day, I promise!"

"Well, here's hoping! Have a safe journey, take care Vic, I miss you!"

"I miss you too! I'll text you when I get there! Lots of Love! Bye!"

"Bye!"

As she put down the phone a pang of anxiety pinched at her chest. She glanced around the room at the bare walls, and she felt completely lost. She thought Vicki would be a crutch to lean on when she got here, someone to help her on her road to recovery.

"Maybe that's why she was leaving, moving to the other side of the world to make sure I don't drag her down."

She quickly counteracted her paranoia. "Don't be daft!" she just explained why she did it! She loves you - maybe it wasn't the best approach, but she doesn't know the full story and she did it with the best of intentions…and you're talking to yourself again Melissa!"

She took a deep breath and threw herself dramatically onto the bed. She stayed there for a few minutes only to remember that she was still lying down on an unmade bed, although at least now she knew, if it wasn't brand new at least it was Lewis's and not a complete randoms. She quickly sat up and went over to her suitcase, pulling out the one set of bedding that she had managed to pack before she left. When she pulled it out, that smell hit her again and she was instantly back in the bedroom she shared with Chris; remembering the lifeless sex she endured, and the nights spent on the floor. She rushed over to the bin and stuffed it in. She needed to buy some new bedding, she needed to start fresh, ready to make new memories. She put on her shoes and realised that she didn't really like what she was wearing either. Everything reminded her of him, everything had to be what he approved of…but not anymore! She snapped herself out of going into a hole and she rolled her shoulders back, put on some lip gloss and mascara and decided to make a bold move and open her bedroom door. She turned the doorknob, taking a deep breath and she stepped back out of her room again. It was even more daunting coming out of it now than it had been earlier in the morning as she knew that most likely people would be awake by now. She felt like she was about to meet them all again. She was already nervous without the added embarrassment of not quite remembering how she behaved or what she said at the end of the night.

She had only taken two steps out of her door, when the door next to her started to open and out

40

walked Ashlyn. She wasn't quite as polished as last night. It secretly reassured Melissa that she wouldn't have to continuously be made up and looking fabulous. Yet even with her bleary eyes and no makeup Ashlyn was still somehow looked stunningly beautiful.

"Arr, good morning to you hun, how was your first night sleep in your new abode!"

Melissa quickly remembered how charmed she was by Ashlyn's strong Irish accent.

"Oh, hi Ashlyn! I'm sorry, I hope I didn't disturb you, I didn't mean to, I've just forgotten a few things so I need to go out and try and buy a few things."

"Don't be daft hun, you haven't disturbed me at all! No need to apologise. I'm saying good morning, but it could be the afternoon for all I know!" she laughed and placed an arm around Melissa as she ushered her downstairs. "Have you had any breakfast? I'm starving!"

"Oh no, I didn't eat anything honestly, I didn't bring anything with me so I wouldn't eat anyone's food, don't worry."

"That wasn't why I was asking! Don't be daft! You're extremely cute!"

She was hoping that being seen as cute was a positive thing. She wanted to fit in more than ever now that Vicki wasn't going to be around. As they got to the front door, Melissa tried to leave to go to the shops, but Ash insisted that she have some breakfast first.

"Just have a quick bacon sandwich and then you can go out shopping, ok hun. We can't have you going out hungry."

"I just feel really cheeky and I'm honestly fine."

"There's no need to feel cheeky Melissa, it's a couple of slices of bacon and bread, it won't break the bank you know, and you haven't eaten since you arrived last night. You need something to eat, now come on!"

"Ok, thank you, you're very kind. I really appreciate it!"

They went down to the kitchen and she could see Kieran sat out on the patio smoking. The glasses and bottles had all been moved and the chairs were back in place.

"Morning Kieran!" Ashlyn shouted out to him. "Oh, morning ladies, well afternoon actually Ash!"

"It's not afternoon, I'm up early for a Saturday!"

Kieran laughed as he got up from his chair and wandered back into the house. "Is Giorgio not out of his pit yet?" Ash asked.

"What do you think?" They both laughed, Melissa smiled.

Ash turned to her to explain, "It's a standing joke as Giorgio never rises before late afternoon, unless he's got work or a hair appointment."

Melissa laughed, "He seems so nice and so much fun."

"Oh, he's the best, honestly, you'll have the best time here hun."

"Yes, and if anyone knocks on your bedroom door after midnight, it will be G trying to get you to go on a midnight adventure!" Kieran added, laughing, "You'll learn to ignore that!"

"Yes, he will do that! He goes round the whole house, once he's decided he wants to go out. He's very spontaneous! Sit down, I'll pop the bacon on. Do you want a coffee?"

"Yes please, as long as you don't mind."

"I wouldn't have offered it if I'd have minded!" Ash turned to Kieran, "She's so bloody sweet isn't she."

About five minutes later Ash brought the bacon sandwiches over to the table and the three of them tucked in. "Now it's up to you, but we have a kitty for food and drink that we all just put into each week and we're supposed to take turns doing the shopping, but it seems like the guys have decided it's my job! Which doesn't frustrate me at all!" Ash rolled her eyes as she explained.

"I don't mind doing the shopping. Anything I can do to help just let me know." Melissa was eager to make herself useful, "especially as I don't have a job yet, I need to keep myself busy."

"We'll all keep an eye out for a job for you won't we Kieran? Don't worry you'll find your feet in no time. I remember how daunting it was for me when I first moved here, I think we all felt like that at first, well apart from Giorgio he grew up here obviously."

Kieran had stopped participating in the conversation and had seemingly zoned out whilst he read the paper and munched on his sandwich.

Melissa was so grateful that Ashlyn had insisted that she ate something as she really was starving. She ate it in a flash. "Thanks so much for that, Ashlyn. I really do appreciate it. I better get going to the shops now. Where are they again? Do I need to go in my car?"

"It's literally just down this road, cross over at the lights and you'll see the supermarket and a couple of other shops next to it. You don't need your car, but you just need to be able to make sure you can carry your bags home, so I'd take your car if you're planning on buying a lot."

"Oh, I think I'll walk down then, I can always go back for stuff and I'm not sure I'm brave enough to face the London roads again just yet! I'll see you later."

Melissa then remembered that she didn't have a key yet, "I don't have my key yet, will someone be in to let me back in. Sorry to be a pain."

"We'll be here no problem. I'll tell Giorgio to give you your key when he gets up."

"Thank you. See you in a bit."

"Bye hun,"

"Bye" Kieran finally looked up from his paper.

As she shut the front door behind her she took in everything around her, the noise, the cars, the perfect rows of beautiful Victorian houses. She could feel the beating heart of the capital, pulsing through her. There was something in the atmosphere, something about London that made her feel instantly more alive. With each stride she was breathing in the freedom, it felt good and really liberating. She was excited to go shopping and buy whatever she wanted clothes wise, interior wise and make up wise, not forgetting food, she could finally eat whatever she wanted too without worrying about rearing off the path of the regimented food timetable that she had to adhere to for him, or having a treat and putting on weight. All that was behind her now, the only way she wanted to try to look now is forward, 'I'm not being stuck in the past any longer, I've turned a page, that's it, this is a new and exciting chapter of my life and I can do this. I don't need anyone, as long as I can make myself happy, I'll be fine, so that's what I've got to do'

She pondered over the not needing anyone part; she did need people. She needed people to have fun with and to keep her from having too much time on her hands with only her negative thoughts. She started to wonder what her housemates thought of her so far. They most probably thought that she was lightweight or boring going to bed so early. She thought about this morning though and how lovely Ashlyn had been making her breakfast and she did say she was cute. She wasn't sure about Kieran though he barely looked up from his paper this morning. She started to worry that she had offended him or maybe smoked too much of his weed? She couldn't judge Giorgio as she hadn't seen him yet, or Charlie and Maddy but thankfully they went to bed whilst she was still compos mentis.

As Melissa reached the supermarket she noticed herself in the glass windows, she glanced down at her grey baggy jogging bottoms and sweat top. Both were incredibly drab and unflattering. Her hair looked completely wild, her curls were frayed with frizz and wispy bits. Her make up skills were not good enough to help her shine either, the signs of exhaustion were there for the world to see. She sighed as she looked at herself in the reflection of the shop window and she suddenly felt very down. After a minute of just standing still examining her reflection, feeling both sadness and anger, she realised that she could change that very quickly. The inside of her was one thing, but she could quickly change how she felt and how she was perceived by other people, by changing how she looked on the outside. So, she began striding towards the shop doors determined to buy at least one outfit that looks effortlessly chic. She didn't want to be the only one in that house that didn't have a sense of style, you could guess things about each of their personalities by what they wear, it's like they use fashion to project the parts of them that they want on show.

She wanted to choose what parts of her were on show too. She wanted to hide the parts of herself that she was ashamed of, behind the parts of her that she didn't mind the world seeing.

She went to the changing room with items that she had seen put together on the manikin, she had just gone for the look she liked the most and decided to copy the manikin from top to toe to make sure she got it right. She put each of the items on, including the shoes and turned towards the mirror. She took a step back; she hadn't seen herself in anything other than dark grey tracksuits for weeks now and she was surprised by how nice she looked. It was a rare occasion that she ever thought of herself as 'looking nice' but she couldn't not think that, because she felt good. It felt wonderful to see herself looking good. She was less impressed by her face and hair, but she would have to try and sort that out too. She asked the sales assistant if she could just pull the tags off to pay so that she could keep the clothes on. She also asked if she could put her tracksuit and trainers in the bin. She paid for clothes and headed out of the shop on the hunt for some make up. She had no clue what products were the best ones for her and the selection wasn't huge, so she decided just to grab the basic's at the most expensive price point and hope for the best. As she paid for the make up she became lost in a trance, she began thinking of the times that Chris had hid her makeup, or the time that he threw it away. She remembered buying a replacement of each item and creating a hiding place for it in a false drawer; so that she never had to go to work without it again. Her memories then switched to how she used to be able to break off the shackles of her home life, with each stride as she headed to work. If she could emulate the way she used to feel at work and channelled that into her new life, then she could create a veil of confidence. She was sure she was going to need to at least pretend to have it to survive here. Everyone was so cool here, she almost needed to stand out in order to fit in.

Determined to look the part she also went to the hair aisle and decided it was time to show her hair what gel felt like again and tame her mass of wild frizzy curls. She reached out for an expensive curling jelly that she hadn't bought since before she went to Cyprus. She wanted to erase the past three and a half years and go back to the person she was before that trip. She wanted to be bubbly, fun, flirty and free again. Free from torturous thoughts, fear and stress; Free from secretly hating herself because of how she had allowed him to treat her. How could she have let herself lose so many precious years living so unhappily. She quickly blinked away her thoughts and switched to focusing on the positives.

'These might only be small steps, but you're taking them, and they're in the right direction - stop looking back!'.

After she left the shop she lifted the lid off her hair gel and scrunched a bit into her curls, she tried to gage how she looked in the reflection of the shop window. She felt a million miles away from looking flawless, but it was a vast improvement on how she looked and felt earlier.

She walked back up towards the house, she had got everything she needed. Thank goodness she got her last paycheck just before she moved here. She had real spring in her step despite struggling to carry the umpteen bags she had now acquired. As she reached the front door she dropped the bags dramatically to the floor, hoping she hadn't smashed any of the wine she had just bought and her hands were covered in red marks from where the plastic handles had dug in. She paused as she excitedly went to press the doorbell, quickly noticing the difference from how nervous she had felt last night. She couldn't believe the difference she felt in less than 24 hours.

Giorgio opened the door in the most colourful satin robe she had ever seen, it was like a technicolour dream coat.

"Oooh you look nice babe! We're going to the pub in an hour. Do you want to come? I'm just starting to get ready now."

"Are you sure? I don't want to intrude?" Mel said sheepishly.

"You're not intruding! I wouldn't be asking you if we didn't want you to come?"

"Well, as long as you're sure, I'd love to come. I've just bought some wine and beers too, to make up for what I drank last night."

"Fab, well we're only going to the pub for a few hours anyway and then we're going to come back here so we'll crack them open when we get back."

"Does this outfit look ok for going out in?" Melissa was worried about letting the side down in the style-stakes.

"Absolutely, you look gorgeous! We're only going to the local anyway so if anything you'll be overdressed!"

"Oh, should I get changed then?" She didn't know why she suggested that as she didn't have anything else that would have been suitable anyway.

"No! I didn't mean it in a bad way! I'm a stylist and I'm always overdressed - I love it!" Giorgio giggled. "What's the point in going out unless you stand out from the crowd! You get more attention that way!"

She wasn't sure she wanted that attention.

Although she knew she didn't look or feel as fabulous as Giorgio had said she did, he was so nice for suggesting it. She was sure he was just saying it to make her feel better. She felt excited at the prospect of her first night out with her housemates, even if it was just down at the local -

she also liked the idea of having a local as she's never been allowed one before.

"Ok great, I'll just put these drinks in the fridge and then take the rest of my stuff upstairs. Will you let me know when you're ready to go out?"

"Just come to the kitchen when you're ready hun and have a drink, then once we're all ready we'll head out."

This was just the kind of fun, carefree Saturday that she had craved for so long, yet now it was upon her, stomach kept turning. 'Maybe this is too much, too soon' she pondered, whilst she tried to think of things that she could say, to try and get out of going. She decided to push herself to do it anyway, what else was she going to do, sit up in her room and relive the past? No, she was going to put a front on no matter what and dig deep to find 'fun' Melissa once again.

Melissa, Ashlyn, Giorgio and Kieran had a great few hours in 'The Crown', then Kieran met up with his mates from Uni, Kieran was doing his masters in Art at Goldsmiths. Giorgio, Ash and Melissa were calling at the Chinese to pick up a takeaway before singing and swaying their way home.

The Chinese food was delicious, it was like an explosion of wonderful flavours all of which she had never tasted before. She hadn't known what to order as Chris didn't like fast food, especially Chinese so she was never allowed to order it. This was the type of Saturday night that reminded her of being at her nana's house growing up. The TV blasting out the best of Saturday night television. A room filled with love and laughter, whilst eating a chippy tea in their pyjamas'. The only difference being that now she was old enough to wash down her food with a nice cold glass of white wine. They all laughed until their belly's hurt – probably also due to the fact they had completely over indulged in the food. Then it wasn't long before they were dancing around Giorgio's room singing into the remote control, a hairbrush and an empty wine bottle.

"Can we have more nights like this please!" Melissa gushed as she gave them both a hug goodnight.

CHAPTER 3.

DESPAIR

Since she had ended things with Chris, some mornings she would wake up feeling energised, excited and ready to see what the new day would bring. Other days she would wake up feeling completely exhausted, as if she hadn't slept at all. It would often feel like she had spent the night physically fighting and tirelessly battling to keep her demons at bay. It was at night, just before she went to sleep, when her mind would become it's noisiest. Replaying past events and hurtful comments on a loop. It was like she could run away from them all day, keeping busy and occupying herself with other things, then at night when everything was still, they crept out of the shadows and started to attack her as she tirelessly tried to sleep. It would leave her drained of life, reliving being back in that house with him again and again.

Today was one of those mornings. She could see the light trying to sneak into her room, breaking through the cracks in her blinds to come and save her from her nightmares, but she just couldn't find an ounce of energy to get up and let the light in. She felt like her body had turned to cement, her head was fuzzy and her eyelids heavy. She lay there willing herself to get out of bed, but nothing would happen. Her legs wouldn't move at all. It was like her body had completely switched off from her mind, too battered and bruised by all the painful thoughts that it had been fed in the night. It was as if her body and her heart had decided to stay right where they were, safe in bed preventing them from enduring any more pain. How could she be expected to go out into the world, when she knew she needed to recover from not only the mental scars but the fresh bruises her body had endured only a few nights before. And somehow in the mornings more than any other time in the day, they felt more prominent.

Chris had been ringing and texting her constantly since she had left him. It had become unbearable, she was continually looking at her phone to find 15 missed calls and 10 messages. She had begun to almost go into a state of shock each time he rang. Everytime her phone would ring she would dread looking at it in case it was his name flashing up once again. The last thing in the world that she wanted to do was speak to him, the thought of it made her feel physically sick. Of course he knew she didn't want to speak to him, she couldn't have made it any clearer, but the more she ignored him the more his calls increased in volume. There was no respect, it was all about him. He wanted to talk to her at any cost; she knew he didn't like not getting his own way which equally made her feel slightly uneasy.

But the tide had turned this time and no matter how much anxiety it gave her, she wasn't going to give in. There was no way on this earth that she could ever go back. The mere thought of stepping one foot into that house made her inhale sharply and the all too familiar stomach-flip feeling followed.

Her brain had begun torturing her by recalling some of her recent nightmares since she arrived. In them, she was trying to run away, trying to leave her old house. But her feet were stuck and all she could see was a seething turbulent Chris getting closer and closer. She subconsciously knew she was in a half asleep/half-awake state but she couldn't escape the life-like pictures that were antagonising her over and over however much she tried to block them out. She managed to wake herself up, completely out of breath and dripping in sweat. Still delirious for that split second, she started to mourn for her life changing 'London life' and told herself that it had all been a far-fetched dream.

But when realization started to slowly hit, when she came around to find herself in that room, in that bed, it was immeasurable and completely overwhelming. She let out a silent yelp from her relief.

She still lay there unable to move, her thoughts quickly changed course as she started to desperately search for answers her brain had begun to fire at her. 'But what now? What should I do? What if he finds you?' But she had no answers; she just felt completely uneasy and lost.

She had been in London for a week now and following a fantastic first two nights, the rest of the week had just been on a downward spiral. The reality of everything hit had her and she started grieving more and more. Grieving for lost time. Grieving for her loved ones. Grieving for the relationships that she gave her heart to, only to have it stamped on in return. She could barely get out of bed all week, she felt in pain all over her body and she found herself hibernating in her room, only nipping out for the toilet when she knew there was no one around.

Last night was another terrible night's sleep. She had woken up three times, yet again crying out and sweating. She kept dreaming that Chris had followed her to London without her knowing, and that she was waking up to him sitting on the edge of her bed staring at her. She wondered if her nightmares were premonitions, warnings, so that she was prepared for the fact that he had actually followed her and that one day she would wake up and he would be sat there on the edge of her bed for real. 'What if he was just biding his time, waiting for the right moment to catch me alone?' She shuddered at the thought. She had ignored over 50 phone calls from him since she had arrived and 5 texts from him remained unopened. She stared at her phone debating as to whether she should open them or not. Maybe it would give her some reassurance that he hadn't followed her, or maybe it would confirm that he had. She threw the phone to the end of the bed and it bounced off the iron bedstead and back onto the bedding. A sudden waterfall of tears cascaded from her eyes, unexpectedly. She just wanted him to go away, why wouldn't he go away. She wondered what it would take for him to get the message. She didn't close her blinds before she got in bed last night and she noticed the sun wasn't shining today. Reality set in that it wasn't going to be all sunshine and adventures in London and that she was just as afraid here as she was back in Manchester. No matter how many miles she had put between them, he was constantly there in almost every thought she had. When she closed her eyes she could see him, when there was silence, she could hear him. Every move she made she was filled with anguish and fear from the prospect of what was around the corner.

The novelty of the first day had worn off quickly. Now she felt so flat, exhausted, and empty. She lay on the bed just gazing out of the window, lost in the clouds. She had spent hours watching as the raindrops ran down the window pane into each other, or watching the sun play hide and seek with clouds. As the grey clouds rolled on by, she became very aware of how much time she was letting just slip by her, lying there, doing nothing. She already felt like she had lost out on so much time over the last $3^{1/2}$ years. She wasn't able to do half of the things she wanted to do, travel, party, have adventures, yet, here she was with both time on her hands and the freedom to explore, yet still she found herself shutting herself away. She could remember vividly how painfully slow the time used to pass, how five minutes could feel like an hour; yet today it felt like the hours were whizzing by. She felt like her life had been packed into a sand timer and all she could do was just watch from a far as it just slipped away in front of her. She wanted so much to make the most of her new life but she couldn't find it in herself to put a front on the last couple of days, it would have been impossible, she was just too low.

She questioned herself as to why she didn't instantly feel happy like she thought she would when she got there. Why wasn't she out there getting to know London, eating nice food, drinking whatever and whenever she wanted? Why wasn't she out shopping, treating herself to clothes that she never would have dreamed of wearing before? She could go and buy the biggest makeup collection she had ever owned without fear of it being hidden or thrown away. She lay there listing all of the things that she could be doing with her day, yet still she didn't move. She just felt so tired and found herself continually dozing off to sleep in between her daydreams. She didn't want to go and get something to eat or a drink. If she drank she would need the toilet and she couldn't risk leaving her room and she didn't have any appetite. Being alone in silence was something she was used to and as lonely as it was, it felt safe somehow.

She wasn't sure how long she had been lying there or how long she had been asleep, so she sat up and leaned over to get her phone. Her finger hovered over the button to open the texts of Chris and before she could talk herself out of it she was reading them.

FROM CHRIS - I CAN'T BELIEVE YOU'VE ACTUALLY GONE. I ALWAYS THOUGHT WE WOULD WORK THINGS OUT, THAT'S WHY I FORGAVE YOU FOR BETRAYING ME WITH ANTHONY. NOW YOU'VE ABANDONED ME AND THROWN MY FORGIVENESS BACK IN MY FACE. HOW COULD YOU DO THIS TO ME WHEN I LOVE YOU SO MUCH. XXXX

FROM CHRIS -WHERE ARE YOU? JUST COME HOME NOW, YOU HAVE MADE YOUR POINT. I KNOW I'M NOT PERFECT BUT NEITHER ARE YOU. ALL OF THIS ISN'T MY FAULT WHY CAN'T YOU ACCEPT YOUR PART. JUST COME HOME AND WE CAN START AGAIN. I MISS YOU. I LOVE YOU. XXX

FROM CHRIS- WHY ARE YOU IGNORING ME. I DON'T DESERVE THIS!!!! I'LL KILL MYSELF IF YOU DON'T REPLY. I CAN'T LIVE WITHOUT YOU! CALL ME PLEASE. XXXXX

FROM CHRIS - SO YOU WANT ME TO DIE???
FROM CHRIS - I'M GOING TO DO IT. I WILL. I HOPE YOU CAN LIVE WITH YOURSELF AFTER EVERYTHING YOU'VE DONE!!! HOW CAN YOU BE SO HEARTLESS!

She felt even more numb now than she did before. She didn't know what to say to him nor if she should, or could, even react to his barrage of messages at all. Part of her thought was he just doing it to get her to speak to him? The other part worried could he have meant it? There was also a part of her that wanted him to die - so he would leave her alone. But she felt ashamed to even think it. A huge wave of shame washed over her.

'How could I even wish that on someone? What is wrong with me?' she tormented in her head.

Her mind became flooded with memories of his kind side and moments where he had been nice to her.

She thought back to when she returned back from Cyprus. How fragile she was and how he had made her feel safe. How he reassured her that nothing like that would ever happen again whilst he was around. After his initial outburst he was so nice. He was protective and wanted to be with her all the time, so nothing would happen to her. He assured her he believed her when she'd told him what had happened with the Rep, that it hadn't felt right. He almost showed a glimmer of empathy once. But after a few months, following an argument, he'd always bring it up and call her a slag. He would regret it the next day. He'd always apologised for it in the beginning.

In some ways she thinks maybe she was a bit to blame as she let him make all the decisions at first because she felt so lost, she didn't feel herself so she didn't mind him taking control of everything. 'Maybe that's it, he was only doing what I let him do.'

She wondered whether it was her fault, that he had just taken his control too far because he loved her so much. The first couple of years had been mainly made up of happy times and she smiled as she remembered them. How he always wanted her by his side, taking her everywhere with him because he would miss her when she wasn't there. There were many times she would just sit in the car and wait for him whilst he trained, as he said he didn't want to waste a second after training without her. She found herself crying about Chris, she had an all consuming sense of sadness and pain that what they once had was gone. She found it strange that now she had left, she kept getting flooded with memories of the good times that they had shared, in equal measure of the bad ones and both made her heart ache. She could picture him vividly, crying as she drove away, and the way he sobbed when he found out about her and Anthony. What if that was what he felt like now and she was ignoring him, then he might do something stupid? She didn't want that to happen, she couldn't live with that on her conscience and in a moment of weakness she texted him back.

Almost instantly she regretted messaging him. She had done so well in breaking contact with him. Her head hurt as her thoughts spun out of control. She knew by replying to him, she was giving him a glimmer of hope that he could work his way back to her, yet even in the depths of despair she knew she could never go back.

TO CHRIS - CHRIS PLEASE DON'T DO ANYTHING STUPID. I JUST NEED SOME TIME TO HEAL. I DON'T WANT TO TALK TO ANYONE RIGHT NOW, IT'S NOT JUST YOU. GO AND STAY AT YOUR MUM AND DADS PLEASE YOU

NEED TO BE AROUND PEOPLE THAT LOVE YOU. I CAN'T BE THAT PERSON RIGHT NOW. X

He had found her weak spot though, he knew she was too nice and too caring not to respond to his threats of killing himself and she had played right into his hands. Her phone flashed up with a new message almost immediately.

FROM CHRIS - I KNEW YOU STILL CARED ABOUT ME! DON'T WORRY I WON'T DO ANYTHING STUPID AS LONG AS I KNOW MY MELLY STILL CARES FOR ME. I WILL WAIT FOR YOU. I KNOW IN TIME YOU'LL COME BACK. LOVE YOU XXXX

In one respect she was relieved that he hadn't acted upon his threats, and the next she completely stupid as she knew he had no intention of doing so, she had fallen right into his trap, just as she had for years.

FROM CHRIS - PS I'M NOT BUYING THE HOUSE OFF YOU, I'M GOING TO USE THE MONEY TO BUILD A BIG EXTENSION ON THE SIDE JUST LIKE YOU WANTED AND WE'LL HAVE PLENTY OF ROOM FOR OUR BABIES. WE CAN BE HAPPY JUST LIKE WE USED TO BE XXX

When she recalled the 'happy memories' once again she wondered how happy she truly was at that time. Why could she only remember him taking her training with her? Why couldn't she remember nice days out and nice meals? Or mini breaks and holidays together? Her eyebrows furrowed as she racked her brain for sweet moments. There were plenty of expensive gifts, she could remember those. There were many times that they were meant to go out for meals but they often ended up being cancelled as he came to pick her up so late that instead they just drove around. She was always flattered that he said he was glad that he didn't have to share her with a full restaurant now. He always said that it was so much better when it was just the two of them. That he was happier sharing a bag of chips with her in the car than going for fancy meals. She thought about how many times she had sat there all dressed up making up excuses to her father, as he got more and more angry about him standing her up again. The thing was, at that point, she didn't think of them as excuses. She always understood his reasons for being late and as long as he came in the end she didn't mind. The more she thought about it, the more she had spent an awful lot of time just waiting for him in the early days. She always thought it was so sweet how he would ask her to come with him whilst he did some extra work or training instead of going out with her friends. It never occurred to her that it was anything other than him loving her and not wanting to miss a minute with her. That was when her friends stopped asking her to go though, the more she let them down to go out with him instead, the less they asked her to do anything. Her life revolved around him, waiting for him at home or in the car. She was always waiting for him. Why didn't she see it? She suddenly felt angry at herself for not seeing things for what they were back then. Then she recalled that she did have it out with him once, that she was fed up having to wait around for him in order to spend time with him and that's when he suggested they get a house together. Her issues were instantly gone as she was so pleased that he loved her enough to commit to buying a house together. She can remember her Dad expressing his concerns and her reassuring him she was old enough to make her own decisions. That he needed to stop worrying. But that's when it all changed for the worse. He no longer had to put any time in with her in order to know where she was. He knew exactly where she was all of the time.

Within the first week she had mentioned about them having their joint friends around to the house for a housewarming and out of nowhere he snapped at her.

"What, so you can get drunk and have a threesome with my mates? Isn't it enough that you had one in Cyprus? Now you want to cheat on me in my own house!"

She can remember it like it was yesterday, that comment cut through her like a knife. She couldn't understand why he would say that, why he would think that was what she had planned? It was so unexpected and it wounded her. She wouldn't do that and she still didn't know how she had found herself in that position in Cyprus in the first place.

[FLASHBACK]

"Chris, why would you say that? You know I love you. I would never hurt you. I didn't want that to happen and you know how sorry I am about it, I didn't mean to do it, it must have been the drink."

She can remember begging him to look at her.

"Yeah well, once a slag always a slag. I know your game, I know who you've got your eye on as well. Well just be warned, I'm on to you and you won't be humiliating me again! Especially in my own house!"

A mist of his spit covered her slightly as he was screaming his seething insults at her.

That was the first night he stormed out and left her on her own nearly all night. He wouldn't answer her phone calls. When he finally came home at 4am, she spent over an hour apologising. and she promised that she wouldn't suggest having anyone round again.

Her tears were less frequent, just the occasional lonely one escaped each eye, as she trawled through her memory, recalling each year of their relationship, wondering why she had stuck it out for so long.

How could she have been so gullible to fall for his twisted mind games once again. She went back to wishing he was dead when she relieved all of the hurtful things that he had put her through.

Then came the memory that is one of the hardest for her to bear lately, the night that changed everything, the night her soul started fighting back and the night she opened up about their sham of a relationship for the very first time. It was the night that Anthony walked into her life. Her tears fell hard and fast as her heart ached for him. What she wouldn't give for him to be the one texting and ringing her, begging her to come back. But ever since the day that Chris exposed the affair she still had nothing but radio silence from Anthony and it felt like she had been kicked in the stomach every time she thought of him. It was at that moment she knew that she needed to get out of her head and out of this room. But she couldn't compose herself for long enough and she couldn't risk letting the mask slip in front of her new housemates. For the first time she had stopped still long enough to feel, and she felt like she had gone through every emotion possible today.

[KNOCK KNOCK]

She froze and started to hold her breath so they couldn't hear her exaggerated breath from crying so much. She couldn't answer it, she couldn't let them in. She couldn't let them see what a mess she was. There was no way. Her pillow was soaked with tears.

[KNOCK KNOCK]

"Melissa?"

It was Ashlyn. She couldn't hold her breath any longer, so she turned her face into her bedding. She was sobbing hard now, she couldn't understand why she was hiding in a room of a house full of relative strangers. Something was really wrong with her, there must be? She started grabbing at her hair, rocking back and forward as she attempted to muffle her cries into her pillow.

Ashlyn knocked again, but she still ignored her. Now she was worrying about what everyone would be thinking about her for not answering the door. But she couldn't face anyone, so she stayed exactly where she was until she heard the creak on the floorboards and she knew that she had gone away. She quickly considered she maybe having a breakdown. It felt like she'd skyrocketed right back to the same state she felt when she started to take the pills. She felt so alone. So unable to face the world. So unbelievably sad, that she just couldn't see a way forward. She questioned whether coming to London had been such a wise decision especially as Vicki wasn't going to be around. She didn't know if she had the strength to make new friendships and to let people. She had lay there all day flitting between hysterical tears and staring into space. Consumed by flashbacks and suffering small anxiety attacks when thinking of possible future scenarios. She hadn't eaten or drank, it hadn't even crossed her mind once. She had lost her appetite for food and for life.

It had just turned eight o'clock when there was a knock at her bedroom door again. She panicked, they knew she was in there. She had already ignored them once today, and she ignored them yesterday too, what would they think of her if she ignored them again? She hadn't cried for a while so she thought maybe she could get away with saying she had been asleep most of the day and had felt a bit poorly yesterday. She forced herself to get up and open the door. She had to act now in order to stop herself from spiralling any further. She feared if she didn't face them now it would only get harder.

She opened the door to see Giorgio standing there.

"Hey babe are you ok?"

"Oh yes, I'm fine thank you. Are you ok?"

"Yes fine hun, we just wanted to make sure everything was alright? You don't have to stay up here all the time, you know?"

"Oh, I'm sorry I didn't mean to be rude, I just didn't like to intrude."

"You're not intruding! This is your home now too. We all want to get to know you. You're welcome to come downstairs whenever you want."

"I'm sorry I've just felt really tired today and I felt poorly yesterday."

For so many years it had become second nature to make up excuses; for looking upset or tired, or for being absent from places that she was invited to. For so long her reason for hiding behind the pretence was to protect Chris because she didn't want people to think badly of him. Even though she was still creating a façade now the major difference was that this time she was doing it to protect herself. She wanted to shield herself from looks of concern or pity. She wanted to avoid any questions that would provoke painful memories from rearing their ugly heads and so they wouldn't start destroying her once again. Although deep down she knew it wasn't healthy, for now it was the only way that she could see through this transition, locking away the parts of her life that she couldn't bear to relive. She wondered if it was the weight of those secrets though that had left her chained to the bed all day.

"You must be starving and dying of thirst, why don't you come down for a bit. Kieran made a sunday dinner - he's like a master of Sunday Roasts. There's loads left, why don't you come down and have some?"

"Only if you're sure you don't mind? I am a bit hungry."

In truth she had no appetite whatsoever, not for going downstairs or food. However, she knew that not accepting the invitation could arouse suspicion and she wanted to camouflage her weakened state by acting as normal as possible.

"How many times babe, you're one of the family now so come let's get your arse down these stairs and get some food down you."

He put her arm around her and ushered her out of the door.

She really wanted to embrace her housemates and they couldn't have been more welcoming, but she was so full of fear, she didn't know how to just let go and be in the moment. She was trying so hard to hide how anxious she was, that it left her feeling completely exhausted. She had a fear of people not liking her, the fear of making the wrong choices, the fear of being betrayed; she basically just had an overwhelming fear of everything. If she hid away, then she couldn't make any mistakes. The impact of what she had been through seemed to hit harder each day. She felt so broken inside and she didn't know how to fix it. She longed to find a painkiller that would help to numb the internal agony that she was harbouring.

CHAPTER 4.

MAKEOVER

Mellisa had found herself in a constant battle with her own thoughts which had become a daily struggle. Trying to erase the destructive notions and replace them with things that the counsellor had told her; she needed to remember that everything that had happened in her past wasn't because she wasn't good enough; nor was she unlovable. She needed to remember that they all had their own issues. She often wondered though; Was that really the case, or was the councillor just being nice so that she wouldn't consider taking her own life again.

She was always surprised when people liked her, she found it hard to understand why anyone would. She couldn't believe how quickly her housemates had swept her under their wings, but it was something she expected would come to an abrupt end once they scratched the surface of who she was, and they began to hear her story.

She sat lost in her thoughts, as a cool breeze gently blew her hair and the birds chirped in a loud chorus… one bird chirped up repeatedly and was much louder than the rest. She chuckled to herself as she likened it to Giorgio.

As she embraced the warmth of the sun of the Indian summer, she sat back looking up at the bright blue sky. This was her second full week of coming out of her bedroom. Everyday she had made herself get dressed and do something and she had felt much better. She wasn't able to find a way through those bad days last week. But day by day she gained more strength and more courage to carry on. She wanted to create new memories to replace all of the memories tainted by the last few years.

The sun was low and the brightness of it made her squint. She consequently closed both eyes and took a deep breath. She thought about the whirlwind month that she had enjoyed since arriving in the big city, she smiled before taking another deep breath inhaling the freedom she felt in that moment. She thought about her housemates, her new mini family and she realized just how lucky she had been that Vicki had put her name down for the room. She could not have ended up living with a better bunch of people and she felt immense gratitude for that. She had barely had a minute this week, as they had included her in all their weekly plans and so there was no time to dwell on anything - even if she had wanted to. They had fully embraced her, kept her busy and it was exactly what she needed. She was now known at the 'The Crown' and wine in pjs was a nightly thing at home, catching up in the dining room at the end of each day. It was nice and it was comforting.

"Oh heeeeeeeeeeeeyyyyyyyyy!" her thoughts were suddenly interrupted by a loud greeting that was unmistakably Giorgio. She spun her head around. Back towards the house before she started grinning as she spotted Giorgio dancing and shimmying towards her.

"Hey! What are you doing here? I thought you and Ashlyn had a shoot all day today.

"Well, the bitch who organised it cancelled at the last minute, so here we are darling! Ash is just grabbing the fizz!"

"Fizz oooh, what's the occasion?"

"Well, you'll just have to wait a minute because I can't tell without Ash, you know how excited she gets over things!" Giorgio's hint of sarcasm tickled Melissa, Ash was so cool it was hard to imagine her getting giddy over anything.

"Here she is, New Cross' very own Kate Moss!" Giorgio threw his arms out to welcome Ashlyn to the garden.

Melissa and Ashlyn laughed.

"So what are we celebrating? Melissa was excited to hear their news.

"You've got an interview tomorrow with only one of the biggest event planners in London - to be her PA!" Giorgio popped the cork of the fizz as he finished his sentence.

Melissa couldn't believe it, she was automatically filled with excitement.

"Oh my god! How?"

"Well we're at a ladies brunch this morning doing some of the VIP's make up and Denny Okoro's PA quit, right in front of everyone! So we gave her a minute and then said we knew the perfect person for the job - Melissa Morgan, the fabulous Mancunian that has just moved in with us! Woop, woop!" Giorgio was almost more excited than Melissa.

"Yea, you've got it in the bag, she'll take one look at you and want to give you the job." Ashlyn beamed kindly.

"Oh no! I've not got anything to wear though. I know I got a few new things when I first got here but I've worn them loads now and I don't think they're right for an interview. Not one like this!"

"Well, it's only 12 o'clock, the day is young my friend. You've just sold your car and you have a stylist and a makeup artist at your disposal for the rest of the day!" Giorgio beamed.

She couldn't believe it. She felt so special, their kind gestures were gratefully received.

"OMG! We're going shopping!" Melissa couldn't contain her excitement.

"You're going shopping huni, we're the hired help - not that we want a penny - today it's all about you babe!"

They drank two glasses of fizz each, put their shoes on and headed on out to Oxford Street. The streets were bustling. It was the first time she had been to Oxford Street and it just felt amazing to be there. She walked along proudly, the sun was beaming down in between the tall rows of beautiful shops that lined each side of the street. She felt like she was in a wonderful dream. She could never have even imagined this would be her life a month ago.

They walked into the department store, the cool air conditioning was a welcome addition to the day. Giorgio led confidently, he switched into stylist mode and he was utterly fabulous at his job. Every time he picked something up, she was sure it wouldn't suit her, and each time she tried it on she was amazed at how good she looked. She felt like a star getting this kind of treatment. After they had sorted the clothes, they went to the Make Up department and it was Ash's turn to shine, she too was amazingly talented and very professional. Ashlyn knew one of the MUA artists on one of the counters really well and she assisted them too. They showed Melissa in the mirror and she couldn't believe who was staring back at her. She had never seen herself look this way ever before and it felt amazing. All the put downs and name calling were firmly at the back of her mind in that moment.

Now she could decorate herself in clothes, make up and jewellery, use them as the perfect disguise and make up feel the best version of herself that she can be. She once thought that dressing up would make her stand out, but now she realised it was so much easier to hide in plain sight. And hide her internal scars behind a fabulous and extravagant exterior. Nobody will ask prying questions when I look as together as this. She was so grateful to have Ashlyn and Giorgio's help, she would never have picked such bold colours and accessories by herself.

"Now, what are we going to do about your hair?" Giorgio pondered out loud, intently looking at Melissa as they rounded off their styling session.

"My hair? What do you mean?"

"Well darling, natural curls are fabulous n-all, but yours are looking a bit more like 'mi dinner' than Madonna!"

Melissa, although slightly insulted, couldn't help but laugh. Giorgio was so straight talking, he just said exactly what he thought without thinking. It reminded her of Liz, and it was a quality she admired. That may just have been the best insult that she has ever received, and she took it in the light hearted way in which it was delivered; she loved Giorgio, she thought he was tremendous!

Ashlyn was a little more demure. Melissa was intrigued by Ash, she had spent the same amount of time with the both of them, yet she felt like she had known Giorgio her whole life. She really enjoyed Ash's company and was enchanted by her style and beauty, yet she felt like she had so many layers beyond the one on the surface. Maybe she could see that there were hidden layers to Ash, as she was hiding so many herself. Ash was guarded too, and she couldn't help but feel intrigued as to why.

The guys had already booked her yet another surprise, an appointment with one of their Hairstylist friends for a cut and colour and told her that 'it was on them.' Her hair looked the best it had ever looked, they had magically transformed the heaviness out of her curls and made them light and bouncy again, her hair was a caramel blonde that weaved different shades between her curls. After her make over was complete and she had changed into one of her new fabulous outfits, they headed to the bar. They said it would have been a tragedy for her to go straight home looking like that. They'd had a lovely afternoon and she felt like she had bonded with them more than ever. What they had done for her was really special, it showed her that they truly care and she appreciated it more than they could ever know. When they got back home they all headed to their rooms. Ash and Giorgio had work the next day and she could hardly forget that she had her interview. She was nervous. She didn't want to let the guys down when they had been so kind in getting her an interview. She couldn't believe the opportunity, she almost felt unworthy and undeserving of it. She started to question whether she would be capable of doing a good job or not. As she closed the door behind her the doubt set in and the confidence she had felt earlier was fading fast. She went over to her dressing table to take her makeup off. She couldn't escape her reflection, she looked quite beautiful and it made her smile. The confidence that had escaped her, started to trickle back in.

At that moment she began to see visions of the little girl that she used to be. That little girl was brimming with confidence – she had lead roles in all of the school plays, she had an unwavering love for Art; with a real flair for drawing. She played on every sports team possible, winning many medals and trophies that made her burst with pride. Whatever she did, she gave it her all. She was so kind, polite and fun. She always strived to be the best that she could be at anything she did. When she looked at that little girl she smiled, she wanted to tell her that she loved her and that she was sorry that she had forgotten her but wasn't going forget her again. She remembered exactly who she was at her core, she wanted to be more like her again. She wanted to feel proud again of who she was, and she wanted to have others who loved her to share in her pride.

When she began to think about how far-removed she was from the young girl that she used to be, she fell into an extreme sadness. Her younger self had disappeared from her sight, and she'd became stranded again in the sea of self-doubt that she kept finding herself in. She felt like every time the lifeboat was in reach, that she would be swept out to sea again before she could climb aboard.

She was finding herself drowning daily in the memories of put downs, rejection and overwhelmed by flashbacks of her sobbing alone for hours each day. All those days wasted, just desperately searching to find even an ounce of love within her own home. Those feelings of weakness consumed her body all over again, as if she were back there once more. Just as she reached the depths of despair, she tried to pull herself out, telling herself she wasn't in that place anymore, she had escaped. She was free. So why didn't she feel free? Why couldn't she just move on.

As she went through this thought process, she remembered what helped her to wake up and begin to see the light at the end of the dark tunnel that she'd been trapped in for so long. A picture of Anthony's face glowed warmly within her thoughts, replacing the dark visions of Chris. She could see him smiling at her and the memories made her feel happy and warm inside. Her heart started to beat properly again, just as it did that first night when he began to revive her. She had believed that she was truly, madly, and deeply in love with him – in fact deep down she probably still was. Even if it wasn't ever real for him, it was certainly real for her. She reiterated the councillor's words about not actually being in love with him, that maybe she was just in love with the feelings he stirred up in her. That feeling of being alive and wanted. But how could she possibly know for sure? How could she distinguish between the two just by talking to her? After all, if he walked up to her right now, she knew she would struggle not to just fall straight back in her arms. Melissa glanced at her phone and longed for it to ring, what she wouldn't give for Anthony to see her like this. For his name to flash up. She still couldn't understand why he didn't call or message. She was sure he had loved her too. It can't all just have been pretence, it just couldn't have been, she was there, she felt it. She shook her head, annoyed at herself for falling into this whirlpool of destructive thoughts once again. She hated the fact that given the opportunity, she would allow him back into her heart instantly. The way he threw her under the bus and laid all the blame on her was unforgivable, so why was she longing to see him again? The anger she felt towards him and herself raged inside her. 'Why do I keep thinking and acting like this? Stop being a pushover! You are worth more than that Melissa!.' She needed to find a way to stop looking back and start looking forward.

She needed to show the world a new version of herself. The original version of herself, her true self that was fierce and capable. She needed to look after the little girl that she knew was still there inside her. She just wanted to erase the parts of herself that cared about other people too much. She wanted to stop herself from putting other people's thoughts and feelings above her own. She wanted to stop apologising for everything she said, and everything she did. She looked in the mirror again. She needed to get dressed up everyday, to remind herself of how capable she was.

She started to feel too warm and droplets of sweat started to run down her nose. She took her makeup off and stripped off her clothes. She wanted to get a good night's sleep so she was refreshed and ready to smash her interview the next day. She felt positive and she wanted to go to sleep feeling positive for a change.

She tossed and turned unable to get comfortable. Feeling more tired and irritable with each passing minute. The room was stifling, she got up to open the window a little further in an attempt to let in a little more breeze. She wouldn't be able to sleep with it wide open; the chances of anyone being able to climb up the three stories outside and come into her window were second to none but she didn't want to take the chance.

She threw herself back onto her bed and stripped off the t-shirt she had just put on to wear for bed.

She lay there naked, on top of her sheets and let the cool air breeze over her. She had desperately wanted to go to sleep with all the positivity of the day on her mind, but the longer she stayed awake the harder it was to keep the demons at bay. She didn't want to fight with her mind all night, so she needed a little distraction. It was late so she turned the TV down as low as it would go, but at the point where she could still hear it. Just as she started to engross herself in the film, there was a faint knock at the door. She looked at the clock, it was five past twelve. The faint knocking began again. She threw her T-shirt back on, pulling it down slightly to ensure her bottom half was covered and she tiptoed over to the door to see who it was.

It was Ash.

"Hey! I can't sleep, do you mind if I lie with you for a bit and talk?"

"Er, yeah, sure, it's roasting in here though, I can't sleep myself so I've just put the telly on."

"Yeah I heard you'd put it on, that's how I knew you were awake." She teased.

Ash only had an oversized t-shirt on too. Melissa became quite conscious that her t-shirt was a lot shorter than Ash's though, so she discreetly popped on some knickers before whipping her legs back round onto the bed.

They sat there in silence for 10 minutes.

"Are you ok Ash, you seem a little down?" Ash was never this quiet and Melissa couldn't help but wonder why she wanted to lie with her - apart from the heat, she could see that there was another reason, much like her own, as to why Ash couldn't sleep.

"I'll be ok, thanks babe." Ash took hold of Melissa's hand. Melissa didn't press any further and they just lay in silence, watching the film together until they fell asleep.

They woke up feeling refreshed, they both slept really well, like they were comforted by each other's presence. It was her big interview and she couldn't have had a better start to the day, than waking up feeling rested.

Melissa was slightly distracted though, as she couldn't help but wonder what had been on Ash's mind, and why for the first time had she seen one of Ash's hidden layers. It was a layer she could tell Ash didn't really want to show, but for some reason she had allowed Mellissa a glimpse of it. Melissa feared that, much like her, that Ash had a heavy heart that carried around huge weight, that for some reason she kept locked up inside

CHAPTER 5.

DRESSED UP IN ARMOUR

Already late for her first day at work, Melissa dashed towards the underground, frantically weaving her way in and out of the crowds on the bustling streets. As she ran past a large glass building on her left, she caught a glimpse of herself, and it stopped her in her tracks. She could hardly believe it was her. The reflection she found herself looking at these past few weeks, was a far cry from the one she saw in the mirror only a month earlier. She had got up at 6am to get start getting ready for her big day, but time had run away with her as she continuously titivated her look, she refused to turn up at her new job looking anything less than perfect – her image had become a big thing for her since she embarked on her new life. She no longer wants to hide herself in the shadows, afraid to be seen, she had found a new way to hide her inner torment.

With the help of her new friends, she had created a flawless exterior, an armour that hid all her scars. She smiled proudly, before someone knocking into her reminded her that she had a tube to catch and a new job to get to.

After a few stops, she left the tube to change lines, as the time ticked away and the crowds on the platform gradually increased with no sign of a tube anywhere, her nervous neck rash began to rage, her palms began to sweat, as she was suffocated by the warm air and masses of people. She felt trapped. As people pushed forward to squeeze onto the platform, she slowly found herself closer and closer to the edge.

'Someone's going to push me onto the track' she nervously thought. 'I need to move back. Oh god, what if he's here, watching and he pushes me!'

She found herself short of breath and her heart was racing. She was swirling into a whirlpool of panic again and she needed to pull herself out of it quickly. She desperately tried to focus, remembering some of the techniques she had been learning. 'Breathe through any moments of worry' she told herself. But before she could put them into practice, she was interrupted by a well-spoken lady who began to speak over the tannoid.

"Ladies & Gentleman, due to a person on the tracks at Oxford Circus, this line is now closed - please make alternative travel arrangements."

She was instantly pulled out of one anxiety, only to be catapulted into another. 'What do I do now? Where do I go?' She was still only just getting used to the intricate, overwhelming transport system in London and as the hordes of people on the platform began to barge past her, knocking her shoulders back and forth, she suddenly found herself swept up in a sea of people heading for what she could only guess was another form of transport.

Before she knew it, she had reached the top of the escalators, and the mob started to disperse. She felt a little vulnerable and worried as she didn't have a clue where to go next. She just hoped she wasn't giving off that 'worried-tourist' aura. She was so desperate to look strong and in control just like everyone else she seemed to come across in London.

'New job, new city, new you, remember! You've got this come on Liss, just calm down, deep breaths!' she told herself.

She fumbled around in her handbag to find her phone. Although the crowds had lessened, she still felt like she was in the way, as people continued to knock her from pillar to post as they hurried along on their daily commute. She managed to make it over to the entrance of the station and stand back against the wall to phone her new boss. Once the ringing tone kicked in, she could feel a lump begin to form in her throat, 'Don't cry Melissa, for god's sake, please don't cry!' The ringing ceased as a strong, rather abrupt voice just oozing with confidence put an end to the ringing.

"Denny Okoro, OKORO Events"

"D..D..Denny, hi….I ..erm…"

"Spit it out. Who is this?" she quizzed.

"Liss…er I mean Melissa, Melissa Morgan."

"Ah, Melissa, I was expecting you 10 minutes ago...not the best start on your first day"

'OMG!!!' she screamed inside and longed for the ground to swallow her up, she had messed it up before she had got there.

"No …Denny, it's not and I'm so sorry. I've been told to make alternative arrangements, someone's on the track and…and, well, I just don't know where to go now and I'm just. I'm really sorry…but I, I…"

Melissa looked upwards desperately trying to fight back the tears that were trying to escape from her eyes.

"Breathe Melissa, Christ!!' Denny joked to her. "Listen it's fine honey, I was only teasing, you'll get used to me! Were you on the Central Line? A few of the team are stuck too. Inconsiderate bastards, always killing themselves on my time! I'm going to take an early coffee break whilst everyone is on their way in but just get here as soon as you can, ok?"

Before Melissa could answer, the dialing tone played out. She couldn't decide if that was as bad as she thought it was going to be or not?

As she slowly composed herself, she replayed Denny's remark about the person on the track. Surely, it must have been a bad joke? At least she hoped she was joking?

"Woahhh!" Just as Melissa had turned to attempt to gain her bearings, a 6ft tall (and wide) man had knocked her to the floor without so much as a backward glance.

"Wanker!" she shouted, forgetting herself as she glared up from the dusty station floor.

"Yes, he was!" someone behind her said in reply.

As she looked up, she was met with a warm smile and a lovely looking, well-groomed man who was holding out his hand to her. As he pulled her up to her feet, her smile mirrored his.

"…are you ok?" he asked.

She felt a little flutter in her stomach as he continued to just stand there, smiling, and holding onto her hand. Having been so starved of affection for as many years as she was, it didn't take much to start her imagination racing when she was shown even the smallest bit of attention.

"Thank you! Honestly, I can't tell you how nice it is to see a smiling face, I'm having the worst day. I'm starting a new job today and…."

As Melissa continued to nervously 'waffle-on' (in a way that most people in London wouldn't dream of.) She suddenly took stock of this rather endearing man in front of her, who seemed utterly enchanted by her every word. She was well-aware she was still speaking, but she couldn't seem to stop herself from rambling on. She secretly inspected his face for any signs of boredom, but his big smile remained throughout. Although now it seemed as though her words were getting lost amongst the sounds of the city, as she could barely hear herself speaking. She paused for breath. Their eyes remained locked together as they waited for the background noise to fade. She quickly noticed the slightly awkward silence, she had finally stopped talking, the background noise had gone, and he still hadn't uttered a word. Suddenly the lingering eye contact made her feel uncomfortable. She released her hand from his and stepped back, she was now slightly unnerved by his seemingly 'odd' behavior.

"Anyway, I better go, as I said, it's my first day and I'm ridiculously late, so thanks anyway... bye!" Melissa swiftly spun round to walk away, when finally, he spoke. As she turned back towards him, she was drawn into his amazing eyes once again.

"Wait, don't go! I mean, you said you don't know where you're going, do you?"

"Oh yes! Ha, ha, no I don't! Can you help me please?"

"Of course, where do you need to get to?" His accent was very charming, almost prince-like.

"Marble Arch... please"

"Right, well, let me think. Well, it will cost you a ton in a taxi, so I'd get on the 346 bus"

"Great, thanks - take care then".

"Just a moment, sorry. I know this may seem a little forward, as we've literally just met, but could I have your number please? I would really like to take you for dinner one evening. I think you're lovely!" Melissa blushed and her heart quickened.

But she soon shut down the 'fantasy' that was already playing out in her mind, as the thought of dating a stranger terrified her, no matter how nice he seemed! The 'old-romantic' inside of her was screaming to give him her number but her fear was far stronger and took over her willingness to give it him. So, she did what she always did when she didn't want to be impolite, she gave a number but with one digit at the end different from hers.

"What's your name?"

"My name?"

"Yes, your name, you do have one, don't you?" he joked playfully.

"Of course, I have, well, it's just Melissa."

He placed her name in his phone, unable to contain his smile, "Well I'll look forward to seeing you soon, just Melissa."

She smiled awkwardly and began to walk away. She felt bad, knowing that he wouldn't be seeing her soon.

"Mine's James, by the way..."

Melissa turned her head back towards the ever so dreamy – James – and smiled.

"...just in case you wondered", he winked before turning away to go through the turnstiles.

His wink sent flutters flying throughout her stomach and she wanted to kick herself as she watched him walk away, "No I've done the right thing." She tried to assure herself. "Just because he seemed nice, doesn't mean he actually is nice, and anyway, even if he is as nice as he seems, now is not the time to start dating!" At that moment she realised she was talking out loud and she hurried away quickly in case anyone had heard her. She'd gotten in a bad habit of talking to herself of late, as pre-London there wasn't many other people to talk to.

A bus was approaching from further down the road, it was the 346, she started running as fast as she could towards the bus stop. She was flustered and sweaty, but she had made it in time and managed to jump on to the bus just before the doors closed. There was only one seat left, which she slumped down into with a sigh. She glanced at her watch; it was 9.45 am.

"Oh, for fucks sake!" she blurted out loudly, as onlookers turned towards the sound of her loud Mancunian voice. She blushed and grimaced slightly by way of an apology. She couldn't believe the time and how late she was for her first day. She had so desperately wanted to make a good impression, but she was off to a disastrous start. She took her pocket mirror out of her handbag and checked to see whether the beads of sweat that decorated her nose had ruined her makeup yet. Her hair looked wild and wispy, and she had smudged mascara on her eyelids. She took her wash bag out of her handbag and tidied herself up. At least then when she entered the building, she would be able to do so with confidence - when she finally arrived that was!

***

She was three days into her new job and the pain of her first day was finally behind her. She was surprised at how quickly she felt comfortable there. The story of her first day had tickled everyone in the office, even her boss Denny, and it seemed to ensure that everyone knew who she was. Although she had been successful in catching her bus, Melissa didn't arrive at work until 11.40am!

When she had frantically ran for the bus, she hadn't even thought about the direction she needed to go in and so she travelled for 45 mins through the rush hour traffic, cramped like tin of sardines, on the right number bus, but in the wrong direction! By the time she arrived she looked a far cry from the picture of togetherness that she had so desperately wanted to present. Denny had seemingly taken pity on Melissa and took her out for drinks after her first day, (or rather her first afternoon) and Melissa quickly realised that under that quite abrupt and intimidating exterior, Denny was really nice actually, and she had made sure that she felt looked after.

Melissa ended up sharing a heart to heart with Denny during the night; she only opened enough to share that she had just gone through a messy break up and was still finding her feet in London. After a few too many French Martini's and very little to eat and she had coincidentally ended up crashing out on Denny's apartment floor. Denny joked she at least could make sure she didn't take the piss the next day and roll in at dinner! She had certainly made quite an impression, and she felt extremely embarrassed when she woke up on her new boss' floor the next day.

Denny was the owner of OKARA Events and was a widely respected name in the events business. Melissa couldn't believe her luck at landing the role as Denny's personal assistant; whilst she figured out how to take charge of her own life, she couldn't think of a better way to spend her days than organising someone else's life instead, During their heart to heart, Denny had hinted that things hadn't always been easy for her, much like the conversations she had with Giorgio and Ash she realised that everyone is on a journey of some sort and that reassured her.

Over coffee earlier that morning. Denny had told Melissa that several the men of the office had been arguing over who would be asking her out first, which had ruffled the feathers of Stephanie, the company's front of house manager. Who up until Melissa's arrival had reveled in all the male attention herself.

Denny was incredibly beautiful, she was tall and slim, with very short afro-hair, she looked like she belonged on the catwalk rather than an office. She was super stylish, like she had just stepped out of a magazine, and she had brains and beauty in equal measure. The fact she was the boss, meant that no one dared to flirt with her at work let, alone ask her out.

Melissa found herself looking in the mirror trying to see what they could see, just as she was practicing a confident sultry look, in walked Stephanie. She had impeccable long, shiny mahogany hair and legs that went on forever. Denny had pre-warned Melissa about her, she was excellent at her job, but she had a reputation of being the office bike, whether the blokes were married or not, she considered them fair game. Denny had made it clear that Stephanie was not a 'girls' girl', a quality that she did not admire - nor did Melissa.

"Admiring yourself Melissa, that's not like you" Stephanie scowled, throwing her a dirty look as she waltzed past.

"Yes, I am actually you caught me; we all have to check ourselves in the mirror from time to time don't we Steph!" Melissa felt extremely intimidated, but she was determined not to let her know that. The one thing she set out to do every day at work was not show any weakness to anyone anymore.

"It's Stephanie actually, not Steph!"

"Sorry - Stephanie" 'Shit! Why have I just apologised to that bitch!' Melissa was annoyed at herself for allowing herself to feel belittled by some girl who has never even given her a chance. With her arms folded. Stephanie slowly started to strut towards Melissa.

"Listen!" Melissa felt herself being pulled round by Stephanie, as she gripped her arm just above the elbow. "You might be the youngest in the office now, but you are certainly not the prettiest, ok?!"

Melissa was completely taken aback by this woman, she had never even laid eyes on her before starting work, how could she have such a problem with her. She looked at her, completely dumbfounded. Surely that comment must have been joke. That, or despite Melissa's armour she could still smell her blood.

"I said, ok?" Stephanie glared at Melissa.

"Ok!" Melissa responded with a nervous laugh. She just wanted her to get off. She was desperately trying to stop herself from shaking, as flashbacks of Chris flashed through her mind as soon as she had grabbed her. Stephanie loosened her grip and released her blood red talons from around Melissa's arm.

"Well good because you can't just waltz in here playing besties with the boss and flirting with every guy in the building, so just remember your place!" Stephanie spoke with venom; she was not joking.

Melissa watched as she turned on her stiletto heels and marched back out of the toilets. Melissa was in shock; she couldn't believe that had just happened. She turned back to the mirror and watched as tears unexpectedly cascaded off her eyelashes. One by one they fell, and they kept on falling, she couldn't stop them. She rushed into the toilet cubicle and closed the door. She threw her arms around herself, she started rocking slightly. She bowed her head as the streams of tears continued. Images of Chris grabbing her played on loop in her head, with intermittent flashes of what just actually happened. 'Why did she do that? Why did you let her do that to you?!' An anger started swirling up inside her. She had been taken so off guard by what had just happened, she felt crazed with a mixture of emotions. She took some time to let the rush of upset and anger out. Then she made sure she composed herself once again before she headed back out of the cubicle. She had left her handbag by the sink, and she whipped it open quickly to grab her make up bag. She didn't want anyone to know that she'd been crying; especially Stephanie, she would probably take great satisfaction from thinking she had made her cry.

She had done her best to cover up the fact that she had been crying, but she was ready and armed with several excuses just in case anyone asked if she had. She had plenty of practice of hiding what was really happening. She didn't want Denny to see her as a wimp, so she had already decided that wasn't going to mention Stephanie's playground-like actions. She just wanted to forget it, along with all the horrible memories that had invaded her thoughts once again.

Melissa returned to her desk, relieved that Denny wasn't currently at hers. She was so disappointed in herself, she started to wonder, 'What was the point in coming to London if I'm just going to continue to let people push me around!' She needed to distract herself before she began to spiral, so she logged back into her computer and decided to throw herself into her work. She didn't need the rest of her lunch hour anymore; it wasn't like she could stomach any food now anyway. As she checked through her emails, one grabbed her attention...

From: James Dawson

To: Melissa Morgan

Re: Dinner Date

Hi, Just Melissa,

I hope you don't mind, I remembered you said you worked at OKORO, not hard for me to forget really seeing as Denny is one of my mate's sisters - small world! Anyway, I tried to call you, but it seems I have the wrong number? (I'm guessing you know that already? ;))

Again, I'm being forward, but I've found myself not being able to stop thinking about you and I would love to see you again, if you'd been kind enough to take me up on that offer of dinner one night.

- James (from the tube station) x

OMG!! A flurry of butterflies felt as though they'd danced into her stomach! Melissa had almost forgotten about her rendezvous with Prince Charming, but now the feeling rushed back and all she could picture was his gorgeous big smile and his enchanting green/blue eyes staring int?o hers. 'What should I do?' She couldn't believe that she hadn't given him the correct number because he was a total stranger, yet here he is telling her that he knows her new boss! Was it fate? Despite her newfound hard exterior, on the inside she was still yearning for affection and love as much as she ever was. At least the surprise email had brought a smile back to her face. She decided she would quiz Denny when she got back and see if she could find out a little more about James Dawson.

Melissa was so intrigued by James, she jumped on Denny as soon as she sat down.

"Denny?"

"Ah, Melissa, what can I help you with? Is it the venue change? They are letting us cancel, aren't they? We are within 90 days, so they better not be kicking off!"

"Er ...no, that's all fine, I cancelled that this morning. No, it's not work… It's about James, James Dawson, do you know him?"

"James, yes of course! He's been one of my little brothers' mates since forever...why do you ask? Do you know him?"

Melissa reminded her of her 'first day' story and the handsome stranger that picked her up off the floor. "The one I gave the wrong number to?" Melissa cringed as she said it.

"That was James!" Denny laughed. Denny insisted Melissa should go for it. Apparently, James was the perfect guy, who is everyone's friend and would be a 'big hit' with anyone's parents.

Melissa had her doubts thought. Surely no one is that perfect? Anyway, she had literally been in London for one month and she reminded herself that she needed to find herself before she found Mr Perfect. She needed to keep reiterating the pact that she had made with herself, to stay single for at least a year. Melissa replayed the conversations she had with her councilor, "Learn to love and respect yourself first, then the rest will follow."

Melissa's thoughts took her away from her conversation with Denny, and her hesitancy became transparent,

"What's wrong? Do you not like him? I thought you said you thought he was handsome?"

"Oh no! I did - he is handsome. I thought he was lovely. I'm just not looking to be in a relationship at the minute – not saying that's what he wants, but it could lead there, and I just need a bit of time...you know...to be on my own for a bit!"

"Look darling, I know you've only just come out of a long-term relationship, but, you know, you deserve some fun, going on dates doesn't have to turn into dating. And anyway, look, I've known James since he was a boy, he's never had a long-term girlfriend, it's always been a few dates max, so I'm pretty sure he won't be looking for that either! You should go for it, you're too young and gorgeous to be off the market completely my dear!" Melissa still didn't look convinced, especially now Denny had seemingly confirmed he was a player – if he never had more than few dates with a girl.

"Yeah, I don't know, I'm fine as I am at the minute, honestly."

Denny continued, unaware of the true reason for Melissa's strong reluctance.

"I've got an idea! Why don't you come out with us all, as a group, we've got something planned in a couple of weeks. Just come along as my friend, not James' date and see how you feel! You've got to get yourself back out there at some point or you'll forget how to play the field."

That was another reason that Melissa wanted to stay clear of dating, all the drama and game playing that came with it was just exhausting. She was so tired of second-guessing people's feelings and worrying about upsetting them. The only person she wanted to worry about right now was herself. She was finding it hard enough to stop herself from overthinking about her housemates and work colleagues, without throwing a love interest into the mix. She didn't want Denny to probe any further and make her think there was more going on than what she had told her, so she agreed to go along in a few weeks, and she told

James in a polite email that she would see him there.

To: James Dawson
From: Melissa Morgan
Re: Dinner Date
Hey James,
Wow, how strange is that! Small world indeed! I'm sorry about the phone number, I was so flustered that day!
I've just spoken to Denny actually and she has asked me to join you all in a couple of weeks when you are going to the clubhouse? So, I'll see you there. Thank you so much for the dinner offer, but after thinking about it, I've just got out of a long relationship and well, I just need to focus on me for a while.
Melissa x

Send.

She didn't want to let her past control her future, but she knew she needed to remain guarded. It had taken so much strength to claw her way out of her last relationship, all she wanted right now was to enjoy this new chapter of her life of being a single, successful woman, in an amazing city, without any complications. It seemed clear from her experiences that relationships caused her nothing, but pain and complications and she didn't want to go back down that road again. As thoughts of her past flooded her thoughts Melissa became lost in a trance, repeatedly tapping her fingertips on her desk and staring at the computer screen. Every time the past crept into her present it disturbed all her progress.

The sound of the phone on her desk ringing, jolted her back to the here and now, she jumped a little and leant over quickly to pick up the handset.

"Melissa Morgan, OKORO Events, how may I help you?"

"Ah Melissa, aren't we trying to be posh today?"

'Stephanie', Melissa's heart sank a little, she leaned back on her chair, focusing her eyes through the glass partition that separated the office from reception. She watched as Stephanie smoothed down her hair continuously, with a smug look on her face.

"You know Melissa, you are not allowed to make personal calls or send or receive personal emails during working hours?".

How did she know she'd just sent a personal email? Could she see her emails? It felt like a phone call from Chris.

"I'm sorry…" She automatically went into her apologetic mode, then something pricked at her thoughts and forced her to retract, 'Who does this girl think she is? I don't even know her?' Melissa felt infuriated and the anger she felt earlier bubbled to the surface, "...I wasn't aware that you was my manager now!"

"Excuse me, what do you mean by that exactly?"

"I was just apologising, as I didn't realise that you were my new manager. It's just that I was actually looking forward to speaking to my manager about some inappropriate behavior from another member of staff towards me in the toilets earlier today."

"Are you being sarcastic Melissa?"

"Me, no Steph."

"My name is Stephanie, and I was just saying, I was trying to look out for you, it's up to you if you want to get the sack! Just forget I said anything ok!"

She watched as Stephanie slammed the phone down and flicked her hair dramatically. Melissa felt amazing. She felt awash with pride and smiled to herself. It was only a small stand, but she had made a stand nonetheless and she was proud of herself. She needed to nip Stephanie's crazy behaviour in the bud. She leant in towards her desk and smiled! She felt a little less angry at herself about the incident in the toilets. She wasn't sure where her newfound courage had come from, considering that only an hour earlier she had felt like she was losing control again, maybe it was to do with the email from James that had boosted her confidence at precisely the right moment.

When Melissa returned home from work, she flipped off her shoes at the front door. Her feet were aching, she never realised how much walking she would do once she got to London. She removed her blazer and started unbuttoning her shirt. As she made her way upstairs to her room, she knew she was the only one at home as the house was so quiet. She untucked her shirt out of her pants and unbuttoned her top button. She reached her bedroom and removed the rest of her clothes. It was such a relief to remove her padded bra and pants that had been digging in her all day whilst she was sat down. Her heels were smarting with blisters and she couldn't wait to jump into a big baggy t-shirt and pj bottoms, they were still coordinated like everything she owned now, but they were comfy, oh so comfy. She piled her hair on top of her head and sat down at her dressing table. She pulled some cotton wool balls from one the jars dresser and soaked them in a cleanser. She paused and looked at herself, piece by piece she had removed her armour and all that was left to remove was her mask. She recalled how it had slipped today, but also, she had managed to reapply it without anyone noticing. She was doing a good job at playing the exciting new role that her life had led her to, but as she started to wipe the city off her face, tears gathered in both hers, her reflection became blurred until she blinked and she saw a true picture of herself, she was still broken, she was still fighting, she was still scared, and she was still hiding her true self. 'Will I ever feel like me again?'.

CHAPTER 6.

THE KISS

I t was Saturday morning and she had survived her first week at work, despite the disastrous start. Melissa was sat at the table with Ash and Giorgio - who only up because he had a hair appointment and Kieran was outside smoking.

"Hey I never told you guys, yesterday I got an email from that guy that helped me when I fell over on the tube. He knows Denny. He asked me to go out with him, I said no, but I'm going to go out with them all as a group in a few weeks."

"What's his name? If he knows Denny we might know him?" Ash asked.

"James Dawson?"

"OHHH he's that hot producer guy!"

"Giorgio, you make me laugh, you think everyone is hot!"

"Only if they're hot I do and he is HOT!"

They all giggled.

"Yeah, he is quite handsome and very successful, he's a nice guy from I know of him hun. Why don't you want to go out with him?"

"Oh you know, I'm just not ready for dating again. He was lovely but I just don't want to go down that road again yet."

"Well I've got to go to an sex toy party tonight and you my dear are coming with me! If you're single you need some toys to keep you happy!"

Ashlyn winked at her playfully.

"Me? But I don't know anyone?"

"You know me don't you?"

"I know but you don't want to be stuck talking to me all night because I don't know anyone else there."

"Honey, do you think I would be bringing you if I thought you would just sit there all night not saying a word to anyone? You always get on with everyone, you'll be fine!"

"Okay then, if you're sure."

"I'm sure."

"What should I wear?"

"Something sexy. It's in a bar so it will be like a proper party with a DJ etc."

"Oh ok."

"Bitches! Going out without me!" Giorgio was joking but not. "And I'm getting my hair done today, I'll be looking all fabulous with nowhere to go!"

"I'm sorry G, you know it's girls only. I wouldn't go anywhere without you normally - you know that!"

"Aww, can you not come Giorgio; I feel bad now. Shall we not just stay here instead, or go out all together?"

"Yes! Now there's a plan!" Giorgio exclaimed.

"No! I can't not go. We'll come back and have drinks with you when it's finished G and we can have a laugh about all the things we buy!"

"Fine! But make sure you bring me some goodies back!" Giorgio was unable to hide his disappointed face. He hated it when he wasn't allowed to join in on girls night.

"Sorry Giorgio!" she felt really bad for him.

"It's fine babe, I'm only joking, you have fun and I'll see you later. I'll prob go down to the club anyway and show off my amazing blue hair!" Giorgio put on a smile and gave a wink.

"Blue?" Ash looked unsure.

"Yes babe, blue!"

Melissa started worrying about the party. She wasn't just thinking of Giorgio when she was trying to get out of going, she didn't really want to go herself. She just wasn't sure she was ready to be in a room full of women where the topic was mainly sex and sex toys that she knew nothing about. She didn't want to let Ash down though after she had been so good with her.

The evening was actually a lot more fun than Melissa had anticipated. They had played some hen party style games, watched a presentation on sex toys, bought several items of sex toys and drank lots of shots. Now they were dancing away on the dance floor.

The club was really dark apart from the momentary strobe lights flashing on and off. The smoke machine also added to the sense of drama in the club. She'd seen another new side of Ashlyn tonight, she was so relaxed, quite daring and lots of fun. They were in their element dancing to one good track after another, the songs were getting sexier and sexier in the lyrics and the beat and they started dancing close together, laughing as they bumped and grinded with each other. Then Ashlyn took her completely by surprise as she kissed her. It was like the music was switched off and everything had gone into slow motion. She felt rude not kissing her back, although she wasn't entirely sure whether she wanted to or not. Yet she proceeded to do so anyway. For a moment she was stunned but then …she was surprised that she actually found herself enjoying the kiss. Her lips were soft, and her kiss was so sensual and gentle. This kiss lasted for quite a while, it was like a marathon in kissing. When they finally stopped kissing, they carried on dancing and didn't say a word about it.

Melissa felt a little awkward when they got back home. Has their relationship changed now? Was Ashlyn Gay or Bi-Sexual? She didn't know, she hadn't asked her. Now she'd kissed a girl, did it mean she was bi-sexual? As they got to the top of the stairs, both swaying from all the shots they had consumed, Ashlyn leaned in for a cuddle and kissed her on the cheek.

"Night hon! Great night!" Ashlyn waved as she stumbled into her room, closing the door behind her as her eyes started to close.

Melissa was a little relieved. When Ash had stayed over the other night it was completely plutonic, she was confused now though. She decided it was just to go to bed and try and forget it. Perhaps thats what your meant to do at a sex toy party? Who knows? They were both really drunk so it was probably down to that. She climbed in bed and snuggled into the pillows.

KNOCK, KNOCK!

"Oh shit!" Melissa's heart raced as she was woken by a gentle knock on the door.

"Oh, fuck it's her" she whispered to herself.

She lay frozen to the spot as she tried to rush through a conversation with herself. 'She's here because she wants to sleep with me! Do I want to sleep with her…no, no, I don't. What if we do it and then I realise I don't want that then I will ruin everything! I'll have to move again! I can't move again! Where would I move to?"

KNOCK, KNOCK

'She knows you're in here, you daft cow. So open the door, just open the door. It will all be fine!'

"Shit, ok!" Melissa jumped off the bed, giving her hair a quick ruffle as she rushed past the mirror above the fireplace towards the door. Thoughts whirling through her head as she reached out her trembling hand to open the door.

As she opened the door the light from the landing blinded her temporarily

"YO, BITCH! I won't ask what took you so long!"

"Oh, it's you!" Melissa sighed with relief, and a little disappointment as Giorgio proceeded to enter her room.

"I'm in the mood for an adventure! So come on, get dressed!"

"What now?!"

"Yes, now bitch! You don't need to get dressed up; you'll be fine like that. Just throw your trainers on and your coat! I've got a plan!"

"What about Ash, are we not asking her to come too?"

"No, I've not had a midnight adventure with you yet. So it's just you and me babe!"

"She hopped as she attempted to put her trainers on. Although she was still a little worse for wear from all of the shots she'd had earlier so that didn't help. She threw on her big coat to cover up her loungewear.

"OK, I'm ready!"

"Woo hoo!" Giorgio scooped her up and swung her round,

"Let's go bitch!"

They both laughed.

They got off the tube and there were some bikes parked up that had a two-seater seat on them and lights and music.

"Oh my god, I've always wanted to get on one of these! Let's get one to take us to the palace!"

Melissa smiled, "Oh yes let's!"

There was something exhilarating and terrifying in equal measure about being on one of them bikes weaving in and out of the London traffic. The cheesy pop music blasted out from the bike and they laughed nonstop together in between screaming as they frequently thought that they would get squashed in between a bus and a black cab. The bike went much faster than they imagined, and the wind blew their hair all over. Giorgio kept shouting out to any groups of lads that they passed and Melissa was in hysterics every time.

When the driver pulled over and said that was as far as he could take them, they were sad to get off.

"Aww, that was so much fun! It went too fast!"

"I know I thought we'd have been on longer than that for twenty quid! But at least I won't get blisters on my feet now from walking. Although it still looks like a bit of a walk from here!"

Melissa laughed, Giorgio's shoes were just as flamboyant as everything else he wore, and she loved everything about him. She loved how outrageous he was, how confident he was. The air was quite cold tonight, and they could see their breath as they chatted.

"Gosh, it's colder than I thought it would be!"

"That means you haven't had enough alcohol; we need to get your beer coat on! Where's the shop?"

Giorgio was turning rapidly from side to side, trying to spot somewhere that they could get some alcohol from. "There!" he exclaimed, pointing further up the street to a convenience store and linking her before strutting towards it.

When they got there the man behind the counter said he wasn't allowed to serve them alcohol now as it was too late. Giorgio was not about to let any rules get in his way of his adventure, he started to plead with the man and offered him some extra cash if he would let us have some discreetly. Melissa admired his determination not to let anything get in the way of the fun that he wanted them to have. So she too joined in the pleading. Eventually he said they could have half a bottle of vodka if they popped it up their sleeve and they bought some other things too.

"Go grab us some Coke hun…oh no know you don't like vodka, do you?"

"I don't mind it, just not with Coke. I'll get some Orange juice or something, don't worry it's fine."

She grabbed the bottles of pop and juice, and Giorgio asked for some cigarettes. Then they scurried out of the shop door like a pair of teenagers who had just got away with being served despite being underage.

They set off walking across the park, the paths were only slightly lit by some rather dim lights.

"Where are we going Giorgio?"

"I told you to the palace!"

"What is Buckingham Palace? I'm not sure that the Queen will thank us for calling on her at this time of night!"

"Who needs the Queen when you're with the King darling!" Giorgio laughed out loud, his laugh was infectious, and it was impossible not to join in, even when you weren't exactly sure what he was laughing at.

"Ok, so we're going to the palace to do what exactly?"

"To soak up the royal atmosphere babe, whilst drinking on the steps of the statue, well, until the police chase us off!"

"Ok, sounds fun!" Melissa really did feel like a teenager again when she heard that and it felt good, it was like she was doing some of the silly things that she should have been doing during the years that she had lost. It made her feel hopeful that she could claw back some of the experiences she missed out on in the years gone by.

Giorgio stopped on the path and pulled the vodka out from his sleeve, as they both giggled. "Right, let's sort these drinks out! Drink some of that so that we can pour some Vodka in it." Melissa struggled to drink the drink and stop it from going down her nose at the same time, as she could stop laughing. She wasn't sure why she found the whole thing so hilarious, other than the night was just so silly and daft. There was not one ounce of seriousness, she didn't have to second guess anything, she didn't question whether she was good enough company, or whether she was dressed right. She felt at complete ease in Giorgio's company and it felt so refreshing.

"Let's spin round, it will go to our heads faster!" Melissa blurted out, still laughing freely.

"Excellent idea!"

They both started spinning around as fast as they could whilst drinking from their bottles, before they went dizzy and started falling into each other, making them howl as they ended up entangled in a ball together on the ground. They helped each other up, chuckling non stop.

"To the palace, let's go!" They linked each other again as they swayed their way towards Buckingham Palace.

Giorgio was right, this place did have an atmosphere. It was magical, like a place where dreams could come true. Just like when she first stepped out of the house when she first arrived, once again it was as if London's pulse was pumping through her veins and providing her with a lifeline.

"Do you come here often?"

"Now listen babe, I like you a lot, but don't start chatting me up because I'm not that way inclined, ok!" Giorgio couldn't help but laugh at his own joke and Melissa shook her head at his daftness and joined him in laughing.

"Do you want a cigarette?"

"Yes please!"

Giorgio leant forward to light Melissa's cigarette for her, before lighting his own. He inhaled deeply and then exhaled.

"I do like to come here sometimes, yes, usually when I'm feeling a bit lost. It reminds me of my parents, they are big on the royal family. That's part of the reason they moved to London in the first place, so that my mum could say we lived in the same city as the queen! They used to bring me and my brothers and sisters down here most weeks and we'd sit with a picnic and wait until they changed the guards."

"Aww that's cute. You don't feel lost today though, do you Giorgio?"

"A bit...I don't really like to admit it but yes, somedays I do. I'm just good at hiding it behind the bravado."

"Why do you feel lost?"

"Oh you know, just life sometimes it can feel overwhelming, some days I miss my family, somedays I want to be someone else."

"Why would you want to be anyone else? You're amazing! I admire you so much!"

"Why thank you my darling! You too are amazing! I just wish everyone thought I was amazing. I can't help but feel my family would be happier if I was a straight guy, running the family restaurant and wearing normal clothes with a bunch of kids dangling from their legs. Sometimes I feel like I have let them down, you know!"

"Oh I'm sure that's not the case, I'm sure they are immensely proud of you, just as you are!"

"Maybe, maybe not,they say there, they have never said anything to make me feel otherwise. But you know sometimes you can't help but wonder, but hey ho, I am what I am darling, I can't run away from it and I don't want to most of the time, so I just get on with it and try and live my best life!"

Melissa could sense that Giorgio wanted to end the conversation there, so she helped to change the subject. "Here, let's top up the vodka in these bottles!"

"I'll drink to that my darling!"

As Giorgio poured the vodka into the bottles, they heard someone shouting.

"Excuse me ladies!" It was a policeman heading over their way.

"Oh shit!"

"I told you they would come chasing us off! Run!"

They both laughed hysterically as they jumped down the steps of the statue and started running back towards the park. They had to stop running after a while to catch their breath.

"Shall we go home now?" Melissa asked.

"Yes, we'll take this party back to my room!"

They got back home and partied in Giorgio's bedroom, until she passed out drunk on his bed.

CHAPTER 7.

HOLDING BACK

She was so excited to be attending her first professional event. She couldn't believe Denny had asked her to join her when she had only been there a couple of weeks. As she walked into the room she was stunned to James Dawson standing there.

"Hi!" he gasped.

"Oh hi! I didn't know you was going to be here." Melissa was glad she got that whole new wardrobe of clothes now so that she always dressed for the occasion should surprise encounters like this occur. She couldn't help but smile. The same flurry of feelings that she got when she met him came flooding back and she knew she was in dangerous territory when it came to James. There was something about him that made her feel happy. Every time he sent an email, he had managed to make her smile. He had a great sense of humour, and it was like his warmth radiated through the computer screen. She only met him once, yet she felt like she had known him for a long time.

"You look beautiful." James smiled with both his mouth and his eyes.

He had kind face, that was handsome too, she felt very attracted to James, seeing him for the second time confirmed that to her.

"Oh, well I wouldn't say that but thank you." Melissa could feel herself blushing. She was getting a bit flustered, she wasn't prepared for this, it had caught her off guard. She wasn't able to put a front on the same way when she wasn't prepared. Her true feelings were harder to hide when she was took by surprise. "Anyway, I best find Denny, I haven't said hello yet. "she needed a reason to move away from James before she fell madly in love with him.

"Okay, hopefully see you throughout the evening anyway." James' smile was almost intoxicating, she could feel herself being pulled into him, it was like she could feel his feelings. He was so open that she could see right inside him and he was letting her know he had feeling for her. She suddenly got a huge smile on face and couldn't help but beam back, "Yes, hopefully."

She walked away knowing they would find a way to start talking again and it unnerved her. Her gut was telling that there was something about James that was good. But she had only been separated from Chris for just over 2 months and there was no way that she was in the right place to go into a relationship. The thought of putting her heart back out there before it has even properly healed, was just beyond scary. It almost made her feel sick. The idea of feeling heartbroken all over again before she'd even glued the pieces of her heart back together was just too much to bear. Just the mere thought of it made her feel ill and she didn't know if she could ever do it again! That thought of letting go and diving in with two feet, diving into another relationship was just too scary. She knew she wasn't strong enough to survive another heartbreak. She could only hope that one day she would feel differently.

She spotted Denny and went over to her.

"Hi Denny!"

"Hi Melissa, I was just talking about you. Don here was asking me about work, and I was telling him all about my new PA and how she was making my life so much easier!"

"Oh, that's nice to hear thank you!"

It really was, as Melissa had felt like she was stuck in 3rd gear at work, and she couldn't figure out why? Her work ethic was unfaltering, until recently, she knew she wasn't doing the best job she could yet, but somehow, she was doing a good enough job that she'd impressed Denny. She hoped that she would be firing on all cylinders at work again soon as she had missed that sense of achievement and praise you get from doing an amazing job! So it was nice to receive some again she thought.

"Have you seen James yet Melissa? I've just spotted him over there. I love that I get to bump into him at these work things now. He's done so well for himself. Why don't you go and ask him to join us Melissa?

Don, James is a producer. He's a friend of my brother's so I've known him for a very long time, he'd be perfect for your upcoming project you know?" Denny turned back to Don, obviously pitching James to him. 'She must respect him if she is recommending him to people.' Melissa thought. She knew she'd better just go and get James like Denny had suggested. But she just knew she was going to fall for his charm, so she was reluctant to be in his company. She turned back to Denny; she was still deep in conversation with Don. This was her first work event and she wanted to be an asset to Denny, so she needed to be professional and go and invite James over.

She walked over to him boldly. He had just stopped laughing along to something with another guy in a suit.

"James, I'm sorry to disturb you."

"Don't be. Are you ok?"

"Yes, Denny was wondering if you would like to come and join us."

"Denny was wondering?" James had a cheeky glint in his eye.

"Yes. Denny was wondering. She's talking to some guy called Don about you."

"Some guy!" James couldn't help but chuckle, "He's a really well know scriptwriter."

Melissa felt a little foolish, but this world was all new to her and she far from knew everyone in it.

"Yes, well. I didn't know that before, but I know that now! And you are officially going to help me by pointing out anyone that should know and embarrassingly don't on our way to them." Melissa pulled a cringe face, although she felt a bit red faced, it was unusual for her not feel humiliated by making even just a small mistake. It was a breakthrough that she had managed to find the moment humorous too.

"Deal! I won't let you down, don't worry." James winked at her as they walked back over towards Denny, who was sat in a booth with Don and two others that Melissa hadn't been introduced to yet.

"Who are they?" James whispered as they continued across the room.

"I don't know!" Melissa didn't know if he was testing her to see if she needed his help or if he didn't know himself.

"Me either!" James laughed,

Melissa felt relieved in some ways, she felt she was the only one in the room that didn't know everyone and wasn't known by anyone. Like she wasn't really a someone. Now she knew James' didn't know everyone either, it made her feel a little less alienated.

They had a fabulous night. She couldn't believe how lucky she was to be sat around the table with such interesting and successful characters. Including James. She had enjoyed his company so much and his incredible ambition only made him more attractive. She was so pleased that they were in a professional setting though so that things couldn't escalate. She had far too many wines to have been in James company alone, she had pictured kissing him at least once tonight and she knew her walls were crumbling. She thought she may have to cancel their next night out they have planned in a couple of weeks as she didn't trust herself not to fall for James, he was so nice. But every time she thought about how nice he was, an image of Anthony came into her head and she recalled how she'd felt at the beginning when she believed he was a nice guy too.

"Well I've had a fabulous night but I better get going so that I don't miss the last train." Melissa announced.

"You can't go getting the train now. Get a taxi!" Denny insisted.

But Melissa had already checked how much it would cost in a taxi and it was way too much. She needed to calm her spending at the minute. She had spent her last wage and the money from the sale of her car, on two months of rent, a whole new wardrobe, redecorating her room and make-up. She had turned to her credit card now until she her first wage from

OKORO, and of course she was still waiting on Chris buying her out of the house. But she knew from the solicitor's letter that she'd received only that morning saying Chris wasn't responding to his solicitors', from that she knew it was going to drag on. She thought by offering to take less money meant that it would have been over and done with sooner, but Chris had no intention on ending things quickly. She knew he would make it as awkward as possible to be rid of him.

"Oh, I'll be fine." Melissa shrugged off their suggestion of a taxi.

"It's fine I'll give you a lift. The company sorted me a car out for tonight. I just need to phone the driver when I'm ready. So, we'll drop you off." She appreciated James kind offer and she couldn't quite believe he had a driver! She couldn't help but think what is wrong with him. What was he hiding? Like Anthony he must be hiding something? No one is that nice, she's learnt that the hard way.

She just needed to keep her guard up, romantic ride home a driver not!

A black shiny Mercedes pulled up outside the venue and James opened the door for her to get in.

"Thank you!" Melissa was kicking herself that he was a gentleman too! He was ticking too many boxes and it was torturous. Melissa felt a little more drunk than she had when she was in the venue. The fresh air had hit her whilst waiting for the car.

"Thanks so much for taking me home, James, I really appreciate it."

"Of course, it's my pleasure." There he was again, saying all the right things with his prince charming voice!

They chatted all the way home, she was sure James had come majorly out of his way to take her home, but she couldn't ever gage how things were in London, only by tube and train.

"Oh, this is me. Thank you!" Melissa shouted forward so the driver would know where to stop.

"I've really enjoyed tonight, Melissa, I would love to do it again." James looked hopeful that she would agree.

"I know, have too, but I can't go out with you James. I'm sorry it's not that I don't want to because honestly I do, as I've told you it's just not right for me right now."

"I take it a goodnight kiss is out of the question then?" James grinned cheekily.

Melissa smiled and rolled her eyes. "James!" He was leaning in towards her slowly, it was slow enough that could stop him, but she couldn't bring herself to. Apart from that drunken kiss with Ashlyn she hadn't kissed anyone since Anthony and she longed to have a passionate embrace again. She couldn't help it, she leaned in to kiss him too. It was an amazing kiss, not too frantic, not too slow, she could feel their hearts starting to race and she had to stop. She really was in danger of getting swept away by James and she needed to protect herself.

"Goodnight, James." She said as she pulled away and opened the door.

"Goodnight." James couldn't take his eyes off her and he was smiling from ear to ear.

CHAPTER 8.

LOOSING CONTROL

Having maxed out her credit card Melissa now had several outfits to choose from. Some mini Moet's were chilling in the new ice bucket that she had got for her room and her 'getting ready' playlist was blasting from her I-Pod.

Melissa had spent the whole morning shopping with Ashlyn and Giorgio, they had picked out everything for her big evening out and worked their professional magic again. She decided to take her time getting ready throughout the afternoon, so that she could look her absolute best. The only time ever that Melissa's room would be seen with anything out of place was whilst she was getting ready. Her obsessive cleaning had got decidedly worse since moving to London, knowing everything was clean and in place made her feel a bit more in control of things, but in that moment, it was as if a tornado had hit her room and she couldn't have been happier.

Melissa had really started to put her own stamp on her room now that she had begun to feel comfortable there. Giorgio had told her that she could do whatever she wanted with the space. She never even realised that her interior style and colour schemes actually reflected just what she really wanted out of life, for things to be simple, clear cut with no fuss, with a hint of glamour that she secretly craved. It was small, yet perfect. It was just what she needed, it was hers and it felt like home.

Tonight was her first proper night out with her boss and she felt nervous. She was frightened of drinking with her and her friends in case she let her guard down. But in the other breath she really wanted to go and have a drink with them, as she found the best way to break the ice. She especially wanted to bond more with Denny, she really enjoyed herself last week.

She was also looking forward to seeing James again. There was undeniable spark. It was the first time that she had felt like that since Anthony, but she just couldn't embark on a new relationship right now and she especially wouldn't want to have one that was attached to work. Her career was always her saving grace, a reason to focus and the last thing she wanted to do was mess with it. She had emailed James the next morning, after that brilliant Thursday night and that incredible kiss, to just reiterate that as much as he had an amazing time, she really didn't want to date or anything but she would love to keep in touch and become friends. That was easy enough over email, but she just wasn't sure how she would manage tonight, when he would be right there in front of her.

As she walked into the bar and sat down. She noticed James smile instantly, he looked thrilled to see her again, he could hardly take his eyes off her nor stop smiling. She was introduced to a couple of people sat around the table

"And finally, my little brother Callum." Said Denny as she pointed in his direction.

"Charmed to meet you, Melissa!" he reached out for her hand and kissed it like she was playing his queen in an old period drama.

Melissa laughed nervously as he did. She didn't know how to react, so she said nothing back. She sat down at the table still a little nervous, so when Denny said she was getting a round in, she jumped at the chance to get a large glass of wine.

The drinks were flowing, as well as a lot of flirty exchanges between herself and James. Although she wasn't ready for a relationship, there was something about James that kept pulling her in. She had decided that although anything serious was a no go, she was ready to have a bit of fun and as long as she could keep her guard up, she could do a lot worse than to have that fun with James.

He was handsome, charming - maybe a little too charming and he made her laugh. Callum and a few of the other guys from work were also flirting with her and she shamelessly lapped up the attention. It was the first time she had properly felt like she was able to have attention and enjoy it guilt free. She knew that any one of them would have happily accepted an invitation back to her bed and it felt really empowering to feel like she was the one who could decide.

"Right, who's round is it now?"

"Oh it's mine! I haven't bought a drink for anyone yet. What does everyone want." She got up from her chair, by now she was full of confidence and at the point where she should probably stop drinking before she relaxed a little too much and dropped her guard any further. But it was her round, the night was still young, and so was she, so she was not about to make a sensible choice.

"I'll come and help you!" James went to get up from his seat. Melissa smiled at James, before Denny interrupted,

"No! I want to go with her." she insisted, jumping up, as James sat back down. Melissa could only hope that one day she would be as assertive as Denny was.

As Denny and Melissa stood at the bar waiting to be served, Melissa glanced back over at the table they were all sitting at, she had a feeling they were looking over at them, as she turned round, she noticed James gazing over and he smiled at her. She smiled back before taking a deep breath and turning back around, she feared the way she was starting to feel about James was very dangerous..

"Well, I can't imagine anyone being more of a hit than you are Melissa!"

"Oh," she laughed, "I'm sure that's just down to me being the new girl on the scene."

"Well it may be a bit of that I suppose, but honestly I've never seen them all like putty in a girls hands before, I'm a little jealous - what is your secret! And my god especially James, man has he got it bad for you girl!"

"Oh, I'm sure he has and probably every other girl in here too!" she joked back.

"No, honestly I've known James a long time and he doesn't get like this. He's never been with a girl for more than a few weeks. He never gets serious with anyone, not like he is about you."

Denny reassured her, only it didn't reassure her, she wondered what on earth she was going on about? Nothing serious was happening? She had made that clear from the start!

"When you went to the toilet before, he told the guys to stop getting their hopes up, that you were his, that he had seen you first!" Denny laughed, "he made sure he marked their cards!" Denny continued to chuckle, not realising what that comment had just triggered within Melissa.

She could feel the anger bubbling up inside her. 'How dare he! Just because he likes me. It doesn't mean he can lay claim to me. I've already told him I don't want a relationship!'

She glanced over at him, her eyes burning with fury. 'I will not be controlled again! How dare he!' As James caught sight of her, he instantly began to smile just like he had all night, but it was fleeting, and soon faded into a look of confusion as he was taken aback by her deathly glare.

As they made their way back over to the table with the drinks, Melissa felt more and more annoyed as she replayed what James had said to everyone. 'He obviously isn't as nice as he makes out - what a surprise!' Her mind was going into overdrive, as flashbacks of Anthony's & Chris's false promises flooded her thoughts. As she handed everyone's drinks over, she slammed James' pint down in front of him. As she sat down, she turned her chair away from him so that she almost had her back to him. She couldn't even look at him, she was so angry.

"So Callum, tell me about your job again? It sounds really interesting what you do. I like a guy who's good with his hands!" She leant forward as she asked and placed her hand on his inner thigh, smiling with a suggestive glint in her eyes.

Callum looked a little taken aback but reciprocated her flirtation right back.

"Well, yes, I have been told that I'm very good with my hands."

Melissa let out an over the top laugh and gently squeezed his leg.

As the evening continued, herself and Callum grew closer and closer in proximity, sparks were flying between them and it was clear for all to see. Melissa's speech became more and more slurred and her vision was blurry. She had frozen James out completely, ignoring every attempt he made to talk to her until he had eventually given up and sat quietly nursing his pint. She glanced round and saw him looking rather glum. She didn't feel sorry for him in the slightest, she was just relieved she had figured out the type of character he really was before she got too close to him.

She leaned in further towards Callum and whispered in his ear.

"Shall we get out of here?" She had completely forgotten that Callum was Denny's brother, she wasn't thinking about what Denny or anyone might think of her, she wasn't thinking about her job or about anyone else's feelings. She was too many drinks in and too clouded by red mist to care what anyone would think of her outrageous flirting. She wanted to prove a point. She wasn't his property to warn people off and that she could do whatever she wanted. She was the only one in charge of her life and no one else! She felt so angry, she couldn't understand why men thought that they could use her and control her. She was absolutely determined to be an independent and strong woman. She wanted to be in control, she had spent so long spinning out of control, that it was time to reclaim that back.

As she leant back from Callum's ear, she backed up her invitation to leave with a sultry stare. He simply nodded with a smile and got up from his chair, holding Melissa's hand. Melissa stood up too.

"We're going to the bar." Callum announced knowing full well that they were actually leaving.

Melissa didn't even look to see if anyone was reacting; she simply followed Callum's lead making their way to the bar. The stairs out of the club were just to the left of the bar and at this point she couldn't help but look back over at the table. No one was looking at them other than James, he looked so genuinely sad, it pulled at her heart strings momentarily. But that feeling of guilt made her feel weak and she reacted by pulling Callum assertively towards the stairs, looking straight at James as she was doing so. She didn't wait for him to react and quickly turned away. She just wanted to make sure that he could see, so that he would get the message that she was her own person and that she did not belong to anyone.

Melissa stumbled out of the door, onto the street and Callum lifted her up into his arms and carried her as they kissed. His hands were all over her. She could tell how much he wanted her. She felt sexy and confident in the way she did the first time with Anthony.

Melissa pulled away from kissing him for a moment, "Flag down a taxi, let's go to mine!"

Callum spun her around and they giggled as he nearly dropped her.

Their taxi ride home was filled with foreplay, they kept forgetting where they were and nearly taking things too far.

"Right, £16.80." The taxi driver abruptly interrupted a heavy kissing session. Callum reached into his pocket for his wallet, neither of them could stop kissing each other, he threw £20

143

through the opening to the driver and they got out of the black cab. As they walked up the steps to the front door, Melissa fumbled around her bag for her door keys. Once she found them, she lifted her finger to her lips gesturing for Callum to be quiet. She opened the door quietly, she could hear everyone in the kitchen so she grabbed Callums hand, closed the door behind them carefully and led him upstairs, bouncing off the walls as she did.

As soon as they were in her room, they were ripping each other's clothes off. She didn't even get chance to take her top and bra off before they were having sex as he bent her over her couch. It was fast and frantic. She was making all the right moves, but there was a part of her that wasn't there. She stopped and turned around, pushing Callum and down onto the couch and she straddled him, as they started having sex again she felt better in this position, like she was more in control. She was the one who initiated this and she was the one who wanted to take the lead. He pulled down her top and bra and began to suck and pull on her nipples. It was too intense and a little rough, and she didn't didn't like it, so she moved his hands away. He wrapped his arms around her waist and lifted her up as he stood up, he walked over to the bed carrying her and they continued in the missionary position. She wasn't sure how long had passed but they had switched positions numerous times, although neither of them had come yet, she wasn't sure if that was the fact they'd had too much to drink or another reason? It was some of the most adventurous sex she had ever had and never the kind she imagined she would have with someone she had only just met. It was a physical release, mentally it was exciting, it made her feel sexy and powerful as they both fought to take the lead. The sexier she felt, the more confident she became. There was something in the fact that they both knew that it was just sex, nothing more. It felt good that the vulnerability of feelings were not there. Of course, she cared a little about what he thought about her, but for once, all she mainly cared about was how she felt. In those couple of hours no-one else was on her mind, for the first time in a long time and it felt so liberating.

CHAPTER 9.

IN THE LIGHT OF DAY

When she woke up her body felt achy and she stretched out before she opened her eyes, her head was banging and she rubbed her eyes as tried to open them. She realised that they were stuck together with last night's mascara. 'Last night!' Her eyes widened to see Callum lying next to her fast asleep. She replayed the events of the night before and a wave of dread hit the pit of her stomach. She didn't remember falling asleep, but she could remember bits of what had happened. As she recalled various snippets of the night and pieced them together she remembered how brazen and heartless she had actually been.

As she started to relive acting so callously, she felt sick. She wanted to wake Callum, she wanted him out of her bed, but equally she didn't want him to wake up as she didn't want to speak to him. He would be expecting to wake up to the person he met last night, the person he went to bed with, only she wasn't that person. She didn't recognise that person and she didn't want to see her ever again. She felt sick, she had only just met this guy, now he was sleeping in her bed. She lay there wondering what to do, then she realised she had no clothes on. She carefully got out of bed and reached to her bottom drawer to take out a nightie to put on. Even though he had seen it all last night, she didn't feel comfortable with him seeing her today. She had no sooner slipped it on when Callum started stirring. He opened his eyes and looked straight at her with a smile.

"Good morning Sexy!"

The comment made her feel uncomfortable, she didn't want to receive any flattering comments, she felt cheap and she wanted to wallow in that feeling so that she would never do it again..

"Oh, morning, I was just getting ready, I'm in a bit of a rush because I need to go out today, so I best start getting showered and everything."

"Oh ok, no probs." He just lay there, much to Melissa's dismay, and he didn't move. He seemed more than comfortable in her presence, so why wasn't she comfortable in his? He reached for his phone and started reading it.

'Just tell him to go!' Her mind was whirring with an array of thoughts, the main one being she needed him out of her sanctuary and fast. It felt tainted now and she was desperate to eradicate it from her memory.

"Oh, I've got a text from Denny moaning at me." Callum rolled his eyes.

"Why, what has she said?" Melissa's stomach churned. 'Oh god, why would Denny be annoyed?'

To her surprise Callum handed her the phone so that she could read the message.

FROM DENNY - James was really upset after you two left last night. He went home pretty much straight away. He tried to hide it, but he looked gutted. Did you have to do that James? He wouldn't ever do that to you! You're meant to be his best friend Callum, you knew how much he liked her! Are you really going to let a girl you've just met come between you? You've been friends forever. Sort it out!

"Oh no, she sounds really mad. I'm sorry this is all my fault." Melissa hung her head in shame. There had been many times in her life where she wished that she could have turned back the clock and made a different choice and this was one of them.

"Hey, don't worry it will be fine. I'm sure she's just overacting, you know what women are like!" she didn't like that comment, not one bit.

" I'll let James hit me if he wants to and that will be that, don't worry. We haven't done anything wrong. It's not like you two are together is it!"

"No, I know that, but still."

"You girls just overthink everything, don't worry I'll sort it." Melissa felt nothing but coldness from Callum. He didn't seem bothered at all by what they had done. Of course, he was right that her and James weren't together, but surely it bothered him at least a little bit that he had upset one of his best friends. She felt like she wanted to scream at him. It wasn't his fault though, this was all her own doing. Nonetheless she wanted him out of her room and out of the house.

"You best get going now anyway?"

"Oh, I see, you got what you wanted and now you want me gone!" he sarcastically proclaimed.

"No, I didn't mean it like that..."

"I'm joking, it's cool I'll go. Last night was cool though, drop me a text if you want to hook up again. I'll ring you now so that you've got my number."

That was the last thing she wanted to think about right now, she couldn't imagine that she would ever 'hook up' with him again.

"Ok, thanks, we'll see."

All the bravado that she had last night had faded, she was trying to act like she was ok, but she had retreated back into her shell. She just needed him to go as quickly as possible.

"We'll see? Playing hard to get now are we hey!" Callum laughed.

"Callum, I told you what this was last night, I'm pretty sure it won't be happening again." she couldn't help but snap.

'Why doesn't he just take the hint and go!' she told herself

"We'll see!" he winked as he walked out of the door and closed it behind him.

She flung herself back onto the bed, with a mixture of relief that he had gone and despair of her actions last night. She kept replaying it over and over. She had been so ruthless, so determined to make a point, she had acted so out of character and it worried her that she could behave like that. The irony that she wanted to show she was in control, but she couldn't have felt more out of control.

She wasn't sure what to do next. She felt like she needed to reach out to Denny and to James, but she was too embarrassed right now. She just wanted a shower and to climb back into bed and hide away from the world. She waited five minutes in case Callum had lingered around and then she got up and started gathering her things together so she could head to the bathroom. She changed the bedding before she did, she wanted to remove all traces of last night. She dramatically binned the clothes that she had worn, she figured she didn't want to wear them ever again as they would be too much of a reminder. Her emotions were swinging like a pendulum. One moment she felt sick to her stomach over her behaviour and the next she felt like she had made a breakthrough, that she was stepping closer to an independent life. In one way she felt liberated. She wasn't lost in romantic feelings, she just simply wanted sex…and so did he. She wanted to feel the feeling of someone wanting her, to feel like it was up to her what they did and didn't do. In many ways she felt such a sense of empowerment. Although she was ashamed to admit that even to herself as she felt guilty in equal measure.

She knew that she had acted that way to get back at Chris, Anthony and every other guy who thought they could control her or that she was their property. The only problem with her plan was that they couldn't see it. When she had looked at James, all she could see was them. She was so full of anger towards them. She was full of anger about what the Rep had taken from her, stripping away her dignity and filling her with shame, leaving her the perfect target for Chris to mould. She was filled with fear by Chris and her heart was still hurting for Anthony. She still couldn't stop thinking about how he crushed her already fragile heart. In truth after everything she had been through her heart was shattered into thousands of tiny pieces and each day felt like she was eternally scrambling around desperately trying to find a way to put them back together without letting the world know what she was hiding inside. At times she felt like a fraud, like she was hiding who she really was, and, in some ways, she was. She just didn't want to be defined by things that she felt other people wouldn't understand.

After she showered, she returned to her room, thankful that she hadn't run into anyone on the landing. She closed her door and swiftly locked it. She threw her towel into the washing basket and put on her most worn and oversized pyjamas, before climbing under the covers of her freshly made bed. She lay there for a while just staring at the ceiling. Then she reached out for her phone.

She had three messages, one from Ashlyn, one from Denny and one from a number she didn't recognise.

FROM ASH – How was last night lovely? Come down and tell us all the gossip once you're up. Xxx

That was the last thing she felt like doing, she couldn't sit there bragging about what had happened, not when she felt so bad about it. She knew they would think she was overthinking it too, but they didn't know why it worried her so much. It was as if as soon as she was triggered she had a personality transplant, she just felt very uneasy about the whole thing. She pressed the button to open the text off Denny, she felt overwhelmed with anxiety and her thoughts were racing as to what Denny would think of her now.

FROM DENNY – Melissa, I've just spoken to Callum, he said he showed you the text I sent him this morning. I just want you to know I don't judge you. You weren't to know the dynamics, but James has been a big part of our lives so I was annoyed at Callum for hurting him. Callum has told me he likes you though and it's not fair that he can't pursue that just because James does too. So, I just want you to know, this doesn't affect us or work and I don't have a problem with you guys seeing each other. D x

She was hoping that Callum had only said that to get Denny off his back and to make sure she would be ok with Melissa at work, as that sounded way off the 'sex no strings' that they had initially agreed to.

Finally, she opened the text from the number she didn't know, a little edgy at the thought of who it might be.

FROM +447183 734 561 – Hey last night was really cool, let me know what night ur free for a drink. I've squared it with Denny, so she'll be cool don't worry. See you soon, sexy. Xxx

"Brilliant! Just brilliant! So, my new boss is basically only cool with me because her little brother has confided in her that he likes me, so I'm guessing she won't be so cool if I just blow him off after ruining his friendship with James. What. A. Mess! What have I done!" She threw her hands over her eyes and gripped at her hair. She stamped her feet on the bed and stifled a huge scream that she had wanted to let out since she opened her eyes, by throwing her head into her pillow. She didn't reply to any of the texts. She just wanted to go back to sleep, then wake up, and for it all to have gone away. She pulled the duvet up over her shoulder, snuggled in tightly and closed her eyes.

When she awoke, nothing was different. She still felt the same lack of direction, the same disgust in herself that she had before she had closed her eyes. She also felt angry at herself that she was feeling so bad. 'If he hadn't said what he said I wouldn't have acted that way. We're not together, technically I haven't done anything wrong.' She couldn't distinguish what were good points and what were bad about the situation. She wondered whether she should care about someone's feelings so much even when she didn't really know them.

Was it not more important how she felt? Even though she kept having pangs of guilt, in the moment she was completely convinced that she was doing the right thing. That she was embracing her freedom and making a point. But now in the cold light of day, she saw it as someone she didn't want to be. She wanted to find her true self again, not turn into some cold-hearted super bitch. She needed to talk to someone that would understand her to help pull her out of this hole. She knew she secretly wanted reassurance she was doing the right thing but she didn't know Ashlyn or Giorgio well enough yet, they only knew the parts of her that she wanted them to know. So she picked up the phone and called Liz. As the phone was ringing, part of her was desperate for Liz to answer, another part of her prayed that she didn't - how could she tell her that she'd made a mess of everything already and that she'd brought it all on herself?

"Hey you! How's London town?"
"Hey Liz, Are you ok?"
"Yes, honey it's all good here. How are you?"
"Yes, everything's fine. I just missed you and thought I would phone to say hi."
[Even though she had phoned her to confess, she couldn't bring herself to go into it all now that she was actually on the phone to her. She hadn't really

spoken to her for a month so she'd felt bad just ringing her up because she'd felt down.]

"Okay, now how are you really? Not that I don't believe that you don't just miss my fabulous self of course! But come on, tell me what's wrong?"

Liz had always had an inner sixth sense and seemed to know when Melissa was hiding something.

"Honestly I'm fine."

"Melissa, don't forget who you are talking to here."

"Well, there is something…."
As she began to talk she also started to cry.

"I've just made such a mess of everything again, I just don't know what's wrong with me."

"Oh honey don't cry, I'm sure it's not as bad as you think. What happened?"

"Well it was my first work's night out, it was just a few of the people from work, including boss Denny and her brother Callum and their friend James. I'd met James before and he wanted to take me out, but I told him I'd just come out of a long relationship so I didn't want to go out with anyone. And last night whilst I was out we were flirting and a few of the guys including Callum were flirting with me too. It was all fine though just harmless fun but then Denny said James had warned everyone off me, that he had seen me first so I was his. It just made me rage, I was so angry, it jwas like a switch just flicked in me. It took me right back to Chris and I just turned into this awful person, I was horrible to James and I slept with Callum. Now Denny is upset with me and I've hurt this guy James for no reason and I'm just a mess about it. I just feel like such a horrible person."

"Ok honey so first off you are one of the nicest people I've ever met, secondly you've not killed anyone and thirdly what exactly is it that you think you've done wrong other than have a one night stand whilst you're young, free and single?"

"I know when I say it, it doesn't seem that bad and I know I'm single but it was the way I did it I was just ruthless Liz. I wanted to hurt James because I looked at him and I saw Chris and Anthony all rolled into one. It's been niggling at me since the day I met him that he had the same kind of endearing charm of me as Anthony did and I kept telling myself that I'm just not going to fall for that again, I've been that idiot before. But just as I was warming to him, I heard what he had said and I thought he was trying to control me like Chris. But now I'm sober I know he would have said it in a light-hearted way and that's exactly the way Denny told me it was too, but I just got all up in my head and I couldn't get out. I got so wound up and I felt so trapped and at that moment I wanted to make a big statement, so that everyone knew that they couldn't control me. I wanted to make a point, to do something to take charge and feel empowered, and I did at the time, but as soon as I woke up I felt like utter crap. I can't stop thinking about what happened in Cyprus today either, I think it's because I feel so cheap, I just don't think I'm cut out for having one night stands, I just don't think it's for me."

"Oh honey, you're bound to be affected by everything you've been through, you'd have to be a robot not to be. Obviously I wasn't there so I don't know if you behaved as badly as you think you did, but if you can't forgive yourself for it, then why don't you reach out to James and explain - obviously you don't have to go into all the details. That might make you feel better? Have you found someone in London to talk to yet? A new councillor?"

"I could try and talk to James, I honestly don't think he will want to talk to me but I can at least try. And no, I haven't looked for one as I had all six sessions before I left Manchester so I should be fine now, that's why I don't know what's wrong with me, why these things still haunt me!"

"Liss, there's nothing wrong with you, look at what you've achieved so far, you been through such a lot at such a young age maybe six sessions was enough to make you feel a bit stronger and a bit better but maybe it wouldn't do you any harm in just starting those up again."

"Most of the time I'm fine, it's just every now and then. Sometimes I just feel overwhelmed. I don't know. Anyway I will try and talk to James, sorry I bet I've completely depressed you now and ruined your Sunday."

"Not at all, I've actually loved hearing from you, obviously I'd rather you wasn't sad, but you've called me - now that's a breakthrough! One thing I would like to say though, is that obviously if you didn't like it, then don't do it again, but if you want to… then let me tell you: having a one night stand doesn't make you cheap or a slag, it's not the same as what happened in Cyprus with that bastard and there is nothing wrong in having some harmless fun, as long as it was fun? Was it good at least, I bloody hope it was worth it if it's caused you this much drama?"

"It was quite adventurous."

"Sounds promising!" They both laughed, she could always count on Liz to make her smile.

"But did you, you know...come?"

"I'm not sure, I don't think so, I remember the sex but I don't remember...coming, no!"

159

"Well honey, that's a no then, you would have remembered that part I'm sure. I'm going to send you a rabbit. That's what you need in your life."

"Oh, thanks Liz, but you're not allowed pets here and I'm not really that big on having a rabbit anyway, I appreciate the thought though thank you!"

"Not a bunny rabbit!" [Liz was howling down the phone and Melissa was completely confused.]

"A rampant rabbit you daft sod!"

"A rampant rabbit, oh that vibrator of yours! Oh!" Melissa started laughing in chorus with Liz.

"I'd forgotten all about that! I thought it was a strange thing for you to say you were sending me! A rabbit - I remember it at that sex toy party. It's pretty big isn't it!"

"I'm crying! [Liz was still fighting back the fits of laughter] "Oh I've missed you Melissa Morgan! Colette and I were only saying how much we missed you the other day!"

"Really?"

"Really! Liss, I hope one day you realise just how bloody special you are, kid! We love you!"

"I love you both too. Well I guess I better get going and face the music!"

"Face the music and then dance kiddo, don't be too hard on yourself. Oh and send me your address so I can send you a rabbit!"

"I will, thanks Liz, bye!"

"Bye honey!"

She still felt bad for what happened last night, but she didn't feel as worthless and a mess like she did before she called Liz. She was so glad she'd called her. She'd helped her realise that she needed to keep reminding herself to reach out when she needed it more often. And more importantly, that it was ok to.

She didn't know if it would come across as a bit crazy but it was something she needed to do before she could move on. She needed to see James, face to face to explain and apologise. She looked through emails and she found the ones James had been sending her. She looked at the signature at the bottom to see if she could see his mobile number. It was there so she quickly put it in her phone. She went to ring him, but she couldn't face it. She couldn't take him calling her names even though she felt like she deserved to be called names, she was sure she would have a breakdown if he did, so she decided to text him instead.

TO JAMES – Hi James, it's Melissa. I'm sure I'm the last person you want to see right now but I just wondered if you would be kind enough to come and see me. Or can I come to you? I need to talk to you. I want to apologise and explain. X

She took a deep breath and began the waiting game, hoping and praying that he would surpass her expectations and actually be forgiving enough to meet with her. She wouldn't blame him if he didn't come, he didn't owe her anything and he probably despises her now too.

A torturous hour passed and she still didn't have a reply. She wasn't surprised. She lay there and recalled one of the times she had been left completely humiliated by Chris and it wasn't a nice feeling. She felt terrible that she was responsible for inflicting humiliation on someone else.

Chris had been at a lap dancing club and it was revealed in front of everyone that he had paid for dancers all night. While they were all sitting in a pub, all the boys and all of the girls of the group were there all huddled around the table as everyone laughed about how Chris couldn't get enough of the dancers, especially one in particular. The humiliation of sitting there and everyone scanning her face for her reactions was just gut wrenching. People were trying to analyse if she knew or not, if she was upset or not. So she just laughed along with it, as if it didn't bother her at all, yet inside her heart ached and she was holding back the tears. To her, getting a dance was the same as cheating. The fact that he needed to go and pay to get his kicks off someone else and not her, never mind the fact that half of their group of 'friends' were there to witness it - this was just another blow to her self-esteem. Not to mention the fact that they kept laughing at the fact 'he couldn't get enough of this one dancer!' The thought that she could have caused James to feel even the slightest amount of embarrassment and sadness that she felt, made her feel ashamed of herself. She wasn't even aware that she had the ability to be so ruthless. She knew that they weren't in a relationship, so technically she hadn't done anything wrong, but morally and emotionally she knew that she had behaved badly. There was no need for her to hurt James like that, he was simply collateral damage, because deep down it was Chris and Anthony that she wanted to hurt, in the same way that they had hurt her. Once Denny had told her what he had said to everyone, it set alight something inside her that she didn't know was there.

She leaned over to her bedside table to pick up and check her phone. There was a reply. Her heart started thumping and her breath became heavy. 'What is he going to say?' she wondered. Her hands started shaking slightly as she opened the text.

FROM JAMES – Hi Melissa, thanks for your text. You don't need to speak to me. I'm fine thanks.

Melissa instinctively knew that James wasn't fine. She now believed all too late that he truly did have feelings for her, it wasn't an act. He wasn't being a 'charmer' he was just being James. Someone that is liked by everyone and is seemingly one the nicest guys she could have met, and she had just stamped all over his feelings, publicly, brutally with one of his best friends. 'Good god Melissa, no wonder he doesn't want to talk to you.'
Just then her phone flashed 1 New Message.

'Please have changed your mind James, please let me talk to you. I'm sorry!'
she muttered to herself with a tone of desperation and she shut her eyes. She opened the text message to see another message from Ashlyn.

FROM ASHLYN – Are you ok hun? Me and G thought you would have been down here by now.

'Oh no, what do I do?' She didn't want to face them, what if they are annoyed at her as they put her forward for the job and they know James too. Especially as they'd tried to tell her that he wasn't a player. She couldn't face them until she had made amends. She decided to phone James, and she hoped with all her mite that he would answer.

As the phone reached three rings she felt certain that he wouldn't take her call, on the fifth ring he picked up. Her heart raced faster and she could feel her tears flooding to the surface. She didn't want to cry, she would probably come across as an emotional lunatic who doesn't know her own mind from one minute to the next. He would be right in thinking that as that was exactly what she felt like, a complete and utter lunatic.

"Hello"

"Hi. James I'm sorry, I really am and I really need to tell you that. I understand why you don't want to see me in person. I wouldn't want to see me if the shoe was on the other foot. I just hoped that you would so I could explain to you a little about the crazy place I'm in right now and why I behaved so cruelly last night and I'm sorry, I'm just so very sorry James."

"I don't know what you want me to say Melissa. I've got the message loud and clear. I'll be fine, don't worry."

"I know you don't really know me, but if you did know me then you would know that I'm not acting like myself. The messy breakup and long relationship wasn't just like a normal relationship and I'm just spinning out of control at the minute and don't think I can stop myself, but I can at least tell you that I'm sorry, you didn't deserve the anger I directed at you, I looked at you and I saw people who have hurt me and that's who my anger was really directed at and I'm ashamed of myself for treating another person that way, especially someone who has been nothing but nice to me." She couldn't help but let out a cry.

"Look, do you still want me to come and see you? Because if you do I'll come over to yours now,"

"Really? Thanks James I really appreciate that, I really don't want things to be awkward between us. Everyone has told me how nice you are and I'd really like to start again."

"OK, I'll set off shortly."

"Ok see you soon."

"Bye"

She didn't change; she didn't want to. It was an exception to the rule moment where she needed to take off the armour and let him see the person she is behind 'the front.' She didn't want to bare all of her battle wounds but she needed to share some of them at least, in the hope that he could forgive her, and she can forgive herself. She kept fidgeting and her palms were sweaty. She wanted to get a drink to calm her nerves, but this was something she needed to do without any Dutch courage inside her. Last night was enough to prove that drinking wasn't always a good idea.

As the time passed, she felt more anxious, how could she explain that she wanted to show him (and them) that she was the one that would be deciding who she spent time with, she would decide who she kissed, slept with and anything else. That in that moment she didn't give a shit anymore. That she wanted to show the world that it was her life and that she was the one in charge of it, just her and no one else. It was time for her to live confidently and unapologetically and no one was going to stop her. Yet here she was waiting anxiously for James to arrive so that she could apologise, it was ironic. He had gotten the brunt of her anger and determination, he didn't deserve it.

She thought she'd better text Ashlyn back as James would probably arrive soon and they would be wondering what was going on. She was sure at least someone in the house would have also seen Callum leaving this morning, hence the need for 'the gossip'. She thought whilst she was already feeling anxious she might as well tell Ash and Giorgio what had happened so she could just get it out of the way and let everyone hate her all in one go.

TO ASHLYN – Hey, sorry I'm ok. I just made a mistake last night and I feel pretty shit about it. I couldn't face you all this morning. I'm trying to sort it out so James will be coming soon and then I will talk to you both and explain. Sorry. Xx

FROM ASHLYN – Ok hun, let us know when you're ready to talk. I obviously don't know what's happened but I'm sure everything will be fine, don't worry. Xx

TO JAMES – Will you phone me when you're here so that I can come down and let you in. x

She tidied around her bedroom whilst she waited for him to reply. Then there was a knock on her bedroom door. Panic set in as she reached for the door knob to open the door. James stood there. He looked down and tired. She stood there in front of him, completely transparent, not one ounce of make up on her face. For the first time in a long time, she had totally removed her mask. Her remorse had suffocated her need to hide away. She knew now was the time to be honest, she needed to be honest, she needed to be herself, in order to help him understand that it had nothing to do with him and everything to do with her. She knew what it was like to feel rejected and not understand the reason why or what went wrong? That feeling is heart wrenching and she wouldn't wish it on anyone.

"Hi, thanks for coming."

"Hi," he mustered a half smile for her and walked in towards her sofa.

She closed the door and sat at the end of her bed opposite him. She didn't know where to start. "Who let you in, I'd text you to say I would have come and opened the door."

"Oh sorry, I didn't see that. Giorgio let me in, he just told me to go straight up and told me where your room was."

"Oh, don't worry, you don't have to say sorry, I was just saying. I don't know why I said anything about it really, I suppose I was just putting off starting a hard conversation."

James said nothing, he just kept his head down, like he couldn't bear to look at her. She could feel his sadness and she felt even worse than she did before.

"James, I really am sorry, the way I behaved last night was totally out of character and I don't really know what happened to me. The truth is that Denny told me that you had warned everyone off me because 'I was yours' and I just saw red. You are lovely and I know you've made it quite clear that you liked me, but it's just all been too much too soon for me. My ex was very controlling and not very nice at all. It took me all of my strength to leave him and I just thought you were trying to control me too and that you had no right to. I don't mean to sound horrible or blunt, so I'm sorry if I do, I'm just trying to do my best to explain to you why I turned and why…well I'm ashamed to admit it, but I wanted to make a point to you."

"I get it, don't worry, I will back off now. I'm sorry I was a bit full on but I just had never felt that way before and I couldn't play it cool, I couldn't stop myself from telling you and telling everyone how much I liked you, which is what made last night so much harder to take. I had literally told everyone there that I thought I was in love with you."
[She was shocked. He barely knew her, yet he'd used the 'L' word so soon.]

"I'm sorry, you don't deserve it. I've tried to be clear with you from the start that I wasn't ready for anything and I do like you James, so I don't know why I did it? When I'd heard you'd told everyone I was yours, it triggered some painful memories and

170

I was trying to show the world that I won't be controlled ever again. I'm sorry you got caught in the crossfire."

"I'm sorry that was too intense and that you've been through such a rough time. I hope one day you find someone who will treat you right."

She couldn't believe how calm and nice he was being. She waited for the name calling but it didn't happen. She wanted to give him a hug, but she didn't know if he would want that.

"I hope we can stay friends James, I think you're a lovely person and I don't want things to be awkward between us. Especially as we have mutual friends."

"I'm sorry Melissa, maybe in time we can be friends but right now I think it's best that we just keep our distance from each other until the dust settles. Give me chance to get over you."

[She wasn't expecting that answer, but somehow it crushed her, yet she wasn't sure why? She wanted them to be able to be friends eventually, but something about what he had said gave her a 'sinking' feeling.]

"Of course, I understand. Can I give you a hug please? I understand if you don't want one."

"Ok" James reluctantly stood up from the couch, Melissa got up from the bed and cautiously went to hug him. He reciprocated the hug and they ended up hugging each other tightly and it was as if neither one wanted to let go. It felt very strange to her, she felt like she was in a totally safe space with James, yet he was practically a stranger to her. They both stayed silent, all she could hear was his heart beating through his chest. Was his heart a genuine one? It certainly felt that way, and she was responsible for hurting it.

"I need to go now." James said abruptly as he pulled away from their embrace.

"Oh ok."

"Thanks for asking to talk to me." He started to walk towards the door and was talking to her without looking at her again.

"Thanks for coming James, again I really am sorry and I really do hope we can be friends one day soon."

"Yep."

And with that he was gone. He couldn't get out of there quick enough. She felt sad and she couldn't hold back her tears anymore. She collapsed back onto the bed and cried into her pillow. She had only been here eight weeks and she had made a mess of everything already. She felt devastated.

After half an hour, when she had finally cried all that, she could cry. Then there was a knock on her door again. She knew this time it would be Ash and Giorgio coming to find out what has been going on. She wanted to hide under the duvet but instead she knew she had to face them, just like she had James. She let them in and explained everything.

"How can you be a slag? I mean come on! Like how many people have you slept with your whole life? If you don't mind me asking!"

"Three" (she never counted what happened in Cyprus)

"Three! You're more like the virgin mary than a slag hun! You've got some major catching up to do darling!" encouraged Ash mischievously.

"Not if she doesn't want to, though – not everyone is like you!" Giorgio chuckled.

"Heyyy you! I'm hard to get, I'll have you know, but when I like someone, I just don't like to wait!"

They all started laughing.

"I'm just not really into one-night stands, so I don't know why I did it? I feel awful now. It just makes me feel so worthless and cheap."

"Of course, it's fine if you don't like them, but you shouldn't feel cheap or worthless, if you're in control and it's what you want it can be empowering. Sex can be really fun." "Why do you think you feel that way?"

"Well…" she paused as she debated whether to bring up what had happened in her past. She didn't want them to see her as weak, but she wanted to be honest with them about her journey.

Melissa reluctantly opened about Cyprus and the aftermath of it. For the first time she shed tears in front of them and gave them a glimpse of her fragile heart.

"Oh babe, that wasn't a one-night stand, that was rape! You do know that, don't you?" The word rape made her shudder, she felt like she didn't have the right to call it that somehow as she could barely remember it. She felt uncomfortable, she knew that so many people suffer horrendous and violent rapes and she almost felt that in some way she was still responsible.

"I know, I just don't like to say that, I suppose I'm scared it sounds dramatic or people won't believe me. I just feel so ashamed, and I can't seem to shift it. My ex always said it was my fault for drinking and being too flirty, I guess that's why it's hard to shake off the feeling that it wasn't my fault."

Giorgio and Ashlynn exchanged concerned looks, before they both leant forward and placed a comforting hand each on her legs.

"Listen Liss we understand that you don't really want to talk about what happened in your life before you came here and we only see just how fabulous you are, but Vicki said you had, had a rough time and we just want you to know we're here for you."

"Yeah, you know, you're not going to just be ok overnight whatever it is that you've been through, healing takes time, and you don't have to hide it from us when you are hurting.

A tear rolled down Melissa's cheek which she brushed away as quickly as it escaped. "I'm fine really, but thank you, that means a lot. I'm really tired anyway so I'm going to sleep for a bit. You guys go have fun, I'll come back down later."

"Ok babe, see you later." Giorgio smiled warmly as if to reassure her they were there when she was ready.

She lay down and cried silently clutching onto her pillow. She had been trying so hard to portray a certain image since she arrived, but inside she just felt like she was crumbling. It was exhausting. She just didn't know how to navigate her way out of this pain and feel in a place of control again. She was grateful for Ashlynn and Giorgio's concern, but as much as she had started to open up to them, she couldn't let them in fully. She was too ashamed at how broken inside she was. This was a party house, full of people who wanted to have fun. She was sure that the last thing they wanted was someone dampening their mood. She longed to truly be the carefree, confident, and stylish person that she was able to portray. But she knew it was all a lie her clothes and makeup were the armour that hid her wounds and shielded her from letting the outside world in. She was so full of fear and she felt so inadequate in the world.

Each cutting word that Chris had seared into her brain reminded her exactly who she really was, they put her right back 'in her place'. She knew what he'd be saying she could hear him now -

'Who the fuck does she think she is?'

'Empowered! Ha!'

'He would have slept with any girl there, you were just drunk and easy!'

'You're a cheap slag'

'Do you know how lucky you were to be with me?'

'Everyone knew I could do so much better than you! That's why I never took you anywhere with the rugby lads because I was embarrassed of you.'

'I couldn't have you stand there as my girlfriend, next to all their fit girlfriends and wives.'

She smacked her head in desperation trying, but failing to stop thinking about the past. She wanted to shake his words and his voice out of her head. She had felt so much better after her phone call with Liz, but seeing James and going over 'Cyprus' with Ash and Giorgio had completely drained her and she felt so emotional and all over the place again. All she wanted was to look to the future – why was that so hard to do?! After a while all the staring into space sent her into a trance and she finally fell asleep.

KNOCK KNOCK!

"Melissa."

Melissa's eyelids were heavy and she had to force them open. She had forgotten where she was and was confused by the voice. As she woke up properly, she remembered exactly where she was, in her safe haven. She felt a warm glow inside. She had been thinking about Chris so much before she went to sleep, she had been able to hear his voice as if he were in the room with her that for a split second she had expected to wake up in her old house. Hence why the sweet Irish voice calling out to her had confused her.

"Are you ok hon? I've been worried about you I don't want you to think I'm prying, but I just want you to know you can talk to me."

"I'm not ok if I'm honest and ironically I don't have the strength to be anything but 'honest' today"

"is it your ex? Do you want to talk about it?"

Melissa instantly reacted to that question with the truth. She was low, vulnerable and bare of her armour.

"He always said I was a slag, I always thought he was saying it to me just to hurt me, but I am a slag."

"You are NOT a slag by any means honey, and who always said you were?"

"My ex. He knew it all along, no wonder he couldn't stand the sight of me. I'm revolting!"

"Woah, babe, please don't say that about yourseld, whats with all the self hate?"

Melissa took Ash aback as she threw her arms around and started hysterically sobbing. Ash reciprocated the hug, she asked no more questions, she just let her cry.

Melissa felt like she had been crying into Ash's shoulder for hours, when in truth it was 15 minutes. It was a long fifteen minutes where she sobbed like hadn't sobbed with anyone ever before. Her emotions seemed to be trying to escape from every single cell in her body and she couldn't control them any longer. As she pulled away from Ash she kept her head bowed down, she couldn't bear to look at Ash, she didn't want to see that look of pity. She had driven thousands of miles to get away from that look, from everyone feeling sorry for her. She felt so ashamed for breaking down in front of her.

The silence broke.

"Are you ok?"

"Yeah, I'm fine, I'm sorry."

"What are you sorry for? It's ok to get upset. You don't have to be sorry to me for that!"

"I didn't mean to. I'm sorry I couldn't help it. But I'm fine really, really I'm fine."

Ashlyn knew she wasn't fine, she knew there was a lot more to Melissa's sadness, but she didn't probe any further at that moment.

"Well I don't now about you but I need a drink. Do you want one?"

"Yes, please. I can't come downstairs though again. I just…I just can't."

"No, I don't expect you to. Don't worry I'll bring some up here. I'll say we're having a girly night."

"Ok, thank you and I'm sorry again Ash."

"Stop saying sorry! You've got nothing to be sorry for."

"I've ruined your night though, crying all over you!"

"You have not ruined my night! The night is young, so we've got time to turn this bad boy around yet." she winked at Melissa reassuringly as she headed out of the room.

Melissa smiled, she didn't know why Ash was being so kind to her. She was sure that she would have preferred to have stayed downstairs with everyone else, who wasn't a complete mess. But she was grateful that she did want to come back up to her as she wasn't sure she could face being on her own tonight.

"I do understand a little of how you're feeling you know." Melissa waited for Ash to divulge a little more. She could sense she wanted to open up.

"That's how I got into make-up, when I was little I used to help me ma cover up any marks and bruises that my father had given her." A rogue tear escaped Ash's eyes as she recalled painting her mum's face.

"That's awful Ash, I'm so sorry you had to go through that in your childhood. No wonder you're so brave!"

"I'm not brave really, but the war paint makes you feel brave. That's why I love it so much. How it can change how you feel."

"It does, I totally get that, it's something I've used many times over the years to make myself feel better. Especially when you do it for me! I feel like a million dollars!"

"That's what I love to hear, that's why I do what I do. I know every woman that sits in my chair, famous or not, everyone has a story, everyone has baggage and sometimes we all need a little help to make ourselves feel better."

"It's lovely how you've turned something that must have been such a tough thing to go through into such a positive and a way of helping women feel better about themselves."

"Well, you've only got two choices in life haven't you, we can sink, or we can swim. I was determined not to let that bastard win."

"Where's your mum now Ash, if you don't mind me asking? It's just I've never heard you mention her before."

Ash paused and looked straight at Melissa, it looked like she had so much to say, yet she couldn't get her words out.

"Look at the time!"

The question was obviously too hard for her to answer and although Melissa was intrigued as to what happened with Ashlyn's mother, it was not appropriate to keep pressing her when it was obviously something she found too hard to talk about and she had already confided in her so much.

CHAPTER 10.

HOLIDAY HIDEAWAY

"**W**ork was awful today. I went to the canteen for dinner, I was sat at the table with everyone, but I went to the toilet and when I came back they had moved my bag and coat to another table."

Melissa was holding back the tears just like she had done all day.

"I was so humiliated. I didn't know what to do. I was so mad and upset that they could be so cruel. Its like being back at school. I know it was Stephanie, but why didn't the others stop her? I mean what have I ever actually done to them!"

By this point she couldn't stop the tears from falling, she couldn't keep her guard up any longer. She had to put enough of a façade up at work, she was too exhausted to do it at home too.

"Jealous bitches!" Giorgio raged.

"What do you mean?"

"Oh come on hun, you are like one of the most naturally attractive women I've ever met in real life – not counting all the tv or film stars of course!" Giorgio winked.

"Well that's quite the compliment Giorgio! Thank you!" Melissa switched from crying to laughing.

"Well it's true! Look, they like James, that's a given. I mean from what I've heard there's not many that don't – he's a good catch. They also like Callum because let's face it, he is one hot piece of arse. And guess what they both like you! You've swooped in out of nowhere, stole all of the attention and they don't like it simple! Well fuck them babe, just fuck them! There's definitely something about Lissy, let me tell you!"

"Yes, even Ash has got it bad for you!" Ash threw Giorgio an awkward glare.

"Joke!" Giorgio corrected.

"That Stephanie just wants to dim your light, to make hers shine brighter and you can't let her hon. You'll always come across people like that, you just can't let them get to you."

Melissa looked extremely uncomfortable with all the compliments, she smiled shyly without responding.

"You know what we need...we NEED...a holiday!" Giorgio blurted out.

"A holiday? Oh I'm not sure about that?" Her experience of holidays hadn't been that great since hitting her adult life, and her reluctance to commit was visible.

"Oh, come on! Who doesn't like going on holiday?"

"I just, well, I've just never really enjoyed going on holiday that much."

[She had already told them about Cyprus. She didn't feel the need to expand. Thoughts of the night Chris left her alone on holiday raced into her mind too. But she was already feeling down and she didn't want to re-live that experience by explaining that to them too.]

"You just haven't been in the right company babe!" Giorgio pleaded. "Holidays are fabulous, honestly darling! It will do you the world of good. Come on, who else is in?"

"I'm up for it!" Ashlyn said, looking at Melissa waiting to gain her commitment too.

"Oh ok then, fine, I'll come! I better not regret it!" Melissa smiled, but inside she was already riddled with nervousness, just by the thought of it.

"YESSS! Whoop whoop! I'm going to go look at last minute deals now and start packing my suitcase!" Giorgio skipped out the room.

"I know what you're worrying about hon, but you're with us, it will be different this time, I promise." Ash leaned over and squeezed Melissa's knee reassuringly.

Giorgio had found a last-minute deal that night and insisted that they all checked their schedules there and then to make sure that they could make it work.

Melissa texted Denny to check and see it was ok. Part of her was secretly hoping she would say no as it was too short notice, but surprisingly she said it was fine. Giorgio excitedly booked it. She wasn't sure she was ready for it, but needed to try and be, and fast! As one week and she'd be there.

***

They arrived in Majorca and the hot air engulfed them as soon as they stepped off the plane. It was so hot it was almost suffocating. Her heart started to beat a little faster and breathing became heavier.

"You ok babe?" Giorgio noticed the shift in Melissa's appearance as her face drained of her colour.

"Me?" She snapped out of her thoughts, "oh yes, I'm fine, it's just so hot isn't it!"

She wasn't fine, memories of holidays gone by flooded her thoughts and she could feel the pangs of a panic attack starting, but she was too embarrassed to say. Everyone was so excited, giddy and already a little drunk, she didn't want to spoil the holiday before it had even begun.

"When we get off the coach, let's just dump our bags in our rooms and go find the nearest bar shall we?" Giorgio suggested.

"Hell yeah, I can't even be arsed getting changed. I just wanna get out and dance on the tables!" Ash agreed as they laughed in chorus.

Melissa attempted to laugh along convincingly. But her head was spinning, her body was tingling and she was struggling to take a breath. The air seemed different abroad and her body seem to reject the new change in environment. There was something about being in a foreign country and not being able to speak the language that made her feel even more vulnerable and nervous than she usually does.

As they stood waiting for their luggage to appear inside the airport, Ash and Giorgio cracked open the alcohol that they had bought from the duty free and began to swig it. They handed Melissa a bottle which she quickly grabbed and started downing to help calm her nerves.

"Go on girl!" Giorgio cheered.

She was glad she could pass off her nervous drinking as being 'up for partying'!

"Get a picture of me on here." Giorgio pulled out a disposable camera and handed it to Ashlyn as Melissa continued gulping down her drink as quickly as possible. Giorgio proceeded to start posing on the conveyor belt of the luggage station. Just as Ash clicked the camera button, the conveyor belt started moving and Giorgio fell backwards, spilling some of his drink over onto it and landing on his bottom. He started roaring with laughter. A group of onlookers looked over disapprovingly, whilst another group of holiday goers cheered loudly! Melissa and Ash fell about laughing, taking Melissa out of her head and back in the moment, 'Nothing is going to go wrong, just enjoy yourself' Melissa reassured herself as she continued to laugh on the outside. Through her self-talk she reminded herself that Chris had no idea she was going away, so there was no way that he could be here. She could fully let her hair down without the worry that he could walk into a bar or she could bump into him at any given moment. The rep from *that* holiday wouldn't be there either. All she had to do was stick with her friends and everything would be ok. She could feel her heart slowing down. As she'd started to feel a little less apprehensive.

"Do ya want us to take a picture of the three of ya's" One the lads from the group that had cheered as Giorgio fell over, approached them and reached out his hand gesturing to take the camera.

"Yes, please! That would be fabulous, sexy!" Giorgio winked cheekily at the young guy standing in front of them as he clambered off the conveyor belt.

"Calm down man, I've only got eyes for the ladies, me!" The Geordie holiday maker laughed nervously as he didn't know how to take Giorgios flirty comments.

They all laughed as Ash handed over the camera to him and the three of them posed up a storm. It was funny how confident Melissa could be in group photos and with a drink inside her, yet the thought of posing for a photo alone was something she would never entertain. The coach was stifling, everyone became adorned with mass patches of sweat very quickly. A rep boarded the coach and began the holiday introductions. Melissa was taken aback when she looked up. She hadn't realised they'd booked with the same company that she went to Cyprus with and suddenly the sight of the reps' uniform triggered her anxiety once again.

"Have you got another bottle Ash?" Melissa asked as she hurriedly drank the remaining contents of her bottle.

"I'll buy you some more when we get there." Ash seemed a little taken back by the franticness of Melissa's request.

"Yeah, sure hon, I've only got one bottle left, I'll pour half in yours, give it here."

"Yes, that's great, anything will do…" realising the desperation in her voice, she attempted to cover her tracks, "I just want to head to the bar as tipsy as possible so I'm not buying loads of expensive drinks that are watered down anyway. I should have gotten more from the duty free, I'm sorry I didn't think."

Ash didn't look completely convinced, Melissa knew she was about to ask her if she was ok and she couldn't bear that, so she swiftly changed the subject, spinning around on her seat to look at Giorgio who was behind them outrageously flirting with the large group of lads from Newcastle.

"Look at him! Only Giorgio could get away with that!"

Ash turned her head to watch Giorgio dancing away to the group of lads, they were lapping it up cheering him along!

"I know, he's one in a million isn't he!" Ash smiled, before continuing, "Just like you!" she said, squeezing Melissa's hand. Melissa felt a lump form in her throat and she knew she needed to move away from any serious conversation before she fell apart. "Cheers!" she gestured with her bottle then proceeded to start off a chant "Go G! Go G! Go G!" Much to Giorgio's delight, upping his dancing game even further.

As the coach pulled over and the rep called their names, the three of them jumped up from their seats and started to walk down the coach to get off. Giorgio gave the lads at the back one last shake of his arse and they all cheered.

"What can I say, they love me!" Giorgio laughed as he clambered down the coach steps.

The driver pulled their suitcases out from underneath the coach and they started lugging them onto the pavement. The apartment was basic as expected and there was only one bedroom.

There were two single beds in the bedroom and a sofa bed in the living area.

"Right you're on there G! Me and Liss are in the bedroom."

"Fine by me honey! I won't be spending much time in my own bed anyway!" He winked playfully.

Melissa still felt a little bit on edge but she was doing well at riding the waves of anxiety that kept crashing over her.

"Are we getting changed or not? I might just change my top as I'm so sticky! I can't believe they didn't have air conditioning on the coach, I thought I was going to pass out!" Melissa exclaimed.

"I know you've looked a bit peaky a few times since we got off the plane, are you sure you're alright going out for a drink?" Ash couldn't hide her concern for Melissa.

"Yeah, of course I'll be fine. I just need to adjust to the heat. A few cold beers and I'll be fine."

"What's she gonna do otherwise Ash, sit in the apartment, we're on our holidays that is not allowed!" Giorgio joked.

"I just meant we could have chilled round the pool for a bit first, it's only lunchtime isn't it?"

"Yes, which means we're already behind schedule so if you're changing then change quick ladies because we've got to go and find the perfect bar that will become our local for the next week and sort out our hangovers each day! Let's go!"

"Ok, two ticks!" Melissa wheeled her case into the bedroom, flung it open and quickly swapped her current vest top for another. "Ok, I'm ready!" She shouted as she heard Ashlyn race into the bedroom behind her.

"I'm just going to stay casual today too Liss. We'll get dressed up and go to the clubs tomorrow once we've had a bit of sun on us!"

"Yes, good idea!"

"Are you sure you're ok? You can talk to me if you need to know. I saw your face when you saw the rep get on the coach." Now they were alone, Ash wanted to check that Melissa was really 'ok'.

"Oh yes, it just threw me for a second as it was the same uniform from when, well you know. But I'm fine now, I've shook it off and honestly I'm fine! Melissa suddenly became aware she'd kept repeating the same answer to that question instantaneously by default. 'I'm fine.' So she calmed herself, took a breath and decided to try and say something more convincing.

"I'm looking forward to replacing the bad holiday memories with some fabulous new ones, which I know for sure I will make with you two!"

"Oh we most certainly will! That's one thing I can promise you."

Ash smiled reassuringly and squeezed Melissa's hand once again.

"Right bitches stop chit chatting, I need some sex on the beach - the cocktail obvs, I will wait until after dark for the other type!"

"G!" Ashlyn and Melissa giggled away as they headed out of the apartment door.

Their apartment was right at the top of the main strip, it was in the perfect position for falling back home when the bars closed. About halfway down they stumbled across an Irish Bar.

"This is it! Ash will feel at home here and they serve an all day breakfast and beer! Ladies, our new local!" He welcomed them into the bar with a theatrical arm gesture leading the way for them to make their way in.

"You better not start with any Irish jokes G!" Ashlyn raised her eyebrow.

"Would I?!" Giorgio replied mischievously.

"Are we getting something to eat now or not? I don't think I'm hungry."

Mellisa couldn't stomach the thought of food at the minute. That nervous feeling had quashed any little appetite she'd had.

"No, I'm just going to get a kebab later I think!"

"Yeah, why don't we just get a few drinks here and then get some sun round the pool and just have some drinks there, we can always come back out later, I just want to get some sun on my face." Ash suggested.

"I know you need it hun!" Giorgio joked.

"You've only got a tan because of your Italian genes!"

"Jealous?!"

Giorgio and Ashlyn always joked with each other and bickered like they were brother and sister. They had lived together for 5 years now and had known each other for 11 years; you could see how strong their bond was.

They spent the afternoon people watching, putting the world to rights and challenging each other with drinking tasks. They spent a lot longer at the Irish bar than intended and so they decided to stay for the duration once they'd found out it was karaoke night. They had the perfect spot looking out onto the strip and the sun was beaming down for the majority of the day. The homely and casual bar suited their laid back looks and outfits perfectly.

"Right what are you singing, Liss?" Giorgio turned to her beaming holding up the booklet with the list of songs.

"Me! Oh no! I do **not** do Karaoke!"

"Well there's a first time for everything and tonight is going to be your first time honey!"

"Ohhh nooo please don't make me, I'll just freeze, there's no way I will be able to get my words out."

Giorgio jumped up and went over with his song requests.

"Too late!" he announced as he shimmied back over to the table.

Melissa eventually gave in when their names were called out. But despite her reluctancy, she enjoyed every minute of it. After a few rounds of karaoke they decided to call it a night. They wanted to be all refreshed for their big night out at the clubs tomorrow. But all in all, their first day and night had been a total success and she went to bed feeling happy and excited for the next day.

***

"We'll meet you downstairs at the bar." Melissa shouted through Giorgios closed door.

Giorgio was still getting ready so they headed down to the bar for a couple of cocktails whilst they waited for him. They went down in the lift and had just got into the bar downstairs when Melissa's face dropped.

"Oh my god! I can't believe this." Melissa bowed her head down as she gasped in anguish.

"What? You can't believe what?" Ash could see by Melissa's facial expression as she looked back up that it wasn't good.

"Over in the corner, those three guys." Melissa gestured discreetly with her eyes.

Ashlyn sensed this and turned round as if she was just glancing around the bar. She turned back to Melissa once she had seen them. "Yes, what about them? It isn't Chris, is it?"

"No but it's three of his teammates!"

"Shit, really! Jeez, what are the odds!"

"I know! Melissa's mind was working overdrive as she fired questions at Ash like torpedoes.

"Do you think that means he's here too? What should I do? Oh god, it's only the second day of the holiday, how am I meant to enjoy it now? How would he know I'm here? I can't believe this!" Melissa went into a frenzied panic. She felt that it didn't matter where she was, Manchester, London, out of the country - he'd always find a way to make sure she can never truly escape him. He was always there.

"It's ok, calm down. It might just be them, he's not with them now so he's probably not even on holiday with 'em!" Ash desperately tried to reassure Melissa as her panic became more and more visible.

"Well, I hope so, but Giorgio isn't sat here with us right now is he? But he's on holiday with us isn't he?" Melissa had a point, she only hoped that Ashlyn's scenario was true rather than one that she was already tormenting herself with.

"Hey sisters! Don't panic the fun has arrived now!" Giorgio burst into the bar and was striding over to them. "And thank goodness I'm here, you two are making the air turn cold with them stony faces! What's the matter with you both?"

"G! Just sit down a minute and stop being so loud!" Ash pointed at the chair, willing him to sit down quickly.

"Charming, what's your problem?" Giorgio's demeanor changed when he saw Melissas face.

"It's my fault Giorgio, my ex's teammates are over there so I'm freaking that it means he's here too!"

"Oh, I see, I get it now. Well of course you're going to feel a bit spooked." Giorgio tried to sound sympathetic. "Fuck'em none of this is your fault is it, so why should you spoil your holiday? And if he is here, I'll scare the bastard off don't you worry – and before you say anything I don't mean with my fists! I'll camp it up and flirt the bastard out of town!"

Melissa laughed, that comment really tickled her and she suddenly had visions of a very uncomfortable Chris running away from Giorgio!

"We can always count you G to lift the mood!" Ash smiled, patting him on the back.

'And they can always rely on me to dampen the mood.' Melissa couldn't help but worry that was what they were thinking.

"It will be fine, they might not even notice you. Although it's unlikely when you look as fire as you do!"

"Thanks G! Hopefully they won't see me. Although part of me wants to talk to them and then I'll know for definite if he's here or not, instead of worrying the whole time that he is!" Her words were coming out as erratic as her thoughts. But the thought that he could walk through the door at any moment made her shudder.

"Don't look up, just act natural, they're getting up!" Ash muttered under her breath.

Giorgio's idea of acting natural was to strike a sultry pose and sit there pouting! Melissa put her head right down and tried to cover her face with her hair, Ashlyn was the only one who coolly sipped on her drink.

"They've gone! Woo hoo!"

Giorgio and Ash seemed pleased with the outcome and Melissa was too, but now she was left with the same question on a loop in her mind – 'Is Chris here too?' She decided to keep her thoughts to herself though. She'd already felt completely neurotic when she talked about him. Although they were always supportive, she was sure she sounded a little crazy to them, paranoid too at times. But she knew that it was only her that knew what he was truly capable of, the lengths he would go to to keep his control over her.

"Well, that's a relief! I just can't believe that, can you?" Melissa had put her guard up and locked the key, she wasn't going to spoil their holiday for anyone. "I think we need a round of shots to get over that near miss!" Melissa tried to convince them that she felt the same relief she did.

"I'll get them in!" Giorgio leapt up from his chair and danced his way to the bar. His Purple spikey hair, with the dustings of glitter in it, shimmered under the neon lights in the bar.

"You sure you're, ok?"

"Of course, they're gone now aren't they and like you said, he wasn't there so he probably isn't even on holiday with them. It was just a bit of a shock, but I'm totally fine now."

"Oh good!" Ash smiled and leant in to cuddle her. Melissa kept feeling that she could open up a bit more to Ashlyn, but she just never felt like the time was right.

It got later and later, she'd managed to put the whole thing to bed in her mind and enjoyed the rest of the night with little worry. So after a fabulous night dancing their hearts out at the club, they decided to walk back up the strip towards the apartment. They were bouncing into things as they zig zagged across the pavements when she spotted Chris' team mates walking straight towards them. It was still just three of them. She got an instant pang of dread - but as her confidence had increased tenfold by the amount of alcohol she'd had, the dread quickly evaporated. She felt certain now that Chris wasn't with them. In her confident drunken state she let out huge "Woo hoo!"

Giorgio and Ashlyn chuckled, "What you 'woo hooing' at!"

"He's not here look! Woo hoo!" Melissa laughed with pure relief and pointed in the direction of the three of them.

198

"Ey! You're Chris' bird aren't you!" One of the guys shouted over as they got closer.

"Number one I'm not a bird and two I'm not Chris' anything, I'm not with him anymore!" She barked at them.

They all looked at each other puzzled, as if they were completely unaware that her and Chris had split up. "Oh right, he never said anything." One of them replied.

The six of them began chatting for a while when a debate broke following Giorgio's drunked slur professing his love for a cheese roll.

"it's a barmcake"

"it's a roll or a sandwich…"

The 4 of them continued their drunken debate when one of them broke off to speak to Melissa.

"I'm Kenny by the way, I don't think Chris ever introduced us properly, but I used to see you at the matches."

"Well, he wouldn't introduce us would he, because then I might have slept with you or run off with you!" Melissa sarcastically jested at him. Her confidence had grown even more along with her drunken state.

"Would you!" Kenny laughed, notably surprised by her response.

"Well not just you, I mean anyone! Not that you're not lovely! I'm sure your very lovely, I just mean I wasn't allowed to talk to anyone!" Melissa was trying to make as much sense as she could in her half cut state.

"Come on, we're going in here!" Giorgio started walking into the Irish bar.

"I thought we were going back to the apartment G!" Ash questioned looking a bit worse for wear.

"We'll just have one for the road." Giorgio waved his arms, gesturing for them all to follow him and they did.

One for the road, turned into two and they were all having a great time. Melissa had surprised herself at how relaxed she felt, seeing as though they were friends of Chris' after all.

"I thought I was going to bump into Chris when I saw you three, I was gutted!"

"Oh no, he's alright Chris, but we don't know him enough to go away with him, he's a teammate yes, but us three are mates too."

"Oh right, so you don't like him then?" she quickly quizzed.

"No," he laughed, "I didn't say I didn't like him."

"Well, I don't! There I said it! I don't like him and haven't for a very long time!" She confessed to them.

"Funny, we'd asked him where you were the other week as you'd not been to any games for ages. But he never said you'd split up, he said you'd got a new job, so you couldn't come to the games anymore as you always had to work."

Melissa started laughing, she thought it was comical that he had spent years telling her he couldn't speak to her at the matches as he was too embarrassed of her, but now he didn't want to tell anyone that they weren't together.

"Well, well, isn't that funny! Well, it's not funny it's sad. The whole thing is just sad." Melissa was rambling more and more after becoming lost in her thoughts. But he made a joke about it and quickly changed the subject. He continued making her laugh at his jokes which had made her forget the whole thing. She looked at Kenny and smiled.

"...Anyway, do you know what Kenny; I think you're funny and very nice and I think we should go and have sex."

Melissa's offer visibly came as a shock to Kenny, but he didn't take long to accept.

"I think I would like that." He chuckled.

"Come on then!" Melissa stood up and got hold of his hand. Kenny stood up straight after her. "Ash, Giorgio I'll see you back at the apartment." She didn't explain, she didn't need to and the others just watched and sniggered knowingly as Melissa and Kenny strolled up the hill hand in hand.

Kenny wasn't exactly handsome, he had obviously taken a few knocks to his face playing rugby and his hair was red and a little crazy, but she didn't really see any of that anyway. Yes, Kenny had been nice to her, but it wasn't like she fancied him.

This was simply a case of doing something because she could, because she felt like having sex and she felt like having it with Kenny. The fact he was Chris' teammate didn't even enter her inebriated head.

The sex was a little awkward and 'fumbly', they were both so drunk. But she was enjoying the feeling of being free to do what she wanted, and it was nice to feel sexy. Kenny was obviously enjoying himself to and wanted her to stay over at his apartment, but she insisted that she needed to go. As soon as she left the apartment, she regretted it and she wondered when she was ever going to learn that this wasn't the answer to feeling whole again.

They were near the end of their holiday and Melissa had managed to get over her embarrassment at how bold she'd been with Kenny. She'd had moments where she'd worry about how Chris would react. But her new lease for holiday-life had her fed up of worrying about 'what if's' so she quickly kept putting it to the back of her mind.

That night they went back to the club for their end of season party. Typically, they were drunk and dancing with their arms draped all over each other. Giorgio was up on stage with yet another fabulous guy whom he was in a world of his own with. Ash & Melissa had danced and giggled all night. Their euphoria was ecstatic. Then out of nowhere in the middle of the dance floor, Ash stopped dancing, reached in, and kissed Melissa. Melissa instantly kissed her back without any hesitation, after all they'd kissed each other before. But she suddenly realised where they were. Giorgio was there, Chris's team mates were there, they were standing smack bang in the middle of one the largest clubs in Majorca, kissing each other in front of everyone. She played ping pong with her conscience in her head. Part of her cared, part of her didn't. Her paranoia grew as she continued the game in her head. 'So what if it got back to Chris? So what if it got back to Anthony?' As soon as she had entertained that thought, she pulled away and starting dancing, giving Ash enough of a reassuring smile so not to arouse suspicion as to why she'd really pulled away. She wondered when the pain of wanting Anthony back, back when they were in their own bubble, would it ever leave you?

They were so sweaty when they got back, that they stripped off their dresses, as soon as they walked through the apartment door.

"Oh my god it is sooo hot!" Ashlyn walked straight into the bedroom and they lay back onto the bed wearing only her tiny sheer thong. "Speaking of hot, you looked gorgeous tonight Liss! Honestly, unbelievably gorgeous!"

"Yes, well Rose tinted glasses will do that to you!"

"They're not tinted, I don't have glasses." Ash's speech was getting a little more slurred now. "Liss, sleep with me tonight! Please! I want to! I don't want to be on my own, I don't want a man. I just want to sleep with you."

"Of course I will Ash, we're sharing a room. I've not copped off with anyone I'm right here."

Melissa held Ash's hand to reassure her. She wasn't sure how to handle it, she loved Ash so much and she didn't want her to feel alone, but she was so confused about how she felt about the 'kissing' situation.

"Just need a wee" Melissa tiptoed to the bathroom and sat on the toilet as she pondered whether sharing a bed with Ash was a good idea. She didn't want anything to happen that they both might regret or equally affect their friendship. She washed her hands then tiptoed back to her bed and found Ash fast asleep. Melissa fell into her bed next to her and fell asleep as soon as her head hit the pillow.

She woke up early, the sun was hot all ready and the heat in the room was becoming unbearable. She looked over at Ashlyn, who was lying in her knickers with her back to Melissa. She wasn't sure she could face Ashlyn yet, she knew the kiss had been passed off as harmless fun, but she couldn't help but wonder did Ash want more? Does *she* want more? Her head was clouded with a huge hangover but she forced herself to get up out of bed. She needed to get out of the stuffy, stale room and clear her head. She didn't want Ash or Giorgio to worry when they woke up so she wrote a note on the back of the welcome pack:

'Hey! I've been awake for hours; my head is banging. I need food and a dip in the water so I've gone out. I didn't want to wake you both but I'll stop at the local on the way back and see if you're there if you're not I'll come back here.

See you both later,
Liss xx'

She wanted to reiterate the word both so that Ash wouldn't get the beer fear and worry that she had spoiled their relationship. Ash may have made the first move, but Melissa knew that she had been flirting back leading up to it. She closed the heavy wooden door behind her as quietly as she could and she made her way along the terracotta tiled hallway out onto the main strip. She was immediately hit with an abundance of heat and the rays of sunshine were blinding. She squinted and wondered why she still hadn't purchased any sunglasses. It was a mistake that she wouldn't be making the next time she went on holiday, that was for sure. She walked down the street, passing the bars that they had drunkenly fallen out of most nights, smiling at the majority of the memories and cringing at the memories of walking home hand in hand with Kenny. It wasn't his fault but she just wanted to erase that night from her memory. She passed the local as they were cleaning the tables and getting ready to open. The owner recognised her and shouted over.

"Top of the morning to you Liss! You're up with the lark aren't you, or are you just getting home!"

"Hey cheeky! Ha ha, no it's not the walk of shame honest - I'm going in the wrong direction for that. I just woke early so thought I'd head out for a swim in the sea and cool down. It's boiling today, isn't it? "

"Ey tis, we've never known it this hot at the end of season before!"

"I'll be back for some breakfast and a cheeky pint once I've dried off."

"Ok darling, you want me to reserve your favourite table?"

"Oh yes please, I'm sure Ashlyn and Giorgio will be down for some food once they wake up. It was a heavy one last night!"

They both laughed.

"Ok darling, enjoy your swim and I'll see you later."

"See you later!" Melissa proceeded to walk down the strip, she could feel her skin heating up already, and she realised she hadn't put any suncream on. She convinced herself that there was no need to turn around as it was only early so

206

she wouldn't get sunburnt. She noticed that she was walking tall today, the night after she'd been with Kenny she wanted to hide away and did everything she could to blend into her surroundings. Today she was ready to embrace the moment, jump in the sea and she was smiling. Although her head was filled with questions, she wondered whether her feelings were letting her know the answers. 'I was willing to.' she deliberated to herself. The straps on her bright red bikini top were cutting into her slightly, and her bottom was sweating in her bikini bottoms that were hidden by her denim skirt. She was nearly at the beach now and she couldn't wait to kick off her flip flops, feel the sand between her toes and paddle in the sea. As she reached the sand she did exactly that along with taking a deep breath of the fresh sea air. The gentle breeze blew her hair across her face and she whipped the bobble off her wrist and threw her hair up into a pony. As she stood at the edge of the sea, the tide washing in and out over her feet, she closed her eyes and lifted her face up towards the sky, embracing the warmth of the sun on her face. She got lost in the sounds of the waves and the seagulls. She felt completely serene, relaxed, it was as if each time that the tide came in it washed some of her painful memories out to sea. She sank further and further into the moment. She put her head back down and opened her eyes, she smiled as the light of the sun danced on the ripples of the water below her. She looked around, the beach was so quiet there was barely anyone else on there apart from her. She inhaled deeply as the sea breeze stroked her face. She was really pleased she had decided to come on this holiday and she'd made new memories to eradicate the old ones. Every time she did something new, something that she didn't think she was capable of, it gave her confidence such a boost and slowly started to renew faith back in herself.

CHAPTER 11.

HE'S BACK

After the taxi driver dropped them off outside their house of course the first port of call would be 'The Crown'. They literally threw their suitcases into the hall and set off for the pub.

"Kieran and Charlie will kill us if they come in and trip over all of our cases!" Melissa worried.

They all laughed as they walked down the road arm in arm, still dressed in their holiday clothes ready to show off their tan; even though the temperature was a lot cooler in the UK and it definitely would have been wise to put their jackets on. However, each of them would have rather been a little chilly than miss out on the opportunity to showcase their sun kissed glowing skin.

Giorgio as always was first to the bar, he was so generous. You had to fight him in order to pay at times. He got them three pints with a shot to chase.

"Right ladies, this is still classed as one of our holiday days, so we've got to make the most of it. Plus the fact that we are not falling straight into bed means that we didn't party hard enough, so let's try and do better shall we!" He smiled as wide as a cheshire cat as he raised his glass for them to all cheers.

Six hours later they were suitably drunk and making sure that they were partying hard as instructed, they had already been told off for dancing on the tables and they were on their last warning from the landlord that they would be barred until the weekend if they did it again. (He never barred them for any longer than that, as they were some of his best customers, despite them regularly getting a little too carried away, he knew they were harmless.) As they fell out of the pub, the cold air hit all of them.

"Oh my god its freezing!" Giorgio shuddered.

"I know I wish I'd have brought my jacket now!" Ash agreed.

They linked arms to attempt to generate some warmth. They started stumbling down the main road, laughing as each one of them took a tumble respectively, falling into a big pile.

As Melissa got up from the pavement with a little help from Giorgio, she noticed a white car drive past. As drunk as she was, the end of number plate seemed familiar. Then her heart sank as she'd also noticed it was a white Subaru Impreza. Her eyes may have been blurry, but she was certain it was *him*. She remembered how excited Chris was when he'd got his red alloy wheels. The car continued to drive past but she started to question if it was just her mind playing tricks on her. 'Surely there was more than one car enthusiast who had the same 'boy racer' taste?' she nervously questioned herself. But she couldn't see who was driving as the windows were blacked out.

"Who was that?" Ash asked, as she noticed Melissas face following the car speeding past.

"Who was what?" Melissa quickly tried to shield what she thought she'd seen by quickly changing her facial expression and turning the question back to Ash. (She remembered how she'd panicked unnecessary on holiday and didn't want to keep coming across as a paranoid lunatic.)

"Liss, what do you mean?" worried Ash.

"Oh, no one. I thought someone waved at us as they went past that's all."

As they got back home she was inundated by flash backs and video replay in her head of the car going past.

"Hey, don't be sick out there Liss!" Giorgio laughed. As Melissa was frantically grappling with handles trying to open the patio doors.

"What? No, I'm not going to be sick. I just need a cigarette!" She started pulling and pushing at the door handles, as the doors seemed to be stuck together, she was desperate to get outside. She felt like she couldn't breath and was being suffocated by her heavy thoughts.

"Hey, calm down, here let me do it! Are you sure you're not going to be sick? You look like you've seen a ghost, you've gone white babe!"

"I'm fine, I just need to get out for some air!" She burst through the doors as soon as Giorgio opened them. Ash and Giorgio exchanged looks, they could tell something was bothering her but they decided to give her some space.

She sat down on the wall outside and put her head in her hands, she felt like she was spinning. When she lifted her head back up she threw it back and glanced at the stars. She pulled a cigarette from the packet and placed it in her trembling lips. She could barely light it as the lighter was shaking so much and the cigarette was vibrating frantically with each tremor of her lips. She felt like she was falling to pieces but she desperately tried to compose herself. She didn't want anyone to see her turmoil, especially as everyone was still in holiday mode. But she couldn't stop her hands from shaking. She kept seeing the car over and over. It flashed by so fast but she was positive it was *him*. She inhaled and exhaled deeply on her cigarette just trying to calm her nerves, but it wasn't working. She jumped as she heard a noise at the bottom of the garden. She spun round to see what it was, her heart was thumping so loud she felt like it was about to burst out of her chest. As she glanced around the garden, she saw a pair of beady eyes staring right at her from the undergrowth. Her fear quickly diminished and felt relieved when she noticed it was just a fox. It stood still in the dark watching her from a far. Ironically that's what she felt like Chris was doing, watching her from the shadows without her knowing. She felt sick at the very thought and began to cry. She'd naively thought all her fears and worries would've left her once she'd arrived in London. But the realisation and knowing feeling that they hadn't, made her feel crushed inside. She wondered if it would ever go away. She contemplated whether she should pour herself another drink as she tried to stop herself from crying and wiped her eyes. The shock had almost certainly drained all the alcohol from her body. She turned back to look at the fox but it fled just as the patio door opened.

"Hey Liss, are you ok honey?" Ashlyn approached cautiously.

"I'm fine Ash, I said I was fine didn't I! Why does nobody listen to me! Why does no one take me seriously!" She barked at Ash then began sobbing uncontrollably.

Ash was taken aback by the way Melissa had snapped at her, but she knew it was completely out of character. She could see that she was upset so she didn't retaliate to her outburst.

"I know honey, I know you're fine, I'm just asking in case you wanted to talk, we're friends remember, that's what friends do."

"I'm sorry, I didn't mean to snap, I'm so sorry, please don't hate me!"

Ash rushed to Melissa's side and hugged her. "Hey, it's ok, whatever it is it will be ok. I could never hate you, so don't even think that. Come on Liss, it's ok."

"No it's not ok, I don't think it will ever be ok, he just won't go away!

"Who won't, Chris?" Ash looked confused.

Melissa realised she had said too much, "No-one, I don't know what I'm saying, I'm just tired and drunk. I just need to go to bed, I'm fine, honestly I'm fine. Just ignore me."

Melissa stood up quickly and retreated back into the house to avoid any further questioning.

"Liss wait, whats happened?" Ash shouted after her but Melissa pretended she hadn't heard. She dashed past Giorgio and Kieran with her head down and raced all the way upstairs as quickly as she could. Ash decided to give her some space.

Melissa tossed and turned all night. Replaying the car passing by, over and over in her mind, desperately hoping to create a clear memory of who was behind the wheel and rationalize the whole thing. (Just like she'd done when she'd thought she'd seen him on the tube.)

'He wouldn't be driving around a huge city like this just looking for me…surely?'

She felt frustrated that he was back in her head, consuming her erratic thoughts. She hadn't even been back from holiday 24 hours and had already found herself shackled to her chains of anxiety – not that she'd completely escaped them on holiday, but she thought she'd at least cut her way through a few of them.

She jumped up and headed over to the bedroom to splash her face when she noticed the window was open. There was an alleyway that ran alongside the back of the gardens that the kids used to get to the neighbouring high school. 'What if he's hiding there?' Her paranoia had intensified. By now she knew she needed to get to sleep. So, shut the window, brushed off her suspicion and decided to go straight to bed.

***

She woke up and sat bolt upright, she was sweating from head to toe. Her body was trembling, and she was crying uncontrollably. She couldn't remember exactly what she was dreaming about but it all came back to Chris.

She lay back on her bed, rubbing her cheek gently into the pillow as she nestled in for comfort. She could hear at least two voices echoing down the hall, along with the sound of raindrops intermittently dripping onto her windowpane. She lay there for a while before she decided she needed to get out of bed and face the day. She headed to the window to open the blinds. She usually loved Saturday's at the house, it would begin with a super long lie in so she always felt super rested. Followed by afternoon drinks in the 'The Crown', that pretty much began as soon as the pub opened its doors. Then they would head to their favourite chinese to pick up some food to take home, followed by a party in the kitchen or Giorgio's room. She walked away from the window towards her bedside table and picked up her phone. She looked at the screen and noticed she had a text message. It was from her sister who'd sent it 2 hours ago.

FROM JENNIFER – HEY SIS, I HOPE YOU'RE GOOD. I NEED TO TELL YOU SOMETHING I DON'T KNOW IF IT'S IMPORTANT OR NOT BUT I THOUGHT THAT YOU BEST KNOW. XX

Her heart sank, 'what could that be?' she wondered. Why would she text her at eight o'clock on a Saturday morning unless something was wrong? If it was something bad she wasn't sure she could cope, especially after last night. She'd wanted to have a good day. She didn't want anything to distract her from that, she needed to stay on course but she replied:

FROM MELISSA – I'M GREAT THANKS SIS. WHAT'S THE MATTER? ARE YOU OK? XXX

All anyone back home thought was that it was just one adventure after the next in London for Melissa, that she was living the dream and that was exactly the way she wanted to keep it.

FROM JENNIFER – SHOULD I CALL YOU? IT'S ABOUT CHRIS. XXX

She texted her sister back, she knew she wouldn't be able to hold it together over a phone call with her and she swore she wouldn't shed any more tears where he was concerned, so she told a white lie...

FROM MELISSA – I'M WITH PEOPLE SO I CAN'T REALLY TALK, JUST TEXT ME IF YOU CAN. XXX

FROM JENNIFER – HE'S BEEN GOING OUT WITH A FRIEND OF MINE CHARLOTTE. ONLY A FEW DATES, SHE DIDN'T TELL ME AT FIRST BUT NOW SHE HAS, SHE SAID SHE'S NOT GOING OUT WITH HIM AGAIN AS ALL HE DOES IS TALK ABOUT YOU AND ASK HER QUESTIONS ABOUT YOU. I JUST THOUGHT YOU SHOULD KNOW AS SHE FOUND IT A BIT WEIRD AND SO DO I. XXX

FROM MELISSA - CHARLOTTE DOESN'T KNOW WHERE I LIVE DOES SHE SIS? XX

FROM JENNIFER – NO, NOT THE EXACT ADDRESS BUT I HAVE TOLD HER WHERE

ABOUTS IN LONDON YOU'RE LIVING. I'M SORRY, I DIDN'T THINK IT WOULD MATTER. SHE NEVER TOLD ME SHE WAS GOING OUT WITH HIM. I'M SURE SHE WOULDN'T HAVE SAID ANYTHING LIKE THAT TO HIM THOUGH. XX

'So he **has** been following me, watching me. It must have been him?' In one breath she was pleased she wasn't going insane, but in the next she felt crippled by fear. If he was going to such lengths to find her, what exactly was his plan?

FROM MELISSA – DON'T WORRY, YOU WEREN'T TO KNOW. I JUST NEED TO KNOW IF HE KNOWS. PLEASE CAN YOU CHECK FOR ME? XX

FROM JENNIFER – OK, I WILL. LOVE YOU XXX

FROM MELISSA – LOVE YOU TOO XXX

Melissa didn't want her sister to feel guilty, she wasn't to know that her friend would end up going out with Chris. Nor would she know the seriousness of him knowing where she lives could be; as even now, she still hadn't shared everything that had happened between them. So her sister couldn't possibly have known the severity of the situation. So she didn't want to worry her with it either. She couldn't bear the thought of unloading her pain and upset onto her loved ones. She could see it in their eyes whenever she had ever touched on the subject and it went against every fibre of her being to burden her loved ones with her 'problems' too.

She felt helpless, it felt like there was no escape. No escaping him. No escaping the past and no escaping her feelings. She longed for someone to swoop in and wave a magic wand, knowing that no one could. She'd had no real proof that he had been watching her, she just knew in her gut that he had. But now this had fed her inner lunacy and had given her all the proof that she needed. Equally she began to rationalise and knew it wasn't enough to take any action in terms of contacting a solicitor or the police. Her sadness turned to anger, 'Why can't he just disappear! Why can't he just go away and leave me to live my life! He didn't even want me when he had me? What the fuck is wrong with him!' She paced around her bedroom not knowing what to do next. She became fearful of him taking her by surprise, what if he was just waiting for the right moment to catch her alone. She still felt that he wouldn't harm her, but in the next breath the fear of what if consumed her? 'What if he's so angry now he does flip! What if he can't stand being out of control so much that the thought of her living her own life has driven him insane? Going out with her sister's friend just to blatantly try and get information about her wasn't exactly the behaviour of someone who is sane. But what if he knows about Kenny and it had pushed him over the edge?'

She lay back onto her bed, thinking about the times she thought she had seen him whilst in London. It made her question if all the times that she thought she'd walked care-free around London without fear – were they just times she was under his surveillance, biding his time, waiting for the right moment? The excessive self-questioning continued in her head.

'The right moment for what though? Why exactly does he need to watch me, what is he waiting for? Did the last text I sent him push him over the edge? What if he wants to hurt me? Would he hurt me? No, no no… he wouldn't, would he?' Her conflicting questions she'd started to mutter were beginning to be laced with anxiety. "He's just desperate, that's all. It's fine, it's completely fine, it's all fine!" She attempted to shut down her thoughts on it and desperately tried to reassure herself that she was in fact 'fine.'

She thought that she'd better distract herself by getting ready to go out. Then the thought of him being out there watching her last night made her recoil. 'Maybe I should just stay at home today just in case.' She tried to justify her desire to stay home further. 'At least until I know exactly how much Chris knows.' Then the optimist in her momentarily broke free and she started to put it down to it being just a bad coincidence. But eventually after battling it out in her head, playing a rematch of the ping pong game, the fear had taken over. She decided to get back under the covers and stay in her safe zone.

Just as she was drifting off to sleep after lying there aimlessly for so long, her phone bleeped. She instantly sat forward to pick it up from the end of the bed where she had dropped it after her sister had text earlier. She was hoping it was her sister Jennifer again and that she would be able to satisfy the hundreds of scenarios Melissa had played out earlier in her head. But it wasn't her, it was Callum.

FROM CALLUM - Hey sexy, do you fancy a drink tomorrow? I'm at a loose end so I thought it would be cool if we chilled having a few drinks and then you know, maybe have a repeat performance of last time? ;) xx

Callum had text at the right time for him, but the wrong time for her. She felt scared and vulnerable and wanted to feel safe again. Despite her prior reluctancy, the thought of being around a strong man that could easily fight off Chris if needed, really appealed to her.

But once again instead of dealing with her feelings, she buried them deep and turned her attention to flirting. It gave her that instant dose of 'feel-good' she desperately craved.

TO CALLUM - YES, SOUNDS GOOD. LET ME KNOW WHERE AND WHAT TIME? LOOK FORWARD TO IT XX

***

Melissa sat confidently waiting for Callum to arrive at the pub, it was a nice day, she felt good and she was looking forward to relaxing and watching the band at the pub. Callum walked in and his eyes lit up when he saw Melissa.

"You look nice…sexy! A tan suits you!"

Melissa blushed and put her head down, even though she felt a little better and more confident each day, receiving compliments still felt so alien to her.

They got some drinks in and the band had been playing for around half an hour, Melissa was having a great time, they both were, well at least she thought they were.

"Will you stop staring at him?!" Callum had a slight grip on her arm and he leaned in speaking intensely.

Melissa was confused. "Who? Who am I staring at? The band?"

"Don't act like you're stupid! You know exactly what you are doing and you're making me look like a right dick head!"

"What? Callum, what on earth are you talking about? I'm looking at the band, because we came here to watch the band?"

"Don't start being cocky, it doesn't suit you!"

"What!" Melissa was completely taken aback by this sudden irrational behaviour and her instinct was to try and sort it out and apologise.

"Look I'm sorry if it looks like I'm staring at someone, I'm genuinely not and I don't really understand where this is coming from, but can't we just forget it and have a nice time?" She looked into his eyes, hopeful that this was a complete misunderstanding that would blow over quickly. "I mean to be fair, I can't really see anyone else anyway past this group of old men and they're not really my type!" She smiled as she looked around and tried to make light of the situation.

"Are you taking the piss?! You've just done it again, when I've just asked you not to?" Callum's eyes had enlarged and he was now talking through gritted teeth, "we're leaving – now!"

"What!" Melissa could not believe how he was acting! She felt very unnerved, she could see the anger in his eyes and she knew she didn't want to go anywhere with him.

"Get up now, we're going!" he demanded.

A wave of rage and defiance rushed through her body. This relationship was meant to be casual and fun, yet here she was being accused of something she hadn't done and feeling embarrassed in public. A red flag went up in her mind and started waving frantically. "I'm not going anywhere! I've still got a drink and I'm enjoying myself. If you want to go, then go!"

Callum seemed dumbstruck by her reaction. "If I go and you don't come with me, then you won't see me again. I can't have you embarrassing me like this!"

"Me embarrassing you! You're embarrassing yourself and I'm going nowhere!" She felt so proud of herself, she nearly gave in to old ways, apologising when she didn't even know what she was supposed to have done wrong, but she clawed it back, she took control. So what if she didn't see him again, it might be awkward with Denny, but there are other jobs out there and she was not about to be pushed about by anyone. If Callum could react like this when they were meant to be in a casual relationship, she could only imagine how he would behave if she were to continue seeing him.

She watched as he made his way through the crowds and didn't look back. She did worry for a second what everyone would be thinking about her, why had her date stormed off. But as quick as the thought entered her head, she quickly shrugged it off and sat dancing in her chair to the band, sipping her drink and feeling more liberated than she ever had in her life.

After around half an hour she felt a little deflated. She was concerned by Callums behaviour and wondered how she had attracted someone like that again. She worried that maybe that was just how all men were. Maybe that was just what she would have to put up with should she ever want to settle down with someone. That thought completely depressed her and she decided to stay clear of guys for a while however casual their offers may be. With that she decided to go home and just hibernate in her room until she needed to resurface for work.

As she left the pub, she glanced around. It had suddenly dawned on her that Callum may have been waiting for her outside. That was something Chris would have done to try and catch her in the act. She had seen how angry Callum had gotten and it worried her. She couldn't see him, so started to walk home. She felt comforted by the fact she was on a busy road and so near to home, that even if he had decided to wait for her, he would be unlikely to act out in such a public place. As she reached her front door, she glanced round once more, she was relieved that there was no sign of Callum, or Chris for that matter. She still couldn't shake off the feeling that she was being watched. She turned her key slowly and walked through the door. She could hear everyone in the kitchen chatting and laughing and she closed the door as quietly as she could. She didn't want to know that she was home, she didn't feel in the mood to explain things, or hear I told you so from Ash, so she tiptoed upstairs to her room.

She came in, kicked off her shoes and switched on the radio before she flopped down onto the bed. Ironically Ne- Yo 'So sick of love songs' was playing and she rolled her eyes. She had turned on her music to try and drown out the sound of her own voice singing 'I told you so' repeatedly throughout her head. The song was only halfway through when there was a knock on her bedroom door. She sighed heavily and rolled her eyes again; she wasn't in the mood for company and she had zero energy to muster up a fake smile.

"Who is it?" she asked, trying not to sound miffed at the person knocking.

"It's Ash babe…can I come in?"

"Yeah sure, it's open, come in."

Ash walked in, she was in her pyjamas with her hair and make up still all perfectly in place from work. "Hey, are you ok?" she asked as she joined Melissa by sitting on the bed and placed her arm around her. She looked concerned. "We're all in the kitchen you know?" she continued.

"Yea I know, sorry".

"You don't have to be sorry babe, it's just it's not like not to come down and say hi…or grab a glass of wine – are you feeling well?" She winked with a playful smile.

Melissa smiled back and they both had a little chuckle, " I know I'm sorry I don't mean to be ignorant I'm just a bit fed up! I don't want to bore you with all of the details, I"

Ash interrupted "How many times do I have to tell you hun, you don't have to be sorry; we all get a bit fed up at times, but it's good to talk about it. You will hear us all moan enough – we live together, we need to look out for each other. You don't have to bottle everything up and hide away up here when you feel fed up – you know what I mean?"

Melissa nodded as a tiny tear formed in the corner of her eye, it wasn't particularly a sad tear, more of a happy one. It was a realisation that she wasn't alone anymore, that she had to change her old habits and let people in as hard as that maybe.

"Let us have a chat – you'll feel better babe. I promise. You get your pjs on and I'll go down and grab us a couple of glasses and a bottle – or two" she winked again, "I won't be a minute".

Melissa and Ashlyn sat crossed legged on her bed, the music was playing, and they had been putting the world to rights for the last hour and were already one bottle of wine down.

"I just give up honestly! I mean I don't even know why I went out with him anyway – I told myself that I was going to be single for at least a year, I don't even want a boyfriend so what was I doing?" Melissa shook her head at herself and reached out to pour another glass of wine before realising the bottle was empty, as one drop hit the bottom of her glass.

"Here!" Ash passed her the other bottle to open before she returned to the conversation "It's hard when you're on your own, trying to figure things out, it's hard not to fall for the compliments or an attractive offer trust me I've been there PLENTY of times – we all make mistakes in life, and sometimes we repeat those mistakes in the hope that this time it won't be a mistake because at the end of the day we just want to be loved, you know what I mean?" She took the bottle and poured her own glass.

"Yeah I know exactly what you mean, and you are so right, it's just, we just want to be loved. My counsellor told me that. But I need to learn to love myself first – not to become full of myself kind of way just…well you know what I mean!"

"Why've you had a councillor? If you don't mind me asking? I didn't think you would have had the chance to mess up as much as me, you're at least 5 years younger aren't you and I'm not even at the councillor stage yet" she laughed, "no offence."

"None taken…well basically to keep it brief my ex wasn't very nice to me, at all really, so I fell for someone else and kind of had an affair and he turned out to be not very nice either so along with some other stuff that happened years ago and so to stop myself from doing myself any harm I went to see a councillor!" she inhaled deeply as she had crammed as much into that sentence as possible so she didn't have to think about it too much again.

Ash looked at her with a knowing smile, she knew that there was a lot more to the story, but she could tell how uncomfortable going there was making her, so she did not pry any further.

"She told me I need to know my self-worth and until I know my self-worth then effectively, I'm going to keep ending up with the same guy over and over effectively but like wearing different clothes – kind of!" she took a big swig of wine. "and that Ash is why I have just been out with the same man – and here's me thinking I'm making progress!" Her epiphany along with the fact that the wine had now clearly gone to her head made her laugh it off light heartedly.

"Oh babe" Ash echoed her laugh and gave her a big hug, "shall we go and have a cigarette!"

"Yes! That's a fabulous idea!"

They linked their arms, squeezing through the door and downstairs with difficulty inducing further drunken giggles.

"Hey, come on don't cry" she wiped away her tears, "come here" she gestured for Melissa to join her for a hug as she held out her arms to her. They embraced tightly and Melissa let out all her tears, she was even entirely sure why she was crying; sometimes it just built up like a volcano inside until she could not contain them anymore.

Ashlyn brushed the back of Melissa's head with her hand, reassuring her it was ok to let go.

Melissa felt overcome with a sense of comfort, trust, and warmth. She felt safe and almost instantly stronger than she did merely minutes before. Ashlyn kissed the side of Melissa's head and they continued to hug. Melissa wondered if Ashlyn needed the hug just as much as she did. Ashlyn always seemed so confident and together, but following their heart to heart, Mellissa had come to realise that most people only show one version of themselves to the world, while they harbour their true feelings and fears inside. Ashlyn moved her hands slowly down from Mellissa's shoulders, down her back and along the sides of her waist. She rested her hands on her hips withher fingertips just brushing the top of her bottom. Mellissa felt shivers shoot down her spine. She felt overwhelmed with a sense that Ash wanted more from their embrace. Within that same moment she felt completely stupid for imagining it. Then Ashlyn pulled her body away from Melissa, but left her hands still resting on her hips. She looked straight into Melissa's eyes, the silence meant that Melissa thought that Ash was sure to hear her heart racing. She was not sure if she was picking up the wrong messages, but it seemed that Ash was looking so deeply at Melissa for reassurance that it was ok to make the next move. Melissa said nothing, she just stared right back at Ash trying desperately to work out the situation and how she felt about it. Part of her was thrilled by the thought of becoming more intimate now matter how far it may go. She longed for a genuine, gentle touch of someone who cared for her on her body. Being intimate with a woman was never something that had crossed her mind before, but she admired Ash and she wanted to explore what these vibes were between them, because it felt safe and warm.

CHAPTER 12.

I CAN SEE YOU

The club was dark, warm and stuffy. A strong smell of body odors hit them as soon as they walked down the stairs. It was soon obvious why. As soon as the strobes hit the dancefloor, she could see it dripping off all the scantily clad bodies that were crammed in there.

"Look at the sweat dripping off everyone!" Melissa yelled to Giorgio.

"I know! Isn't it fabulous!" Giorgio threw his head back laughing.

They pushed their way through the mass of bodies and headed towards the stage. They climbed right up onto the stage, and they started laughing and dancing. The darkness of the club mixed with the flashing lights meant that she couldn't really see if anyone was watching them or not, so she didn't feel conscious at all. Melissa became very aware that her and Ashlyn were heavily outnumbered by men in this club. Despite the number of men surrounding them, there weren't getting an ounce of attention. It was all being directed in Giorgio's direction; it felt so freeing. She wasn't dancing to impress; she didn't care what she looked like she was just able to dance her troubles away. She loved the way the beat of the music helped bring her to life and take her away from drowning in her own thoughts. Last weekend had been a complete write off and she was determined this one a good one, the Gay club wasn't disappointing so far.

"Do you need the toilet? I'm going to freshen up a bit!" Ashlyn shouted over the music to Melissa.

"Yeah sure!"

"We'll be back in a minute G!" Ash tried to let Giorgio know where they were going, but he was far too busy lapping up all the attention he was getting to notice.

They pushed open the toilet door and felt instantly cooler. There weren't any queues in the ladies another bonus to being in a Gay Club.

"Ah that's better it's so warm in there tonight. Look at the state of my make up!" Ashlyn pointed toward her smudged make-up.

"I know, I'm roasting!" Melissa reached into her handbag to get her makeup, and instinctively checked her phone at the same time - there was a message of Chris. She paused momentarily before quickly opening it. She thought it was best to just get it over with and read what he had said rather than let it hang over her all night.

FROM CHRIS - I CAN SEE YOU

"What?" Melissa was confused at first and then as she read it again, she became a bit alarmed.

"Ash, what do you think this means?"

Ash read the text, "What, he's here?"

"No, he can't be, can he?"

"Well, he could be hon, it is a public club. What time did he send it?"

"Oh god, half an hour ago. Do you really think he could be here?"

"Honestly I don't know. I don't why you still allow him to contact you anyway. Why don't you change your number?" Melissa could sense the frustration in Ash's tone.

"Because I need to be able to communicate with him about the house don't I? He's not responding to either solicitor. only to me."

"Yes, of course he is, because then he's getting what he wants isn't he – to be able to speak to you!"

Ash was right, but Melissa wasn't sure what else she could do. The next logical thing would be to get court action or contact the police. But somehow Melissa managed to trivialise her situation in her head as not being worthy enough to go to the police. Not only that she didn't feel strong enough to face that right now. She didn't want to admit that the other reason she didn't want to change her number was because she still secretly longed for Anthony to get in touch. She wanted more than anything to discover that she had been wrong about him. That he had a really good reason for abandoning her and that he did really love her, after all. She still needed to hear that she hadn't been naive again. That she hadn't just been used by him. Even if he wasn't going to say he loved her, she still just couldn't understand why? Why did he throw her to the wolves? Why hasn't he contacted her and why did he turn so cold? Did he ever have any real feelings for her? Was it all an act? She still needed that closure. Because all the questions were still there in the back of her mind; 'what is wrong with me and why am I so unlovable?' The feeling of worthlessness swept over her all over again. Then she quickly snapped out of wallowing about the past as the harsh reality of the situation started to hit her hard.

"This can't be real? He must just be sending it to scare me. He can't be here; he just can't be? Can he??" She looked at Ashlyn for reassurance, but she seemed stuck for words. "I want to go home. I just need to get out of here."

She was used to his outbursts, him checking up on her but this felt like another level. It felt creepy. But if he'd done it to frighten her, it had worked.

"I don't even want to come out of the toilets, Ash. What if he's there? I don't want to see him."

"Look, even if he is there, you're with us, we won't let anything happen to you."

"Thank you." Melissa needed that reassurance.

"We're going to have to tell Giorgio why we've got to go though hun. You know yourself, there's no way we'd get him to leave this club without a good reason. We don't have to go into it all, we'll just say your ex is here and we need to leave fast. He'll understand."

"Ok, I'm sorry."

"Don't you be sorry, we'll sort it." Melissa began to feel a little safer with a confident Ash. But they came out of the toilets with caution. Melissa was frantically scanning the room to see if she could see him - she couldn't. The fact that she couldn't see him almost made her feel even more unnerved. The thought of him watching her from the shadowy corners of the club, without her knowing, the thought that he could just appear in front of her at any minute made her whole body shiver. They made their way over to Giorgio, Ashlyn lent into him to explain. Giorgio scanned the room with his eyes as Ash explained, his eyes then they met Melissa's and he mouthed "Let's go." (Much to the dismay of the guy he'd been chatting to at the side of him.)

With a slight air of caution, they all darted towards the exit which seemed it couldn't be anyfurther away to her. Ash & Giorgio had almost formed a human shield around her giving her some slight comfort, as they ushered her out the doors. Melissa was relieved to get outside, but she kept turning back just in case he had already left the club or he had followed them out.

They flagged down a black cab and jumped in. The relief she felt was immense. They'd only been in the cab a couple of minutes when her phone pinged.

FROM CHRIS - LEAVING SO SOON, YOU LOOKED LIKE YOU WERE HAVING FUN?

Her heart sank. He was there, he had been watching her. The colour drained out of her face.

"What is it, Liss? Are you ok?" Ashlyn shouted with concerned.

Melissa just handed her phone to Ashlyn, and turned to look out of the taxi window. She felt like crying and she knew if she'd speak before she could compose herself she wouldn't have been able to stop the tears from falling.

Ashlyn's face said it all. "What? What is is? Let me see!" Giorgio reached out his hand to take the phone. "What a weirdo? That's creepy! It's not normal!" He grimaced and was unable to hide his disgust from his face at Chris' behaviour.

Ash turned to Melissa, "Are you ok?"

She was so lost in thought, staring out of the window that she didn't hear Ash.

"Liss?" Ashlyn nudged her gently to prompt a response.

"What, sorry, I'm just trying to take it in….I just knew he was here. I could feel it!" She shrieked, desperately trying not to cry.

"Are you ok?" Ash asked again, looking more concerned.

She took a deep breath. "Yeah I'll be fine, I'm used to it now." Melissa knew she couldn't brush them off but she could feel tears building up and was fighting with every fibre of her being to stop them from coming out.

She couldn't wait to get into the house. "I'm desperate for a wee, so I might as well get my pjs on whilst I'm up there. I'll meet you in the kitchen." She started racing upstairs, it was only half-way up before her tears spilled out like uncontrollable sprinklers.

"Ok hun, I'll get you a drink ready!" Ash called after her from the bottom stair.

She'd managed to hold in her whaling until she was alone. A sense of complete despair consumed her and she wondered when this was going to end. Whether it would ever truly be over? She stopped herself from crying too much, she needed to compose herself. She knew the guys would already know that she'd been crying, but she went into default mode by 'putting on' her emotional armour once again. She wanted to show as much strength as she could.

Out of nowhere Callum entered her head. She recalled how flirtatious and powerful she felt around him. Even though something inside felt off with him and their last date had been a bit disastrous, she had found herself feeling a little addicted when she remembered how she'd felt around him. Each time she felt like she was losing her grip, she reached out for a life raft and at the moment, that for what ever reason was Callum. She deliberated reaching out to him for a moment only to decide that Callum was exactly what she needed. She knew Chris would never approach her if she was with Callum, he wasn't confrontational enough with other guys; especially not people he didn't know. If he was watching her, then maybe him seeing that would force him to realise that there was no going back for 'them'. She remembered how empty her mind felt that night she slept with Callum, how she was in-control she felt, and she wanted to feel like that again.

TO CALLUM - HEY CALLUM! DO YOU FANCY HOOKING UP TONIGHT? X

FROM CALLUM - HEY SEXY! I THOUGHT YOU'D BEEN AVOIDING ME! TONIGHT SOUNDS GOOD I'M AT A PARTY THOUGH BUT YOU CAN COME IF YOU WANT TO? WORK UP THE FOREPLAY THROUGHOUT THE NIGHT x

She smiled. She had been avoiding him, but maybe she was just reading too much into what happened at the pub last time. Maybe she was expecting him to be the same as Chris, and that she had written him off too soon. He made her feel sexy and wanted and he was already proud to take her to a party, unlike Chris who only ever took her anywhere when he knew he had to keep up appearances.

TO CALLUM - I CAN NEVER SAY NO TO A PARTY, SO COUNT ME IN XX

FROM CALLUM - GREAT! I WILL PICK YOU UP IN A TAXI AT 8 XX

TO CALLUM - SEE YOU LATER! XX

She already felt a little more in control, and it felt good.

CHAPTER 13.

HIT BY FEAR

She felt amazing. Her curls were sleek and shiny, her makeup was natural, but the bold red lip made her look striking. She was wearing a black lacy slip dress and it hugged her figure perfectly. A small part of hoped Chris would see her tonight, looking fabulous on the arm of another handsome man. She needed to send a message that made it loud and clear that she wasn't coming back. She just wanted him to stop playing games, take on the house and set her free. She couldn't take the thought of him hovering in the shadows any longer. She looked at the time and realised Callum would be here in the taxi at any minute. She checked herself in the mirror one last time and headed downstairs. Everyone in the house had already gone out, so she opened the front door and waited for the taxi to arrive. There was a slight chill in the air, she debated putting a jacket on, but she didn't want to take away any of the impact of her outfit so she decided to brave it.

241

She was getting a taxi door to door anyway. There wasn't any sign of the taxi as yet, so she glanced up and down the street to see if she could spot Chris or his car. There was no sign of him. Then just as she thought she would close the front door and wait in Giorgio's room just to be on the safe side, she spotted the taxi. She smiled, closed the door and carefully stepped down the steps towards the taxi.

"Wow! You look amazing!" Callum gushed as she opened the taxi door.

She didn't usually know what to do with compliments, but she accepted this one without a second thought.

"Thank you!" she blushed.

Callum scooted across to the opposite passenger seat to make room for Melissa, and as she shut the door and the taxi drove off he leaned in for a kiss and moved his hand up her inner thigh.

"Later!" she smiled, pulling away and moving his hand, "You're going to smudge my lipstick!" Her confidence increase was immediate in his company.

Callum smirked playfully as if he couldn't wait to get his hands on her. She felt so sexy around him.

They had been at the family do for nearly two hours, Denny was raving about Melissa to everyone and introducing her to all the family. Melissa was having a great time and as one of her favorite songs came on she hit the dance floor, willing anyone that would listen to come and join her. Callum stared at her. She smiled back at him. She was sure that he would be pleased that she was such a hit with everyone. She was dancing away, having a great time when Callum interrupted.

"I need you to come to the toilets with me."

"Aww, no in a minute, I love this song!"

"I can't wait!"

Melissa smiled at him cheekily, "Well if you can't wait!"

Callum took her hand and led her off the dancefloor. She felt little nervous, she wasn't sure she was bold enough to have sex in the toilets at a family party, but knowing Callum wanted her so bad, made her feel like maybe it was time to do something adventurous.

They fell through the toilet doors, she felt a little more drunk than she realised she was. She had left her card with Callum and insisted he keep the drinks flowing for everyone. She knew Callum's family had a bit of money and she didn't want them thinking that she was a gold-digger.

"Hey you!" She put her hand on his neck and went in for a kiss. Callum thrust her up against the wall, it was a little bit hard but she guessed he was just over excited.

He placed his hand on her neck, it was a little bit uncomfortable, but she didn't want to spoil the lustful moment.

"Do you get off on taking the piss out of me in front of my family?!"

She was really taken back. His eyes were red with anger and his grip on her neck had got tighter.

"Callum, what are you doing, you're hurting me?! I don't understand, what have I done wrong?"

"You think I'm fucking stupid don't you! Just because our Denny is here singing your praises. You think you can go off with whoever you want and I won't say a word. Well I'm not having it!"

"Callum, what is wrong with you? I don't understand why you are getting so mad!"

"Dancing with my cousin, showing me up, acting like a right tart!"

"Callum, I've been dancing with everyone even your nana, I'm just having fun, I thought you would be pleased…"

Just as she said it his fist came flying towards her face, she closed her eyes tightly, bracing herself for impact, only for him to divert his fist at the last second and he hit the wall right by the side of her ear instead.

She started trembling; she couldn't move straight away as she was froxen to the spot, in total shock at what had just happened.

"FUCK!!" Callum was clenching his fist as blood poured from his knuckles.

"I'm going!" she said shakily. He didn't react, he was just looking at his knuckles whilst wincing in pain. She ran out of the toilets and through reception as fast as she could. Denny came through the function room doors as Melissa flew towards the entrance.

"Mel, what's wrong? Where are you going?"

"Home! I'm sorry Denny!"

She fled through the venue doors and raced down the street.

After she'd been running for a few minutes, she realised that she had no idea where she was, or where she was going. She reached into her bag to get her bankcard when she remembered that she had given it to Callum when she insisted on buying the drinks. 'A gentleman never lets a lady go to the bar' his words played over through her mind – 'some gentleman.' He was so smooth but his insults had cut her like a knife. She found a few loose pound coins in the bottom of her bag, so she decided to head over to the bus stop and wait for the next bus.

When the bus arrived, she asked the bus driver for help, "I'm sorry I'm a bit lost. I've only got this amount of money and I need to get to New Cross Gate please." He set off driving before she'd even finished talking, causing her to grasp onto the ceiling rail to steady herself. He slid her money down into his tray and without looking at her muttered, "This will only get you so far in that direction. I'll tell you when to get off."

"Oh ok, thank you."

She made her way to one of the seats near the front of the bus, so that she could see the driver and know when to get off.

She didn't feel like she was on the bus for even ten minutes when the driver waved her over. "You need to get off here." He said bluntly.

"Oh, ok, thank you. Is this New Cross Gate?"

"No, but it's as far as I can take you. You need to head that way." He pointed to the right and with that he opened the bus doors.

"Oh, right." She stepped off the bus and looked around to see if she could figure out where she was. Nothing she could see seemed familiar to her and she began to feel very panicky. She reached into her handbag to pull out her phone. She had two missed calls off Callum. He was the last person she wanted to speak to. She was still trembling, she couldn't quite take on what had just happened.

She tried to quickly get Ash's number up on the screen but her hands were shaking so much that she kept pressing the wrong keys. By now tears were rolling down her cheeks and falling from her chin as she finally managed to bring up Ash's number. She started ringing her, but she didn't answer. She tried Giorgio next, and he didn't answer either. "Please, please, please guys, someone answer me!" She wasn't sure what to do other than follow the bus drivers' instructions of heading 'that way'. She started heading down the main road but it suddenly it started to run out of pavement and seemed to turn into a dual carriageway. The cars were whizzing past her, each one making her jump. She was breathing so heavily she began to feel very light-headed.

"Ohhh! What now!" She screamed out in despair. "Please god! Please help me!" She was completely lost and becoming more and more frightened. She just wanted to go home. She tried calling Ash and Giorgio again, but still there was no answer. She knew they never looked at their phones whilst they were partying.

Her tears were falling faster with each minute and her whole body was shaking. She frantically tried to think of other people she knew in London that could help her. She called Kieran and felt a huge wave of relief as he answered.

"Oh, Kieran, hi thank goodness! Where are you? Are you at home?"

"Hi Mel, I'm not. I'm with my parents this weekend aren't I?"

"Oh, of course you are. Yes."

"Are you ok?"

"Me, oh yes, I'm fine. Nothing to worry about I was just wondering if you could pick something up for me on your way home, that's all."

"Well I can but you'll have to wait two days to get it, he laughed."

"Yeah, ha ha!" She forced herself to laugh instead of cry. "Well you have a good weekend, take care."

"You too, see you soon."

"Bye!"

She broke down. She knew she didn't have Charlie or Maddy's numbers, yet technically they lived in the same house but didn't see them a lot so never took their numbers. She didn't know what else to do, suddenly the city didn't seem so busy and it's lights looked dimmer than before. The cabs were few and far between and none of them had the light on so they just drove past her. The fear was overwhelming. She had no other option but to keep walking and hope that none of the cars speeding past would hit her. As she finally reached the pavement again, the relief was palpable. The road was much quieter now and there were a lot less cars. She just hoped that she was still heading in the right direction. She still had no idea where she was. She checked her phone to see if Ash or Giorgio had tried to call her back. She had hoped that maybe the noise from the roads had drowned out the sound of her phone ringing, but there were no missed calls. 'What if Chris has been following me?' her heart raced and it was hard to fight off the tears. How could she feel so isolated and vulnerable in the middle of such a big city. Then she spotted a man across the road and her heart started pounding faster. Her palms felt sweaty, the city was so quiet compared to normal and the sounds of his footsteps were getting louder and faster. She moved to stand under a streetlight. 'He won't attack me here.' With her hands trembling she pretended to answer the phone and attempted to compose herself; she was sure he'd have been able to sense her fear.

"Hiya," she paused in order to sound convincing. "Oh yeah, you're only about two minutes away then. I'll stay on the phone until you get here!"

She watched as the man began to cross the road, she felt like if he came any closer he would hear her heart thumping louder and louder.

"Oh, I can't wait to see you all!"

She continued her fake conversation as she watched the man getting nearer and nearer to her. She kept waiting for him to turn around and attack her at any moment. She felt so exposed and vulnerable as she stood under the spotlight of the streetlight, all dressed up but with a tear stained face. She braced herself for fighting back, but he just carried on walking down the road, he hadn't crossed the road to attack her, he was just a man walking somewhere. She felt a slight sense of relief, but then jumped out of her skin as a car went past filled with lads beeping and jeering out of the window. She started crying again, she didn't know what to do.

"Please ring me back, please!" She sobbed.

Then James popped into her head, she had his number, he lived in London, he's a nice guy - she felt she had little choice but to trust her intuition and phone him, she couldn't stand there any longer so she decided to phone him. She only hoped that he would answer and that he wouldn't hold what happened with Callum against her being one of his friends! She felt so weak, like she was admitting she needed rescuing, but in that moment she did, she just prayed that he would be kind enough to rescue her.

She struggled to get James' number up, as her hands continued to tremble.

The phone started ringing, it rang four times and just as she had convinced herself that he wasn't going to pick up, he answered.

"Hello"

"Hello James, I'm so sorry to bother you" her voice quivered, as she unconvincingly tried to hold back the tears.

"Are you ok Melissa?"

"I'm so sorry, I didn't know who else to call. I'm ok, well I'm not ok. I've got myself in a bit of a stupid situation and I don't know how I'm going to get home, I don't even know where I am properly, I've got no money and no one is answering their phones and well, I'm sorry to have to ask you especially after everything, but I wondered, could you help me please?"

"Of course! Where are you, I'll come right away."

"I don't know," she started crying.

"It's ok. Don't panic. What can you see? Any well-known buildings? Restaurants, shops? Are there any road signs?"

"Erm…"

"Don't worry, just stay calm and I'll be there before you know it - we just need to figure out where that is. But we will, don't worry."

"I can see a pub called The Kings Head. And a clothes shop."

"Ok and what bus stop did the driver tell you to get off at."

"Long lane."

"Ok give me two minutes to look up a few things."

She was so grateful that James had answered, and she already felt so much better just knowing he was on the other end of the phone.

"Ok I think I know where you are but stay on the phone and keep telling me about what you can see. If a black cab comes, flag it down and I will pay for it when I get there."

"Thank you," She was so embarrassed to have gotten herself in this situation. She wondered what James must think of her, just ringing him out of the blue to come and rescue her.

It took at least five minutes, but a black cab passed and to her relief it had it's light on, so she flagged it down and jumped in as quickly as she could. She felt immediately comforted.

"Please can you tell me where the nearest tube station is?"

The taxi driver told her and her location became even clearer to James.

"Ok, ask him to drive you HOTEL PURPLE and I'll meet you there and drive you home."

"Ok," it was only as she said the words ok, she wondered why she had to meet him at a hotel, was he expecting something in return for picking me up? 'Does he think I'm easy after I slept with Callum?' She suddenly started to feel bad for questioning his integrity when he was coming out of his way to help her and deep down she knew he was lovely. She had to got it wrong about him, she never gave him a chance. But she needed to be sure, to feel safe and after the Callum incident, didn't know who to trust.

"Why am I asking him to take me to a hotel?"

"Because it will have a 24-hour reception with staff and maybe a bar and you can wait there with peace of mind until I get there. And it's the only place I can seem to think of around there." He laughed a bit and it made her smile with relief. She knew at that moment and her gut told her not to worry, to trust that he has no ulterior motive. He just wanted to genuinely help her.

"Oh, but what about the taxi? I can't…you know..."

She didn't want to say out loud that she couldn't pay, in case the taxi man heard her and decided to chuck her out.

"Oh, yeah, ok don't worry, just wait in the taxi until I get there, and I will pay. I won't be long."

"Thank you" she said softly, she meant it.

It felt like hours until James arrived, but in reality it was around 15 minutes. It was hard to describe the comfort she felt when she saw his face.

"Thank you again James, I'm so sorry."

"It's fine. Let's get you home."

She barely said a word in the car journey home, she just stared out of the window wondering what a mess she made of everything again. Her great plan to make a point to Chris had backfired and just rocketed her back even further. She was humiliated and felt stupid for feeling so convinced that she was doing the best thing by giving Callum another chance. She'd ignored the all-too-familiar warning signs and felt as though she some how had deserved it all for being so naive.

As they pulled up at the house, Melissa noticed it was still in darkness and there was no sign of anyone being home. She didn't want to go into an empty house and she also felt really bad that she had barely said a word to James since he had picked her up.

"Do you want to come in for a bit? I mean everyone should be back soon. You could have a few drinks with us all. I feel bad I've not really explained anything or barely spoken to you when you have been so kind in coming to get me. You didn't have to.."

"Course, that will be nice." James interrupted. "And you don't need to explain, just as long as you're ok?"

Melissa smiled and sighed at the same time. James had been nothing but nice to her since the moment she met him and she had been nothing short of a nightmare in return.

They were heading down towards the kitchen, when Melissa needed the toilet, so she pointed James in the direction of the kitchen. Melissa caught sight of herself in the hall mirror. She had mascara all down her face and the hard truth was staring back at her.

"Actually, you go and pour us a drink, there's wine in the fridge or red on the side if you'd prefer that. I'm just going to get changed quickly, if that's ok?"

"Sure."

Melissa ran upstairs and closed the bathroom door behind her. She looked in the mirror and had reams of mascara down her face, her lipstick had faded and patchy; the cold had truth was staring right back at her. 'I'm a mess'

She ran up the flight of stairs to her bedroom, pulling off her dress and throwing it to the floor in anger. She went over to her dressing table and reached for the face wipes. She frantically scrubbed at her face, tears streaming down as she did. She removed every scrap of make up, she was tired of pretending. Tired of smiling on the outside when she was crumbling on the inside. She threw on some pyjamas and headed back downstairs. She wondered why she had asked James to come in when she didn't feel like being in anyone's company, but she didn't want to be alone and she couldn't just leave him in the kitchen whilst she sat crying in her bedroom. So she took a deep breath and decided to go and have a drink with him. She wished Ash and Giorgio were home; she wasn't sure she could do this without falling apart.

"Hey, you ok?" James stood up from the dining chair and reached out, with a glass of red for Melissa.

"Thank you, yes, I'm fine now, although I know that I don't look 'fine'!"

"You look fine, I'm just worried about you. What happened tonight?"

Melissa studied James' face and his body language. There was not an ounce of him that made her worried or scared, he had just rescued her when she most needed it and he had remained nothing but a sweet friend in the process. Part of her felt like she shouldn't say a word, he was friends with Callum after all, but another part of her felt like she owed him an explanation and that talking about it may be exactly what she needed.

"I don't even know what to say James. Basically I'm a mess, I keep making one stupid mistake after another and tonight was just another classic example of that."

James listened intently and so Melissa felt reassured to carry on. I just should never have gone tonight. I ignored the red flags with Callum and I only went to prove a point to my ex who I think is watching me. But Callum didn't appreciate my behaviour and he just flipped and it scared me so I ran."

"What do you mean he flipped, what did he do?"

"Doesn't matter, I know he's your friend and I've already come between you enough and I'm so sorry for that. I just, I don't know...anyway you don't want to listen to me rambling on all night. Do you mind if we change the subject? I just want to forget what happened."

"Well I know one way we could take your mind off things."

"Oh no, James, I'm sorry if I gave you the wrong impression asking you to come in.."

"No, I don't mean that! I meant this!" Melissa was relieved and a little surprised to see James holding up a joint.

"You smoke weed?"

"Occasionally, for the right occasion and this just happened to be sitting on the table...it looks like it's asking me to smoke it!"

"Oh!" Melissa chuckled, James had already managed to lighten the mood. "That will be Kieran's, he's such a pothead! He's away this weekend, so I'm sure he won't miss it…why not!"

Melissa and James sat talking and giggling for over an hour, she felt so at ease in his company. She didn't care what she looked liked, or what he knew about her; it was so strange as she barely knew him, yet she felt as though she had known him her whole life. It wasn't long after midnight when they realised the time.

"Ah, I better go, I'm sorry. I've got to head to Ediburgh tomorrow and I've not even packed yet."

"Oh of course, don't worry. I think I'll just have a nice bath and get in bed before Ash and Giorgio get home and before they try to keep me up all night. I'm really tired now."

They walked towards the front door and Melissa felt sad to see him go. She was so relieved he had been around tonight. They hugged each other goodnight and gave each other a kiss on the cheek. She watched as James got in the taxi and then quickly shut the door. She rushed upstairs, she hated being in the house alone, especially at night time. She started running the bath and got undressed as it started to fill up. She started to feel quite down again and lonely. There weren't many moments where she found herself alone in the house, and that had suited her perfectly, as being alone was something she had been running away from continuously for the last 4 months. Now she felt like it was time though, to just stand still for a moment, to be alone with nothing but her thoughts.

She couldn't hide her feelings on a night out tonight, or in yet another kitchen disco. She had masked her feelings at least a little whilst James had been here but now she knew she needed to feel. She needed to discover what she was really feeling - if anything at all, as she worried that her heart and spirit had been so fractured by what had happened this last year that she had now lost her ability to have any real feelings at all. She needed to process everything that had happened to her and start taking smaller steps forward. She had to find a different way to fight her demons now, as moving away hadn't provided the magic wand that she had been hoping for. She glared down at the bath water that submerged her body, she wondered if how she was feeling now felt the same as actually drowning.

"Liss, are you ok? You've been in there for ages?" Ash knocked gently and shouted through the locked door.

Melissa didn't respond.

"Melissa, can you hear me? "

Ash's voice was panicked and she started knocking more frantically on the door, "Melissa!"

When Melissa still didn't respond, she started banging on the door, "Liss!"

Melissa jolted from her tangled web of emotionally charged thoughts that she had been stuck in, whilst the bath water had gone cold without her even noticing.

"Yes! I'm sorry! What's the matter".

"What's the matter? Jesus Melissa, I thought you were dead!

"Dead? Why?"

"You've been in the bloody bath for over two hours and you just ignored me banging and shouting at the door."

"I just, I ended up in a daze. I'm sorry I scared you, I didn't even realise you were home."

"I knocked on to let you know we were home, you answered me, remember?"

"Oh yeah."

"Liss, you don't seem yourself, what's happened?"

"You were right Ash; I shouldn't have gone out with Callum again and I shouldn't be angry at you for trying to look out for me."

"Tell me what happened? Are you ok?"

"I'm ok, it's just he frightened me. Then I was lost and alone and everything around me scared me. I couldn't think straight and felt so scared. I needed rescuing and I hate that I felt vulnerable and needed that again. I think there is something wrong with me! There must be!"

"Let me tell you hun there is nothing wrong with you! Do you hear me!" Ashlyn passionately gripped Melissa, trying to wake her from the zombie-like state she had now morphed into. "Melissa, look at me, you're one of the best people I've ever met. I think you're absolutely amazing. Come on, let's go upstairs to your room, you can tell me what has happened." Ashlyn cuddled her as she walked her up the stairs to Melissa's room. Ash guided her to the sofa and sat her down. She covered her up with a blanket.

"Talk to me honey, what's happened. I hope you know you can tell me anything. You know that now don't you?"

"I know, I know, thank you Ash that means a lot. I just feel so stupid. I just feel like I can never make the right decision. It's like I enjoy being hurt or something, but I don't, I don't want to be hurt, I just want to be happy and loved."

"You are loved Melissa; we all love you. Your family loves you, your friends in Manchester all love you. I thought you were enjoying living here?"

"I am, I love living here, it's just I wanted to be different here, but I'm not. Underneath everything is still the same me and I just keep making the same mistakes. I am so tired of it, I'm just going to stay in this room and never leave."

Ashlyn was desperately trying to keep up with Melissa's emotional rambling; she wanted to understand what had upset her so much. She had seen her upset before, but she had never seen her look this vacant, this emotionless, it was unnerving to see.

"Well, that would be no fun now would it. You can't miss out on what the world has to offer you and nor can we let the world miss out on having you in it."

"I don't offer anything but misery and drama." Melissa was there in person, but it was as if she had run away from her own body, it was like she wasn't inside anymore. Her eyes were glazed over. Ash couldn't hide the concerned look on her face. She looked down for a minute like she was trying to think of the exact right thing to say.

"I've seen someone like this before you know, I've heard someone else I love talk down on themselves as much as you do. It was my beautiful mum that would say these types of things and who would have the same look on her face as you do now."

Melissa turned her head towards Ash but said nothing, she just listened and waited for her to say more.

"Melissa, my ma was scared, she felt worthless and she wasn't."

"What was she scared of?"

"My father." They paused and looked at each other as Ashlyn was overcome with emotion and tears quickly fell down her cheeks. "Saying that out loud is tough, you know. It was a long time ago but sometimes it still feels like yesterday."

"I understand that." Melissa was slowly coming back to earth, seeing Ashlyn so emotional and knowing she was about to reveal more about her traumatic childhood. It pricked at her conscience and snapped her out of the empty hole that she was falling into.

"What are you scared of Liss? If I know, maybe I can help you."

"Everything if I'm honest. I'm scared of my past and my future. More than anything I'm scared of letting anyone in, but I don't want to be scared anymore Ash."

"Your ex, did he hurt you? The way my father hurt my ma?"

Melissa paused before opening the old wound.

"My ex did hurt me, but not like that. Although there were times, I worried he might." Melissa lowered her head. Did it happen a lot with your mum and dad Ash you never really told me what'd happened?"

Ash sighed, "he would beat my mum up a lot, He was a drinker and usually by the end of the night he would be in a rage about something. I can still see her wincing and hiding her tears the next day, for so long she thought I didn't know.

"That's awful Ash"

"What about you?" Did he hurt you mentally and physically? I've seen the signs Liss. I've lived through hiding my abusive past too"

"It wasn't as bad as what your mum must have gone through, I'm sorry I shouldn't be so affected by it." The word 'abusive' had made Melissa want to retreat to her comfort zone by trying to avoid talking about it altogether.

"Liss, please don't apologise. Your pain is no less important because you didn't suffer physical abuse if that's what you mean, it's still abuse!"

The word 'abuse' always made Melissa feel uncomfortable. She felt too uncomfortable being put in that category of someone who had suffered abuse, as much as she deep down knew it was true. She almost felt as though she was a fraud because he hadn't ever really physically hurt her. But the reality was it was too painful to relive. She'd attempted to hold some of the 'bad stuff' in a box in her head. But more recent, they would spill out like an irreparable leak and she couldn't take anymore.

"I, I don't really want to talk about it Ash, I can't."

"Ok. Do you mind if I talk about my experience of abuse then? Because for once in my life I feel like I actually want to."

Melissa nodded for Ash to continue and reached out to hold her hand.

"I was eight years old the first time that I saw it. I couldn't get to sleep that night because I had a bit of a cold. I was thinking of going downstairs to ask my ma for some medicine when I heard the front door slam. It was my father returning from the pub. I stayed in bed as I didn't really like it when he had been to the pub, he was always so short tempered, and he wanted us all out of his way. Then I heard another bang and my ma screamed. I could hear lots of noises, in between my ma's desperate cries and pleas for him to stop, I remember knowing it was my father hitting her. It went on for around half an hour and I just lay frozen in my bed crying. I felt so helpless, I wanted to help my ma, but I was too frightened. That was the night I started grieving for my father. I still loved him, but I could not believe what he was doing, I never looked at him the same way ever again." She paused to wipe her tears, "The next day I ran to give my ma a big hug in the morning and she cried, it hurt her to hug me. Then I found myself unable to go to sleep every night after, I didn't want to hear it happen again, but I couldn't just go to sleep wondering whether it was going to happen again or not. Each night I felt such a huge sense of relief when he went to bed and I hadn't heard any shouting, banging or crying, other nights I would hear it all over again and I would just lie there wishing I was big enough and strong enough to help save my mother."

"Oh, Ash, that's awful! I'm so sorry."

"Yeah, it was pretty heavy. I don't think I really understood just how much I carried on my little shoulders until I was older."

"Oh gosh your poor mum, poor you. Was he hurting her all that time?"

"Yes, on and off. Sometimes I'd hear nothing for weeks then other times it felt like it was happening everyday. I had an older brother, one night he heard it and he tried to help her but our father just beat him up instead. It was awful, my ma cried more that night than I had ever heard her cry before." Ashlyn's tears were freefalling at speed now and reliving the pain seemed to become too much.

"Oh Ash!" Melissa threw her arms around Ashlyn and hugged her tightly. The two of them sat sobbing in each other's arms as they let their emotions pour out of them.

"I hear you crying at night sometimes. I worry about you, but I don't want you to think I'm being nosey or crowding you if you need time and space to deal with something."

Melissa just looked at her, unable to decide the best way to respond to her. She paused and all that would come out was, "Thank you." Thank you for what? Thank you for acknowledging her secret sadness and pain. Thank you for leaving her alone with it or thank you for worrying about her? She wasn't exactly sure.

The more Ashlyn opened up, the more Melissa felt comfortable to open up to her. She found herself sharing things that she hadn't been able to share with anyone else. Saying it out loud before now made her feel even more ashamed that she had allowed it to happen to her. It felt different now, Ashlyn could understand her in a way no one else could have.

"Oh gosh! Look at the time!" It was nearly 4am. "I'm surprised that Giorgio hasn't been up here looking for the party we're having without him!"

"Oh, don't worry, I bet he didn't even notice I wasn't there. He was well gone earlier, it was a free bar tonight. Anyway, we better get some sleep!"

Melissa looked at Ash and she realised that the reason they had ended up kissing a couple of times now was because they shared a deep emotional connection. They had grown to love and need each other, through their shared experiences.

CHAPTER 14.

KNOWING YOUR WORTH

She picked up the phone reluctantly, "What?" She wanted to start strong and with an attitude.

"Hey you, you ok?" Callum asked casually.

"Pardon?" She couldn't believe his tone, acting as if nothing had happened.

"What are you being funny for?"

"Callum, seriously? Are you joking or have you completely forgotten about what happened last night?" She was angry, and she was glad he was making it easy for her to be angry at him.

"Look, I'm sorry about last night. We all lose it from time to time don't we. I'm sorry can't we just forget about it now. I don't want it to stop us from hooking up! You looked insane last night."

"I just...I just, honestly what is wrong with you!" She felt enraged. What is wrong with him? Why

267

does he think his behaviour should just be swept under the carpet? Red flags were constantly flying now with Callum. This wasn't her being paranoid or frightened of letting anyone in. This was her seeing his behaviour for what it was – totally unacceptable and she was worth more. She wasn't going to waste anymore time on a guy that clearly had issues and she wasn't even sure that she truly liked anyway. It was becoming too intense.

"I ended up stranded in London, on my own thanks to you and your appalling behaviour! Thank god for James or god knows what could have happened to me!"

"You what? James? What do you mean ``thank god for James?"

"That doesn't matter. What I meant was you went to hit me Callum and no, we can't just forget that!"

"Yes, but I didn't hit you did I? I wouldn't. I hurt myself instead."

"Whatever Callum, whatever it was that we had, it's over."

"What over so you can get it on with James? That was your plan all along wasn't it! Was you playing some stupid game, playing hard to get with James and using me in the process."

"Using you! We both said right from the start it was just sex. That's all I wanted, that's all you wanted, then you went complicating it with dates and asking me to do family do's! But whatever, it doesn't matter, just sex or not, it won't be happening again!"

She slammed down the phone. He started ringing again straight away. She didn't pick up.

FROM CALLUM - I'M ON WAY TO JAMES, IF YOU WON'T TELL ME WHAT HAPPENED WITH YOU TWO THEN I WILL MAKE HIM TELL ME.

"Oh shit! She knew she had made a mistake as soon as James' name flew out of her mouth. She didn't mean to land James in trouble, especially as nothing had even happened and he had been so nice to her.

She decided to ring James first and then she replied to Callum. She didn't want to get pulled into a trap that she did all too well where she would end up feeling like she had done something wrong and apologising and begging for forgiveness in order to calm someone down.

"Hi, is everything ok?" James asked warmly.

"Hi, well actually, no it's not."

"Callum rang and in short when I was telling him that I didn't want to carry on with whatever it was that we were doing together. I argued with him and I accidently said it was a good job you cared about me or you helped me, or something like that. I think I've made it worse by not explaining what I meant by that when he asked me, because I panicked. But now I think he's pretty mad and he's text to say he's coming to you, to make you tell him what happened. I'm sorry, I really am. God, I bet you wish you'd never met me? All I have done since you met me is cause drama."

"Melissa, slow down. It's fine. I told you last night I know he has a hot temper, and I wasn't saying it for any other reason than I think you deserve better. He's one of my best friends, I've known him my whole life and I do love him, but he does have issues. Look. It's no secret I like you and I'm working on getting over that as I respect you when you say you're not interested, so this isn't me trying to get in with you. I'm saying it because it's the right thing to do. You've made the right decision. And you don't have to worry about him coming over to hit me or anything, as I'm on my way to Edinburgh remember? I'm nearly there actually!" James chuckled, just like he had last night he had managed to lighten the mood quickly and made her feel at ease.

"Oh yeah, I'd forgotten you were going there! That's a relief!" James didn't strike her as the fighting type. "Well, I hope you have a good time, you'll have to let me buy you a drink when you get back - just as friends of course - to say thank you for last night."

"Sounds good, but there's no need to thank me honestly! And don't worry about Callum. I'll speak to him whilst I'm up here. He'll have calmed down by the time I get home. I do need to speak to Denny about him though. He crossed a line last night."

"Denny text me last night to check if I was ok and sorry for Callum's behaviour. But I told her it wasn't for her to apologise." Melissa could feel herself getting annoyed again.

"I'm so sorry but I have to go, I've just got here. See you soon ok?"

"Bye James!"

No sooner had she put the phone down to him, when her phone started ringing again – but it was Chris. She didn't answer but noticed he'd left a voicemail. The mood she was in she didn't particularly want to listen to it, but she decided to listen anyway. If anything, it might've put her mind at ease if he told her his whereabouts. Knowing he was far far away. But it didn't. He was just playing the song 'Lonely' down the phone, he didn't say one word. She put her phone down on her bedside table and it pinged again. She could tell it was going to be one of those days where she needed to keep her phone on silent, to stop it from ruining her day.

FROM CHRIS - I'LL NEVER LET YOU GO. I'M NOT GOING ANYWHERE. I'D ONLY EVER GIVE U UP IF YOU HAD KIDS WITH SOMEONE ELSE. XXX

She threw herself back onto the bed and exhaled loudly, she was exhausted already. She was glad it was Saturday and she didn't have to muster up any energy to go to work. She picked up her phone, turned it on silent and headed down to the kitchen to try and stomach some food.

"You've got a parcel by the way. It arrived earlier, I left it on the table in the hallway." Kieran stated.

"A parcel? Oh, ok, I wasn't expecting anything. Thanks, I'll have a look now."

Melissa left her breakfast on the table and she trotted up the stairs towards the front door. She turned at the table and looked at the package. She ripped off the first layer of packaging to see a Burberry box inside. She was puzzled, she hadn't ordered anything from Burberry, she couldn't afford anything from there. She lifted the lid of the box and inside was a Burberry scarf wrapped in tissue paper. There was also a card. As soon as she saw it her heart sank - it was Chris' handwriting. .

'Melly,

I want to make it up to you, please let me try. I hope you like this, you deserve it. I really am sorry. I love you, just give me another chance.

Love Chris xxxx'

"He does know where I live!" She stumbled as the realisation of her worst fears were confirmed and it knocked her off her feet. She needed to sit down so she collapsed down onto the bottom stair that led upstairs. She held the card in her shaking hands and read it again in disbelief. It had been six whole months since she had left and yet he still didn't seem deterred from trying to win her back, not even slightly. She could hear footsteps coming down the stairs behind her.

"You ok Liss? What are you doing sitting here?" Ash instinctively knew that something was wrong.

"It's from Chris, he does know where I live!" At that point the tears started to roll down her cheeks. Her mind was racing. Would she have to move now? She didn't want to move again. She did not have the strength to start all over again and nor did she want to.

"I don't want to move! I love it here! I can't do it again, I just can't."

"Woah, wait, slow down. You DO NOT have to move. We will sort this out. Text him now and tell him to back off. Tell him straight. If he will not take no for an answer we'll get a solicitor. Don't worry we'll sort this. He won't get away with it."

"What if he comes to the door, what if someone lets him in and they don't realise."

"We need to tell the others what's going on Liss, it's time to let them in. Everyone can help, we can all look out for you but you have to let them in. You don't have to go through this alone anymore."

"I don't want everyone to think of me as some weak victim though Ash. I just don't think I *can* tell them." Melissa could feel herself starting to shake.

"You're not weak! You're so strong hon. He's the one who's weak! He's the one who should be ashamed, not you!" Ash had her hands on either side of her shoulders as she crouched down to her level to look in her eyes reassuringly.

"Well, if you can't and you want me to, I'll do it. But I think we need to Melissa, he probably won't have the guts to come and knock on, he's a coward, but just in case we need the others in the loop he sounds like a proper creep."

"Okay, yes you speak to them if you don't mind?" Melissa could feel her anger starting to bubble over. So, she decided to direct it at the person causing it.

TO CHRIS – WILL YOU PLEASE STOP! STOP CONTACTING ME! STOP SENDING ME GIFTS! IT'S OVER CHRIS AND YOU NEED TO ACCEPT THAT I'M NEVER COMING BACK. NEVER!! PLEASE MOVE ON!!

She was getting angrier by the minute, all those years she'd wasted, everything he put her through and he still thinks he's got the right to ask for another chance!

FROM CHRIS – I WILL NEVER STOP I'VE TOLD YOU, NOT UNTIL YOU HAVE CHILDREN WITH SOMEONE ELSE ONLY THEN WOULD I GIVE U UP. I LOVE YOU XXX

Melissa felt exacerbated. What was what it was going to take to make him stop? Having children with someone else was a world away from where she was now and she wasn't sure how she would cope going forward if he was constantly there in the background, constantly contacting her and knowing he could be watching her at any given moment. She was trying her hardest to stay strong but finding that strength everyday was exhausting.

TO CHRIS – 'I'M GOING TO HAVE TO SPEAK TO MY SOLICITOR THEN CHRIS BECAUSE THIS HAS GOT TO STOP!'

"Come on Liss, let's go talk to the guys, you need to describe them to him, just in case."

She didn't want to but she knew she needed to.

"OK, I just need a minute first please."

"Ok hun, don't worry it will all be ok. I'll make sure Charlie and Maddy are there too." Ashlyn kissed her head before walking off down the hall towards the kitchen.

Melissa took a deep breath and forced herself up from the bottom step. Her legs felt heavy and weak, she seemed to be struggling to put one foot in front of another. She walked down the hall bracing herself for an uncomfortable and emotional conversation with her housemates. As she walked in the room, everyone stopped talking and turned to look at her. Kieran gave her an uncomfortable half smile. Charlie and Maddy shouted out in chorus, an over the top, happy "Good Morning Melissa" and Giorgio and Ash were unable to hide their concern. Her legs buckled slightly and she clung on the back of the chair to steady herself, "Oh sorry Kieran"

"Don't be sorry, are you ok?"

"Sit down hun!" Giorgio rushed over and pulled one of the dining chairs over to her.

"Thank you." she felt a bit dizzy as she waited for Ash to start the conversation.

"I've told them briefly what's going on. He's a bastard, who has treated you like shit for years and now you've left he won't accept it. Now he knows where you live. We need to make sure everyone keeps an eye out in case he's hanging around. All you have to do is describe him hun and then we won't say another word about it, ok?"

"Ok, I'm really sorry about this everyone."

"You've got nothing to be sorry for!" Giorgio insisted, with everyone reiterating the same after him.

Melissa went on to describe Chris and Kierans face, notably dropped.

"What is it Kieran?" Ash probed.

"She just described the guy who dropped off the parcel this morning, I thought it was just a delivery driver."

Melissa took a deep breath. She felt dizzy again, she could hear the sounds of everyone talking, yet she couldn't hear a word they were saying. Her eyes started rolling and she saw Giorgio and Kieran leaving the room.

"Melissa, Melissa? Are you ok?" Charlie and Maddy stood either side of her rubbing her back.

At that moment Giorgio burst back in the room,

"Oh my god, he's sitting in a car outside!"

Everything became too much, she could feel her breath becoming more shallow, before she knew it she had passed out on the floor - much to everyone's   horror.

CHAPTER 15.

EVOLVING

It had been two months since she had heard anything from Chris. She was so relieved that the solicitor's letter threatening a restraining order seemed to have worked. Melissa's weeks were still filled with good and bad days, but on the whole she had built herself back up, in a way she once never believed that she could. Her life now, was something she couldn't even have dreamt up a year ago, as she could never see past the situation she was in. She had started to remind herself of that daily, of how far she had come.

She sat down on her bed after work and flipped her shoes off her throbbing feet. 'I really need to start embracing travelling in trainers and putting my heels in a bag!' she thought.

It had been another long day in the office, where she felt like she had just gone through the motions. She wondered where her conscientious side had gone. She had an exciting job with great opportunities, yet she still wasn't fully embracing it.

She could only muster up the energy to do the basics, never mind going the extra mile. Although Denny was obviously happy with Melissa's work, but Melissa knew she wasn't doing the best job she could, and that bothered her. Work had always been her safety net and the one thing that she had been able to take pride in over recent years, so she couldn't understand why her drive had been so noticeably absent since starting at OKORO. She thought about her old job and how everytime she had another glowing appraisal it gave her such a natural high; they were welcomed moments amongst the many lows that she was enduring at the time. She thought about Colette, how much of a great mentor she had been and just how much she inspired her to always do her best. Her focus and determination was unwavering. It triggered thoughts about how she could move her life forward in a more positive way; she thought about Colette's morning routine and how it seemed to set her up for the day perfectly. She visited the gym each morning without fail, and she always seemed so highly motivated as a result. She decided it was time to throw herself into work instead of alcohol and partying quite so much, as that didn't seem to be working out so well for her so far.

She was grateful for the lessons she had learnt so far within her time in London, along with making some fabulous memories, but she had felt a shift in herself again lately. She craved more from life than just getting by, using the crutches of alcohol, sex and cigarettes to help her keep her emotions at bay. She knew that she had passed through a stage that she had to go through, and she didn't regret it, but now it was time for her to evolve. She was determined to find true independence, to thrive and not just survive. Denny had told her about some hot yoga classes that herself and a friend had started attending. It sounded like something that could be really good for her and she decided she was going to set her morning alarm uncharacteristically early and step out of bed into a new routine. She didn't want to tell Denny or anyone else that she planned on going, as she didn't want them to suggest joining her. It was something she wanted to do for herself and it was important to her that she went alone. She wanted to prove to herself that she could make the switch to self care, without it being for any other reason than she wanted to look after herself and give herself the care she deserved. She didn't want to go because she was meeting someone and she wouldn't want to let them down. This way if she didn't go the only person she was letting down was herself and that was something she wanted to promise herself that she wouldn't do anymore.

She decided to text Ash and Giorgio, to let them know she wouldn't be joining them downstairs tonight. She wanted to get out of her work clothes, have a long bath, drink lots of water and put on one of the facemasks that she had bought last month and not take the time out to actually put it on. She wanted to get an early night and start the day with the same level of desire for life that she felt now.

She pulled off the clothes that had felt like they had been restricting her all day, it was a relief to be stripped of them. She thought about how much clothes had helped her through the last 8 months, how they had become the valuable armour that protected her from revealing the turmoil inside. However, now she felt like it was time to invest in some more comfortable pieces to compliment her current ironclad style. It was time to spend some of her days without hiding behind her clothes and make up, she wanted to be comfortable in her own skin and comfortable in her clothes. She realised she had spent over half an hour talking to herself and smiled as it dawned on her that she hadn't once allowed her self talk to be tainted by worrying what people would think of her, there was no fearing for the future, no looking back, or feeling paralysed by the memories that had haunted her for so long, just excitement. She felt proud. Although her journey had been full of mistakes and wrong turns, she was learning and growing all the time. She was getting there at her own pace and she now realised that was ok. She couldn't rush the process. She had to just take each day at a time and not punish herself for still being affected by everything she had been through. She was going to start praising herself more and giving herself a pat on the back for all of her little wins, even if some days that meant just celebrating getting out of bed. Those were the days that she needed to be even kinder to herself instead of beating herself further. She struggled to remember the last time she felt so much clarity, tears of happiness welled up in her eyes. For the first time in a long time, she had found the ability to have faith in herself.

As she woke to her alarm ringing at 5am she literally sprung out of bed, she had slept really well and felt refreshed and ready for the day ahead. She was out of the house and at Yoga for the 6am class and she was showered, ready and at work for 7.45am. She had the most productive day since she had started and Denny was notably impressed. She knew this was the way forward for her, as she felt the sense of achievement that filled her with pride just like she had in her old job. When she returned home that evening she enjoyed a glass of wine with her tea and then returned to her room. She was tired by 9pm and Giorgio and Ashlyn had teased her about how she had changed. In the past even a little harmless teasing would have worried her, that something was really meant by that but she was so happy with her shift in focus that she just laughed it off and didn't give it another thought. Just as she had settled under her covers her phone pinged. It was James…

FROM JAMES - HEY! DO YOU FANCY A CATCH OVER DINNER TOMORROW NIGHT? I'VE GOT TABLE BOOKED FOR TWO, AT 7PM AT THE IVY. IT WAS FOR A BUSINESS MEETING BUT THE GUY CAN'T MAKE IT NOW, SO IT THOUGHT YOU MIGHT FANCY IT?X

TO JAMES - YES, I WOULD LOVE TO COME, THANK YOU! I'LL MEET YOU THERE STRAIGHT FROM WORK. NIGHT X

Dinner would be lovely, especially at The Ivy! She had never been there before and she couldn't remember the last time that she went out for a meal. She set her alarm clock, as she yawned and reached over to turn out her bedside lamp.

***

THE NEXT NIGHT

"You know after what happened with Callum and I came to see you…"

"Oh no, please don't bring that up. I don't want to go back to that day James. I wasn't myself back then, I was so messed up."

"No, please just listen I wasn't going to say anything about that, that's gone now it's behind us, we're friends now. I just meant, when we were talking and you mentioned everything that you had been through, you never properly explained. I just wondered if you trusted me enough to talk about it now. You don't have to if you don't want to, but i just want you to know that I'm here, I'll always be here."

"Well you can't say you'll always be here James, when you get a girlfriend she might not be a fan of our friendship for a start."

"I'm not getting a girlfriend?"

"Yeah, I don't mean right now but one day you will."

James paused for a moment before offering a half smile, "Yes, well one day hopefully, but anyway, you're changing the subject. So I take it that you don't want to talk about it?" He was very inquisitive and direct. She did like that about him. She liked the fact he was another person that she could be around and not have to second guess what they were thinking all the time.

She furrowed her brows and studied his face. She was taken right back to the moment when Anthony asked her that same question. She had fought so hard to keep her guard up with Anthony but the way he was with her meant it was impossible to do so. He seemed to genuinely take so much interest in her and had convinced her that he was sincere only for her to feel deceived once again. She had believed every word that came out of his mouth and the way he broke her heart left her more guarded than before.

She returned back to the present moment and realised she hadn't said a word for a couple of minutes. James didn't press her, he could see she was thinking, so he gave her the space she needed to decide. She glanced away and stretched her neck out as she took a long breath and looked up. Part of her wanted to talk about it, because somehow it didn't feel quite as raw any more, of course it would never completely go away, but the difference was that she felt on the whole she had made peace with herself for what had happened to her. She had forgiven herself during their couple of months and that is what had made the difference. She was trying to let her guard down more and more each day and she really enjoyed James' company; probably more than any else's if she was honest. She knew he was a good person and he had already proved himself to be a good friend, but still a part of her was worried about giving him personal information and trusting him completely in case he used it against her. She had been wrong about people so many times that she didn't want to be wrong about someone else and it set her back again. She glanced back over in his direction and their eyes met, there was something inside her telling her it was ok to trust him that she wasn't wrong this time. She trusted her instincts with him the night she needed rescuing and he didn't let her down, so she decided to open up. She was trying to evolve and heal and every time she opened up to someone she did feel lighter, so she hoped that by letting another person in, it would help her heal even further.

"I, well. Well, I don't know where to start really?"

"At the beginning? We've got all night, as I said, I'm not going anywhere."

She ignored the subtle and equally not so subtle signs that deep down James would like more than the friendship they shared. This was all she wanted right now. She didn't have any thoughts of romance or men on her mind at the moment. When she'd collapsed that day, it had made her realise she had to start looking after herself. The stress was impacting her body. She had reached out for professional help and she could feel the benefits of it already.

"Ok, well I suppose it started when I was 19 and I went to Cyprus with the girls" she took a deep breath as even though she was stronger now, she knew every time she said it out loud she couldn't help but get emotional.

Melissa spent the next two hours sharing everything with James. Everything from Cyprus to her whole journey with Chris and she even spoke about Anthony and how he had broken her heart. She'd managed to compose herself throughout and only shed a few tears. It had felt like she was describing someone else's life. She even

286

described how some days were too much, she couldn't risk leaving her room and felt too dangerous for her fragile heart.

Throughout the evening James just listened. Letting her talk and when she paused to take a breath before facing the next instalment he would squeeze her hand, reassuring her it was ok.

"And well that's it really." she said with a slight humour in her tone, knowing that she had just released an avalanche of information that was enough to make anyone feel depressed.

"I'm sorry that you had to go through that. I can't imagine how hard everything has been for you. Thank you for trusting me. Can I give you a hug?"

She appreciated him asking and she was also relieved that he had offered, there was nothing that she needed more in the moment. "Yes, please."

He quickly stood up from his chair to in and embrace her, wrapping his strong arms tightly around her. As they hugged, a few stray tears escaped Melissa's eyes and she couldn't see it but a tear rolled down James' cheek too. They hugged, saying nothing for what felt like forever. It was probably the most tender hug she had ever felt. She could feel the sincerity of it and it felt nice to be held in that way. There was something about James that made her feel secure, like she had known him forever. He was possibly one of the most warm-hearted people she had ever met.

Everyone was right when they told her that when she first met him. She felt bad that she had ever doubted his authenticity.

CHAPTER 16.

FRIENDS REUNITED

After leaving for London, Melissa had convinced herself that it would only have been a matter of time before Liz, Collette and Andi would only have gotten fed up with her and her never-ending insecurities if she had stayed in Manchester. That was why she had hardly contacted them since arriving. Anytime she did check in, it was just a quick text to say how fabulous everything was in her life, rather than how she truly felt. She didn't want them to dread hearing from her. As she waited for them to arrive she reflected on how different her life might have looked if she would have stayed in Manchester. Of course, she had her family and Colette & Liz, but she wasn't sure she could have ever opened up to them about everything in the way she had been able to with Ash. She wondered if she had not been able to put that space between her and Chris, and completely throw herself into a new life, would she be the person that she was today? Would the girls be able to see the difference in her? She hoped so. She was so excited to see them, it had been such a long time since she had left her old life, and she couldn't wait to introduce them to her new one.

She eagerly awaited their arrival. As the train stopped and the doors opened, she scanned the platform for them, it was hard to see anyone though through the bustling crowds, then suddenly she heard "Hello London, the ducks are here!" followed by a familiar laugh and a woo hoo! She spotted Andi shortly after hearing her, closely followed behind by Colette and Liz who were obviously enjoying Andi's energy. Each one greeted Melissa with a huge smile and they embraced her with a group hug. Melissa wondered why she had ever doubted their love for her or worried about seeing them. It was like they had never been apart and she could feel the warmth from them instantly. They immediately picked up where they left off and she was reassured that no amount of distance between them would ever affect their bond, she felt silly and a little disloyal for feeling otherwise.

"Right, where's the nearest bar my loves, because our champers ran out three stops ago and this queen is parched!" They all laughed. Melissa was so pleased to see Colette and Liz enjoying Andi's company as much as she does.

"Erm, well we need to hop on a tube but there's a nice bar in London Bridge, shall we go there?"

"Lead the way honey, lead the way!" They all laughed and 'whooped' as they walked into the station linking, whilst trying to push their suitcases at the same time - much to the annoyance of the other commuters.

No sooner had their bums hit the seats in the bar, Liz dived in fishing straight for the gossip. "So tell us then, what have you been up to? We want to know everything! We've barely heard from you since you came to live in the big city!"

Melissa started to explain everything about her new job, Callum, James, the holiday (the teammate of Chris') and touched on some of Chris' recent antics.

"Well, you're doing well with your no one-night-stand rule then honey! I'm sorry I sent you that vibrator now, I've awoken a sex beast - I should have kept it for myself, you've been getting more action than me!" joked Liz.

They all fell about laughing.

Melissa sarcastically commented in return, "Oh yes, I've got myself in perfect order. I know exactly where I'm going and what I'm doing at all times. I'm not a mess at all!"

"Well, who bloody does girl. We're all just winging it most of the time!" Andie added reassuringly.

"Yes, at least I know I am!" said Colette, "I tell you one thing though, you might feel like a mess, but my goodness you don't look it! You look absolutely amazing, sweetie!"

"I know, I was just about to say that! Honestly, London obviously suits you Mel!" Andie agreed.

"Aww, thank you! I can't take credit for it, Giorgio and Ash, my housemates are stylists and makeup artists aren't they, they literally insisted I get a whole new wardrobe the moment I got here. And I have a whole new love for makeup! I just feel so much better stepping out of the house now, even when I don't feel it, at least I look confident!"

"I mean, you always looked great, don't get me wrong honey, but now you look like a bloody a-lister or something!" Colette gushed.

"Oh, I don't know about that but thank you!" Thank you, a word she had found so hard to say following a compliment before, was now something that she was trying her hardest to do. She was slowly learning to accept that when people said nice things to her, most of the time they truly meant it.

"Anyway, enough about me! Tell me what's new with all of you!"

"Well, Colette has just found out that she's been promoted!" Liz beamed proudly as she put her arm around Colette. Colette reciprocated the affection, "And Liz has FINALLY given Stephen a red card!"

"Oh my gosh Colette, that's amazing! Does that mean you're above Ed in Sales now?"

"Oh yes honey, he can't reject my ideas any longer!" They exchanged a playful high five. Melissa was so pleased for Colette; she had always worked so hard, she deserved the recognition.

"And Liz OMG! I never thought that I would see the day! What made you properly end things?"

"Well we might have had a little steak out, just to see if the lines he was spinning me were true or not. Obviously, it was a complete pack of lies and we caught him red handed! So I called him out there and then. Then I cried for about a week, drank too much wine, ate too much chocolate and then I pulled myself together and got back out there. I'm hoping to get my leg over while I'm here actually."

Andie's eyes enlarged and she nearly choked on her champagne. Melissa laughed, "Now you know what I mean about Liz, Andie."

"I most certainly do honey! I most certainly do!" Andie replied, as they burst into laughter.

"And what does that mean!" Liz raised an eyebrow.

"That you are absolutely fabulous darling!" Melissa replied, blowing a kiss in her direction.

"You're so right I am fucking fabulous...and I'm also fabulous at fucking too!" She raised her glass and gave a cheeky wink!

They all laughed before raising their glasses in unison..

Seeing as though the girls were all tipsy already, Melissa thought it was a good idea to take them back to the house to introduce them to her London family!

The noise in the kitchen was deafening, she needn't have worried about anyone feeling awkward or not getting on. Crazy in Love came on and Giorgio jumped off the dining chair, "Kweeen!" with Liz following him only a heartbeat after. They both started performing the routine in tandem.

Liz turned cheekily to Giorgio, "I think you may be the single most fabulous person I have ever met! Are you sure you can't be turned?"

"I think I'm in love!" Giorgio beamed to Melissa.

"I said you would love each other!" she laughed. Their vibe was contagious and everyone ended up off their chairs and dancing round the kitchen.

She was thrilled to see both her old and new friends all getting along so well. They were meant to go to a club later that evening, but instead they all decided they would much rather stay home, drinking and dancing together in the kitchen. It was such a milestone for Melissa, looking at each of friends and recalling the pivotal moments that she had been through with each of them made her realise just how far she has come. They had the best night and the ladies didn't leave for their hotel until around 3am. Melissa waved them off in a taxi and was looking forward to seeing them the next day.

"Well Melissa Morgan, not only are you a beauty, but your friends are beauties too! I absolutely loved them! And Liz, oh well, I think she is a goddess! Night babe!"

Melissa giggled, "I'm glad you liked them! Night G!"

The next morning Melissa jumped in a cab and headed towards the hotel to see the girls. She picked up some hot breakfast barmcakes along the way and headed up towards their room.

KNOCK KNOCK.

Liz opened the door looking a little worse for where.

"Room service!" Melissa joked, as she bounced into the room.

"Oh my god, you're a lifesaver. I have got the worst hangover!" Liz grabbed one of the paper bags off Melissa and started to ravish the bacon sandwich.

They all sat chatting about what a good time they had last night. Melissa was on a real high. Everything in her life was starting to fall into place and it felt really nice having the friends who had seen her so broken, be able to see her doing so well.

"I'm dying, I shouldn't have eaten that, I feel worse now." Liz crawled back into bed and hid under the covers, much to the amusement of the others.

"So what's this party you've been invited to back in Manchester then?"

"Oh it's Lutfa's, do you remember her? She was one of the friends that me and Chris used to hang about with. She went out with one of Chris' friends."

"Oh yes, wasn't she the one who figured out there was something going on with you and Anthony?" Colette asked.

"Yes, she was. She's one of the only ones who has bothered to check in on me from time to time. She never judged me and I really appreciated that.

Especially those first few months." Melissa explained. "That's why I feel like I should go, and this time nine months ago there would have been no way that would have been strong enough. But now I feel like I might be. Maybe it will do me good to bite the bullet and come back for the weekend. I can't stay away from Manchester forever."

"Well if you think you're ready, then maybe you're right, maybe you should go?" Andie encouraged her.

"What about Chris though, won't he be there? And Anthony?" Colette looked a little concerned.

"Possibly, I suppose so. Why should I miss out though, it shouldn't be me that stays away as if I'm the one in the wrong." Melissa started to fire up. "Anyway, even if he was there, he wouldn't be allowed to talk to me, or I could apply for the restraining order."

"I say go and show the bastards that you don't need them!" Liz shouted from under the covers.

"I know, it would feel good to show everyone I'm doing ok. I've always felt like because I moved away it made me look guilty or something. I know I shouldn't but it has always bothered me what people thought about the whole thing, I'm sure I will have been painted as the big bad witch."

"I know, you probably have been honey and it's not nice, but it doesn't matter what they all think, they're in your past now. Like you said they haven't bothered with you have they. I'm just not sure it's a good idea, you're doing so well, why rock the boat?" Colette was unable to hide her concern.

"I know what you're saying Col, and part of me thinks you're right. I don't even know why I'm even considering it. But another part of me wants to go. For Lutfa and for myself. I think I need to face everyone in order to properly move on, you know?" Melissa didn't want to reveal that the possibility of seeing Anthony again was shamefully another reason that was swaying her to say yes.

"I don't know, I'll have to think about it." Melissa concluded, she didn't want to discuss it anymore. Deep down she knew Colette was right and it probably wouldn't be as easy as she thinks, but secretly she had already made her mind up. The opportunity to show everyone that she wasn't broken was too good to miss, even if it may cause her pain in the process, she almost felt that she had to go to make a point.

"What's happening with the house now my love? Has he bought you out yet?" Questioned Andie

"No! I just keep trying to put it to the back of my mind and leave it with the solicitors. He's still not responded with his own solicitors for months now. If he carries on though, my solicitor says we'll have to go to court but I just can't stomach the thought of that; so I'm just hoping he'll start co-operating soon. Although I'm not holding my breath."

Once they all finally got dressed, they headed to The Crown to meet up with everyone. She had invited James down to introduce him to her Manchester friends too. She was glad that he accepted the offer and was such a nig hit with the girls! Overall she was so grateful that all her friends had gotten on so well this weekend. She had felt the most content that she had done in a very long time.

Dressed up in Armour by Lolo Stubbs

CHAPTER 17.

BACK NORTH

The train ride back to Manchester went a lot quicker than she imagined it would and as the train pulled into Piccadilly station, she wasn't sure she was actually ready to get off it. She watched as everyone hurried to leave the train as fast as they could, scrambling to get in front of each other. She looked out of the window and wondered whether she had done the right thing in coming back here in the first place. Although it was only for a couple of days, she was worried that it could send her rocketing back. Was she strong enough to do this? Was it safe? Was she completely stupid for even thinking it might be okay?

As a trainline worker started making her way up the aisle, cleaning up the rubbish that the commuters had left, she wondered if this was her opportunity to clean up any mess she had left behind when she left Manchester, her opportunity to seek closure. It was time to take a deep breath and make the move from her seat.

She walked quickly down the platform towards the turnstiles, she rolled her shoulders back and held her head high. She was here now and if she was going to do this, she was going to do it with confidence in each step she took. She showed her ticket to the staff and as she thanked them, she heard some giddy shrieks, "She's here! She's here!" it was Colette and Liz running right towards her, throwing their arms around her as soon as they reached her. That was just the kind of warm embrace she needed. Colette immediately relieved her of carrying her case and Liz squealed, "Let's get you home girl!" Their warm welcome immediately made her feel better.

As they drove up the street to Liz's house, Melissa had mixed feelings as she was haunted by images of the past. Her body became covered in goosebumps as she recalled some of the moments that had played out on this street. However, from the moment she walked through the front door, she felt the way she always had here - at peace.

"She's been cooking up a storm all afternoon for us in there!" Colette informed Melissa as she kindly took her coat from her to hang it on the banister.

"Thanks Col! And it smells amazing Liz!"

"Well, I thought as it's a special occasion, we should dust the cobwebs off my rather fabulous dining room and eat a nice three course dinner, with candles, around the table tonight! And Col has got us a couple of bottles of Champagne too!"

"Aww, you two always spoil me, thank you both. I've missed you both!"

"We've missed you too kid!" Liz walked through the lounge door onto the kitchen to carry on cooking.

"It was so nice to see you in London last month lovely and we were so giddy when we got your text to say that you were coming back for the weekend, so it was the perfect excuse to celebrate!"

"Are you staying here tonight too, Col?"

"Well actually, I was going to get to that, I'm staying here every night at the moment honey pie."

"Oh?" Melissa paused and waited for further details, just as Liz burst back through the lounge door into the hallway.

"Yes, she's finally left that sap! Thank goodness! Now, will you both come in here as you're making me uncomfortable standing in the hallway and also, I can't hear what you're saying and obviously I can't miss out on any gossip!"

They laughed and made their way into the lounge where she very quickly handed them a cold glass of fizz each.

"So, Col, you've really left him and the house? How are you feeling? Are you ok?"

"Yes, I did it! The house is up for sale so I'm staying here until it's sold. I didn't think I could go through another break up but seeing you in

London, so much happier than I've ever seen you and it inspired me."

"Me?!" Melissa seemed completely shocked at the prospect that she could have inspired anyone.

"Yes, you! You just took a huge leap of faith and it was the best thing you could have done! You're amazing, my lovely!"

"Oh, I'm not amazing! It's not been a bed of Roses and still isn't some days. But I don't regret moving now, not for a minute."

"Why did you initially?" Colette seemed surprised at Melissa's admission.

"Yes, at times."

"We didn't know that? Why didn't you talk to us?"

"I didn't want to burden you, I was fine sometimes but it was hard at first. I felt like an imposter, like I wasn't really meant to be there. Once I got to know everyone and decorated my room etc, it became home and it's my favourite place to be now!"

"Apart from here?!" Liz pulled her infamous face, with her eyebrow raised.

Chuckling, Melissa replied, "Apart from this place, of course! And my nana's house! Well and my Dad's house when the witch isn't at home!"

"Oh yeah, you're going there for lunch tomorrow aren't you?"

"Yeah, I can't wait to see my Dad and the girls, my Nanna will be there too - thankfully the witch is working until 6!"

She was interrupted by her phone pinging.

FROM JAMES - I HOPE EVERYTHING GOES OK THIS WEEKEND. DON'T LET THE FUCKERS DRAG YOU DOWN. JUST REMEMBER HOW FAR YOU HAVE COME AND HOW AMAZING YOU ARE. X

She smiled, that was exactly what she needed to hear in that moment and she was thankful that James had taken time out of his day to message her. After everything that had happened between them he was the most unexpected, amazing friend and she was grateful to him in her life.

"Eh hmm! Who's making you smile like that missy! We've seen that face before!" Liz probed.

"Oh no! It's not anything like that again. It's James, just wishing me luck for this weekend. He's a good friend."

"Well I don't know why you're just friends, I'd be on that quicker than you could drink a shot! - I don't think that's how you say it, but you know what I mean!"

They laughed.

"He is lovely, honey," Colette joined in.

"He is, but it's not like that. Honestly we're just friends now, I told you he liked me to begin with but I made sure I screwed that up by sleeping with his mate. So I'm just glad we've even ended up as mates, we get on so well."

"Well I think you're crazy if you let this one pass you by, but it's up to you my lovely. Anyway, let's go sit down and eat! The starters are ready!" Liz ran towards the kitchen as the oven started beeping.

She had enjoyed a wonderful afternoon with her family, a great night last night with her amazing friends, but now she was filled with dread. Lutfa's party started in an hour and suddenly she wondered what on earth she was doing going along. Yes, Lutfa was one of the few friends that had bothered to keep in touch with her but she was certain tonight would be absolute torture and she questioned why she was putting herself through it.

She felt confident in her outfit and she was really pleased with how she had done her makeup. She couldn't have felt any better about herself on the outside so that was a good start. She was so relieved that Colette was able to come with her for moral support. The thought of seeing all of them 'ghosts' from the past had begin to make her feel rattled.

Within minutes of being in the room she saw Anthony. There he was, he hadn't changed one bit. Just the image of him brought back so many wonderful memories. She looked away quickly, he hadn't seen her and she didn't want him or anyone for that matter to catch her staring.

She couldn't help but watch Anthony dancing with Louisa, trying to analyse their body language. It was making her heart crumble slightly but she couldn't look away. It was like self harm, but she knew she needed to see him with her, in order to close the door in her heart to him and finally move on. She had been in London for nearly 12 months now and he hadn't once tried to contact her. She didn't know why she still kept having moments where she was pining for him? Then, just as she had decided she had seen enough and was about to look away, he looked right at her. His head was resting on Louisa's shoulder, she had her back to Melissa and as they danced slowly, he gave Melissa a smile. At least she thought it was a smile. She couldn't help but show the confused expression on her face. It was a half-smile that seemed to have a tinge of sadness as the corners of his mouth were downward. She had no idea what message he was trying to send her and she decided she didn't want to know. She felt angry at him. How dare he, all these months, all that heartbreak and he gives her a soppy half smile trying to get in her head again.

She needed to go. She had come, showed her face and stood up tall, but enough was enough. She didn't need to put herself through this kind of torment any longer.

"Shall we go Col?" She whispered to Colette who had ended up chatting to a guy there. She felt bad as they were starting to look pretty cosy. She retracted, as she felt selfish making Colette leave when she was obviously having fun, "I don't mean right away. Just letting you know that I'm ready when you are."

"Ok honey, we'll go in a bit, yes!" Colette leaned in to whisper to Melissa, "How cute is he! I think I'm in here!"

"Go for it Col, you deserve a bit of fun."

As Colette turned back to talk to her potential hook up, Melissa decided she couldn't sit there looking like a third wheel nor did she want Anthony and Louisa in her line of sight.

"I'm just going to the bar!"

"Ok honey!" Colette didn't even turn around, her eyes were fixated on the hunky guy she was chatting too.

Melissa trotted across the dancefloor to get to the bar. She glanced around the room, she noticed the group of friends she had shared with Chris all huddled around a table laughing and joking with each other. She felt sad when she saw everyone: she'd broken contact with a lot of them so she had ended up driving herself crazy at times trying to imagine what they were saying about her. She knew that so many people in this room saw her as the 'bad one' - especially as she 'ran away'! Seeing them all triggered her recurring thoughts once again. What did they think about her having the affair? What did they think about her leaving Chris? Did they see the unhappiness or did they think she was a 'heartless slapper'?

"Do you want a drink love?"

She turned to see a very handsome barman smiling right at her.

"Yes, I want a bottle of white wine please, with a straw." Melissa was half joking, all she wanted to do right now was get so drunk, blot this whole party out, click her fingers and wake up back in her room in London.

"Coming up!" The barman laughed and headed over to the fridge.

She wished she had never come here tonight, what good had it done her? Yes she had enjoyed the weekend but she should never have come to this party. Colette had been right and she'd wished she'd listened to her earlier.

The barman passed her the bottle, a glass and a straw. As tempted as she was, she didn't swig it straight from the bottle, nor did she use the straw. She filled her glass and downed it. She filled the glass again and drank it in quick succession. She had been doing so well recently and now she found herself looking for answers in the bottom of a bottle of wine once again. She was just relieved that Chris hadn't turned up, as that would have been the last straw.

She danced on the spot so that she didn't look as lost as she felt. Colette was still chatting away. so Melissa decided to stay propping up the bar, she had no one else to talk to. She didn't want to look like a loner though so she started chatting to the bar man. He was really interested in her life in

London and said he'd been considering moving there himself.

"You should go for it! You'll love it!"

"Ok then I will," he laughed, "Will you go out with me if I do come? That might persuade me to take the leap you see." He winked.

She laughed and glanced round as she did. She saw Anthony looking over at her, he didn't look particularly happy. 'He's jealous' she could tell he was by his expression, and it made her happy to think that he was. She looked back at the barman, he was really handsome, she was sure he must have been a model on the side or something like that.

"Of course I would. I could show you all the sights." She knew he wasn't going to actually move to London, he was just flirting with her and she lapped it up. She finished her third glass of wine and her confidence, along with her rage for Anthony and everyone else who had hurt her, was growing. She started to want a little more than flirting from the barman. Her insides had been battered again tonight and she needed to feel something other than pain and anguish.

"Do you fancy taking a break?" She winked and smiled.

He nervously unbuttoned the top button on his black shirt. He knew full well what she meant and the fact he wasn't as confident as he looked, it made her feel stronger, more powerful somehow.

"Erm, yeah, I'm due one in fifteen minutes actually."

"Ok, well I'm just going to finish this wine and then I'm definitely going to need to use the toilet. Perhaps you could show me where they are?"

"The toilets, yes, sure I will."

She finished her wine and turned to walk towards the toilets. "I'll see you in a minute yeah? Outside the ladies?"

She walked off confidently, leaving the barman a little stunned. She couldn't help herself but glance over in Anthony's direction again. He was still watching her. Louisa went bounding over to him and turned his head towards her. Melissa smiled to herself. She was just fine on her own, she was happy and she didn't need anyone - apart from the barman, right now she really needed the barman.

The toilets were on the corridor towards the entrance, it was cooler and quieter there. Just as she hoped she wasn't standing out here for no reason, the barman came around the corner, he was very sexy, even his walk was sexy. She bit on her lip as he walked towards her, she had never done anything like this before, she didn't even know his name.

"We can go in here instead of the toilets." he held up a key and pointed at another door near the toilets.

She followed him in, he looked around as he opened the door and they went in together. He locked the door behind them and they started kissing immediately, it was fast, frantic and it made her feel alight again. They fell into some shelves as they stumbled from kissing so passionately. This was the wildest thing she had ever done in her life, she had released all her inhibitions and just acted upon them without thinking too much.

She spotted a chair to the side of them. She undid his belt and the buttons on his pants,

"Have you got a condom?"

He pulled one from his pocket, she ripped it open with her teeth, pulled down his pants and rolled the condom seductively onto him. He smiled, as she pushed him onto the chair and straddled him. He began to ride him, up and down, feeling more empowered by every thrust. Her inhibitions had melted away two glasses earlier. Anthony, Chris and all the worries of what people thought of her couldn't have been further from her mind. Their groans were growing and soon enough the sexy barman had come. She didn't, but she didn't need to, she had got what she needed from it.

As they got up, he smiled.

"That was amazing!" The barman let out a sigh and kissed Melissa.

"Yeah, it was." It wasn't amazing, but he had made her feel wanted and desired, and escape her mind and that was all she wanted.

As they left the room, Melissa started to feel a bit uncomfortable, her confidence had drained away.

"I better get back, I'll get sacked if my manager catches me. I'll see you in a minute."

"Yes, see you in a minute."

As he started to walk off down the corridor, the door of the ladies flew open. and Colette walked out.

"Oh there you are honey, I've been looking for you. Are you ok?"

Melissa realised she wasn't ok. "I've just slept with the barman. You were right Colette, it's too hard being here. I should never have come. I'm such a mess."

"Oh honey, come on, let's go."

"But what about the guy you were chatting too, I don't want to spoil that for you?" Melissa's eyes began to well up.

"Oh don't worry about that, I've got his number now anyway. Let's just go home."

Melissa wanted nothing more than to go home, but to her actual home, her sanctuary with Ash and Giorgio. Coming here had sent her rocketing back towards the darkness and she needed to get back home and remind herself of who she had become.

CHAPTER 18.

AN OCEAN AWAY

Tonight was the night, it was James' surprise leaving party and Giorgio had offered to host it at the house for Denny, who thought her apartment wouldn't be big enough.

Melissa thought about the last twelve months, about how she had evolved as a person and how James had been a huge part of her journey. In that moment she felt incredibly grateful that herself and James had crossed paths and a pang of sadness hit her at the thought of him leaving.

She was gutted to hear he was moving when she returned from Manchester. She wasn't in the best place when she came home anyway and hearing that James had got a new job in America was a blow she wasn't expecting. She had gotten used to him being around and she really valued their friendship. She was definitely going to miss him being around.

She looked at herself in the mirror, finally the person on the outside matched the person on the inside. Of course, she had moments, she felt almost certain she always would, but she had fought hard not to let those moments consume her or allow her to look down on herself anymore. Even after the setback of going to Manchester, she managed to get herself back on track, after a few days of going off the rails. She smiled, she felt proud. Granted she didn't feel pride in every part of her journey, but it had all led her to where she was today and she was finally proud of the person that she had become.

KNOCK KNOCK

"It's only me!" Ash walked in, "Well look at you! I tell you whoever has done your makeup is one talented Makeup artist!"

Melissa smiled warmly, "Oh, she is hugely talented, she's a little moody at times but I can put up with that as she's the only one who can make me look this hot!"

"Hey!" They both laughed and then hugged each other.

"Thanks for doing my makeup Ash, I really appreciate it! Do you like this outfit?"

"Yes, you look unbelievably gorgeous - did Giorgio pick it out for you?"

"No, actually, I picked it out all by myself!" Melissa couldn't hide her pride.

"Oh my, well hun, I think our work here is done…finally, thank goodness you've been a little slow on the uptake!"

"Hey!" Melissa chuckled.

"Are you ok anyway?" Ash asked softly, changing the tone of their conversation.

"Yes, I'm fine. Why?"

"Well, I wouldn't blame you for being a bit upset that James is moving so far away. You've been spending a lot more time together recently."

"Oh, of course I'm a bit sad, but I'm so pleased for him. Plus it gives us an excuse to go to America doesn't it. And anyway I've still got you and Giorgio, you two aren't going anywhere."

"No of course we're not, but it's different with James isn't it?"

"Is it? Why does everyone keep thinking that we're just friends? Ok we've kissed once but that was ages ago and a lots happened since then. So let's stop this and go party! Not going to lie I am dreading seeing Callum though. I've not seen him since that night and it's just going to be awkward."

"I'm not sure Denny is letting him come. Between us I've heard he's got a bit of a problem with cocaine, so he's gone a bit off-radar."

"Oh really! Well at least that explains why James hasn't seen much of him. I did worry I'd come between the two of them."

They heard gaggles of laughter coming from downstairs.

"Shit, we better get downstairs, Giorgio will be going mad hosting on his own." Ash panicked and they headed downstairs.

The party was in full swing and she was finding herself getting closer and closer to James. The feelings she had for him when they first met began to resurface once again. The flow of drinks were making her feel even more amorous. She wasn't sure if it was the fact that he was now leaving and soon to be unobtainable, or the fact that everyone kept pointing out how great he was, but she found herself becoming increasingly intoxicated by him. She found herself unknowingly stroking his thigh as they chatted, laughing and then their eyes locked. They both stopped talking and just gazed at each other intensely. If the room were not filled with people, she just knew from the heat between them that they would soon be in a passionate embrace. Memories of their first kiss stirred her arousal even more. At that point she looked down and jumped up quickly, "I'd better get us a top up! I'm not a particularly good host, am I? Can't have the guest of honour sitting there with an empty glass!"

She hurried out of the Giorgio's room and downstairs into the kitchen before he could even say a word. 'What is going on?' James has been a friend for so long now, where have these feelings come from?' she wondered.

"What are you so deep in thought about?" Giorgio questioned, poking at her side to jolt her out of her daydream.

"Oh nothing, well I think me and James just nearly kissed, or at least we both wanted to. I don't know what's happening, we're just friends."

"You're gearing yourself up for a farewell fuck, that's all it is hun. Goodbye sex is hot, enjoy it!" Giorgio winked.

"Well I suppose I don't have to worry about what could happen next then do I? Things can't exactly get complicated or go sour now he's going, can they?"

"Exactly just go for it!" Giorgio smiled and handed over some drinks to a group of people in the kitchen.

She returned to James with their drinks, feeling slightly uncomfortable about the 'non-kiss' 'nearly kissed' moment and she wasn't sure how to strike up the next conversation with James.

"Here you go!" She decided just to focus on handing out the drinks and just see what followed.

"You look really beautiful tonight you know, well you always do actually."

Blushing. Melissa quickly replied. "Oh I'm not sure about that!"

She sensed she had embarrassed him with her reluctance to accept the compliment, so she continued. "But it's genuinely nice of you to say that. Thank you!"

Why do you always do that?" James looked quite serious.

"Do what?"

"You always struggle to accept a compliment no matter how big or small. Why?"

"I, I don't know, it just makes me feel uncomfortable I guess, I don't know why?."

"Because you don't believe it, do you? Even now. Right from the first day that I laid eyes on you, I've had to fight not to think about you. You bowled me over with your beauty, your smile and your personality, but I know that you don't see how that could even be possible. If only you could see yourself through my eyes then you would understand why I am hoping that my last night in the UK will be spent with you."

Melissa didn't know where to begin addressing what he had just said. A tiny part of her was still shouting 'player! He's a player!'. A patient player admittedly but she was still reluctant to fall for the prince charming act. The majority of her knew that she knew him enough though now to know he was genuine. But there were still pieces of her heart that were she was holding back.

"Well it's your lucky night then isn't it because you are already spending your last night here with me! What more could you ask for?" she joked.

"The whole night."

"Pardon?"

James wasn't holding back, he was laying his cards out on the table and she knew exactly what he meant by the comment, she just didn't know how to react to it.

"I would like to spend the whole night with you."

"Oh well...ok." It just fell out of her mouth before she had even properly thought about it. Maybe because she had overthought it for nearly twelve months. Maybe deep down inside she knew exactly what she wanted, so she followed her instincts that had led her to saying ok.

"Really? You're sure?" James looked shocked.

"Yes, we'll call it a going away present shall we, because I forgot to buy you one!" she bit her lip. She was trying to sound confident to mask her nerves.

James said nothing, he just smiled and couldn't stop gazing into her eyes. She stood up and held her hand out to him - it was now or never.

"Now?" James had just taken a swig of his drink which seemingly went down the wrong hole as he tried to respond to Melissa's gesture.

"Well, are you coming or not?" She still astounded herself when she showed this much confidence, whether she was half acting or not. Her sexual rendezvous hadn't especially lived up to expectations since being free and single and she had hoped it would be different with James.

James grabbed hold of her and got up from his chair. The rest of the party were too busy dancing or talking outside to notice them slip away. The Chemistry between them had been electric all evening and they had barely left each other's sides.

She led him all the way up the stairs to her room and when they reached the bedroom it was like everything was switched to slow motion. The music was echoing up the stairs and James reached out his other hand to Melissa, he pulled her into him and they started dancing. He twirled her around and she felt like she was in one of those romantic films that she had watched over and over, during her many duvet days. She went to lean her head onto his shoulder but he stopped her and looked straight into her eyes. She knew this was the moment they were going to kiss again and she suddenly felt very nervous. James didn't seem nervous though now, it was as if the roles had reversed as soon as the door closed and he led the way from there on in.

Each kiss set of fireworks bursting inside her, her heart raced each time their lips locked it became more intense and more passionate than the time before. He moved his hands from her shoulders down towards her breasts, teasing as he moved them away again at the last moment. Her chest rose and fell as she inhaled and exhaled deeply. He reached back up to the top of her shoulders and gently slipped off each strap of her dress. He stopped kissing her just to look into her eyes. The last twelve months had been rocky between them but it had all led them to this moment, finally they were in each other's arms and they were both exactly where they wanted to be. James seemed to want to savour every second of it. She didn't resist the intimacy; it seemed like for the first time in a long time she was doing exactly what she should be doing. She wasn't acting out to make a point, she wasn't too drunk that she didn't know what she was doing, she wanted him more than she had initially realised. Nothing else was whirring around her head, she was completely present in this perfect moment.

James leaned in to kiss her again, he was leading the way and setting pace, and she was happy to let him do both, as it was as if he could read her mind. Each touch, each stroke, each and every kiss was exactly where she wanted it to be and it was exhilarating.

He slowly pulled down her dress; over her breasts, over her stomach and her hips until eventually it fell to the floor. He stopped again, gazing at her adoringly as she stood there in only her heels and briefs. She stepped out of her dress and pulled him in towards her. She wanted to make sure he felt as adored as she did, because right now she did adore him. She adored how gentle and slow he was and how much he cared about her - how much he always had cared about her. She kissed him, their tongues were gently intertwining. She unfastened his belt from around his jeans, she moved her hand down his inner thigh, before swiftly moving back up to unfasten his jeans. They stopped kissing for a moment whilst he unbuttoned his shirt, throwing it to the ground as fast as he could. As she pulled down his jeans, he pulled her in by her hips to kiss her again. He smoothly put his hands on the underside of her knickers, moving them down as he moved his hands lower, slowly brushing his fingertips over her bum, moving them around over her hips and finally stroking in between her legs . She let out a groan, it was the most erotic moment of her whole life, he hadn't even touched her properly yet and somehow she had never felt more aroused. As he slipped off her underwear he stood back to take his boxers off too. They paused for a moment as they stood in front of each other vulnerable, exposed, but in the most beautiful of ways. Then their passion moved up a gear as they embraced again, pressing their naked bodies up against each other, his hard penis pressing against her. She didn't want this feeling to end but equally she was pleased it was only the beginning. He scooped her up in his arms, she kicked off her briefs that were still around her ankles and wrapped her arms around his neck as he carried her over to the bed. All the while their lips never left each other and the groans between them increased. As he lay her down onto the bed, he continued to kiss her but soon left her lips to move down slowly kissing her neck, her body was covered in goosebumps. He then moved further down to kiss and cup her breasts, it was deeply sensual. He left one hand on her right breast as he moved his other one down between her legs. He gently teased around the area moving his fingers from one thigh to another. Her breath was heavy, her heart pumped furiously with excitement.

"Touch me," she whispered, she couldn't wait for him to touch her, to feel him inside her.

James began to kiss her stomach all the way down past her belly button. He moved his hands under her knees and lifted them up as he began to kiss and guide his tongue around her clitoris. She gasped, and gripped the bed cover beneath her. She winced as the pleasure was almost too much to bear. He lifted his head only to break the euphoria momentarily, before he then retraced his steps but this time with his fingers. She gasped and groaned in bursts that got louder each time.

"Oh James, oh my god!"

He pulled her towards him to the edge of the bed, lifting her bum and gently tilting her hips as he did it. This was it, she opened her eyes to look at him and their eyes locked as he entered her. Getting deeper with each tender and loving thrust. It was like a perfectly orchestrated piece of music with each harmony in complete sync with each other. Their groans were in tandem and they intensified each minute. She felt like she would explode if it got any better, yet with every second somehow it did. She didn't want this feeling to ever end. She wasn't far from reaching a climax and she had hoped he wasn't either, as much as she wanted it to last, she couldn't wait any longer. She could tell he was close too and she couldn't contain it any more. In that moment she completely let go, feeling more relaxed and at ease than she ever had with anyone and the orgasmic waves enveloped her whole body. Her body shuddered as she let out gasp after gasp! Almost immediately James shared in her ecstasy as he too reached a climax, further adding to her pleasure as they screamed out in chorus. James collapsed on to her and they lay together trying to catch their breath whilst he was still inside her. The noises from the party continued to echo upstairs and she felt certain that at least someone would have just heard them, but she couldn't have cared less. She wouldn't have changed that last hour for anything.

As their breathing returned to normal, James lifted his head.

"That was incredible! Just like you are!"

Melissa could feel herself blushing.

"I think you're pretty amazing too!" He smiled and kissed her chest. He then continued kissing her all over her neck and breasts before he started sucking gently on her nipple, she could feel that fire ignite inside her again and before long they were enjoying passionate sex once again. With him leaving the next day it was as if they both wanted to make the most of each other before there was an ocean between them.

When morning came, she woke up in James' arms. Her face was nestled into his shoulder, their legs were entwined and he was stroking her hair. She felt him kiss her head and whisper "I love you." He didn't know that she was awake, so she lay there for a while longer so she didn't have to acknowledge what he had just said. As soon as he said it, every fibre of her being wanted to say it back, but she wasn't sure if she did love him or if she was just intoxicated by the mind blowing sex they had enjoyed on and off throughout the night. She had never felt so adored by anyone. Did she love the way he made her feel or did she love him? She felt like she had played with his heart for too long and that it was unfair of her to say anything unless she was 100% certain. After she felt like a sufficient amount of time had passed since he uttered those dangerous three words she stretched out as if she was only just waking up.

"Good Morning you." James went straight in to kiss her, she panicked, it all felt so real and dangerous this morning, as much as she has grown in this last year, she had far from figured everything out and she still wasn't ready to completely open her heart. She let her guard down last night because he was leaving. It felt safe to do so somehow, but now she felt scared and quickly locked the door to her heart up again.

"Oh morning!" she said as she quickly turned over and scrambled to get out of bed. "Sorry, I need to brush my teeth! I had so much to drink last night, my mouth feels so dry!"

She hadn't had 'so much' to drink last night. She was saying it to make up for the fact that she had been so open and free with him. She didn't want to hurt him or taint what they had shared, she just needed to protect her heart. He was leaving and there was no point in any heavy conversations or complicating things with feelings and she had told him it was a going away present.

She quickly put on her dressing gown and turned back towards James, "Do you want me to get you a coffee or anything before you go?"

He looked deflated, his lovely smile was nowhere to be seen. "No thanks, I'm fine." IT was like he knew that the window in which she had let him in had firmly closed again.

"Ok, I'll just nip to the bathroom then. I won't be long." She felt so wrong and uncomfortable giving him the brush off, it was the complete opposite of how she felt last night. If she was doing the right thing for her heart, why did it feel so wrong?

She returned to her room to find James fully dressed and sat on her couch.

"I was just waiting to say goodbye, but I'll get out of your hair now."

"Ok" she replied, but she didn't want him out of her hair, she wanted to climb right back into his nook and stay there. She just didn't know how to express it.

As James headed towards her door, she lay down on her bed just watching him go. She desperately wanted to tell him not to, but she resisted the urge, despite both her head and heart screaming inside her, willing her to say something. To tell him not to leave. The way he paused as he reached for the doorknob made her think that he could hear her thoughts, just like last night. Yet still her lips wouldn't move, she didn't say a word and neither did he. They just looked at each other, their faces fraught with hidden emotions. She urged him to say something first, just to take the onus off her. Their lingering silence became more awkward, and Melissa finally broke it by blurting out, "Well, bye then! Make sure you enjoy every minute – don't be a stranger!"

"I will…and I won't," he replied with a slight smile. His hopeful face melted her heart.

"Yes sure, I'm saving up already!"

"I'll buy you a ticket! You could come in a week or two then, once I've settled in?"

But her walls came up even further at that moment, he was going, where could this possibly go now other than heartache? Long distance relationships never worked. No, she needed to end it now. "Well, there's no rush! You've not even got there yet!"

His face dropped a little, "Yes, of course, there's no rush!"

"Well I guess I'll see you when I see you then."

"Yes, safe flight… bye James!"

And with that he was gone.

She rolled onto her back and stared at the ceiling. There were no thoughts racing around her mind. No crazy over the top conversations with herself. She just felt a sudden emptiness inside. She felt an overwhelming sense of sadness and her heart began to ache almost instantly. The ache in her heart eventually set off a hamster wheel of thoughts and once again her head was whirring with indecision. 'It's not the first time I've felt my heart ache, I've done the right thing. Heartache is better than heartbreak. I'll be just fine. I've definitely done the right thing. Feeling that much can't bring me anything but hurt."

An hour had passed and she was still lying on her bed, replaying everything about their journey, from the moment she first met him until last night. Their complicated friendship had been through the mill, he had seen her through some real low points and yet he is still saying that he loved her. "If he really is the one, why can't he unlock my heart."

KNOCK KNOCK

'Maybe it's him, maybe he's come back. No - why would he, I couldn't have given him a frostier send off! What is wrong with me!'

KNOCK KNOCK

"I'm coming!"

She ran to the door and opened it.

"What's wrong?" Ashlyn tilted her head and asked softly.

"Nothing, I'm fine!"

"Look I pretty much know you inside and out now, and when you stay up here and don't join us downstairs it's usually because something's wrong. Plus, I just saw James leaving!" Ash had now come in and sat down on the sofa.

"Honestly, I'm fine, last night was great, me and James had fun. Now he's gone as planned and I'm feeling just as I did yesterday, absolutely fine!"

"Well I think the whole party knew you had a great time and the only way I could get any sleep was by kipping on G's sofa" she raised her eyebrows. "So I'll accept that. But I'm not buying that you're fine Liss, because you're not. You know you can trust me, so talk to me."

"Ok. I guess I don't want to say it to you because you'll tell me that I'm crazy! Well I am crazy and that's the problem! And I thought I had made so much progress." Melissa threw her hands up into her hair and gripped it.

"Liss, what is it?"

"Well, last night was more than great. It was beautiful, there's no other word for it. I woke up in his arms this morning and he said he loved me, but he didn't know I was awake. I pretended I was still asleep so that I didn't have to deal with it. Because I didn't know how to handle it, I didn't know how I felt - I still don't know how I feel. But I was so cold with him, like I didn't care and I do care, but he's gone to LA now so what's the point in feeling anything anyway. I'm just going to end up hurt, that's how it always ends up so I'm just trying to cut out the drama of it all. I can't do it again Ash, I can't let someone in again. I just can't. I just don't think I ever will"

Finally the tears she had held in for the last hour came pouring out and she collapsed onto the bed holding her head in her hands.

"Aw Liss!" Ash rushed over to comfort her. She knew how long Melissa had spent trying to rebuild her heart, how long it had taken her to put herself back together and she understood completely why she was so petrified of jumping into a relationship again.

"It's ok, you'll figure this out. I promise. You're stronger than you know and I've not seen you like this in ages! So just focus on the positives, ok?"

Melissa cried into the shoulder of the one person that knew her insides and understood her better than she understood herself at times.

"What you need is a good night out or in! I'm going to do your makeup and you are going to feel fabulous."

"Ok, yes that sounds good. Thank you. You're the best friend Ash, I love you."

"See, you let me in and so you're already doing better than you think. You'll get there when you're ready hun. When the time's right you won't have to think so much, you'll just know. Now, stop calling my gorgeous friend crazy and putting her down and let's get ready."

"Get ready now? It's only 11 o'clock?"

"Since when has that ever stopped us? Anyway, have you never heard of a bottomless brunch!"

She had been trying to swap boozy brunches for Yoga and water, but today this was exactly what she needed.

They laughed and Ash kissed her on the head and made her way out of the room. As she did, it took back to James kissing her head, to him saying 'I love you.' He must have meant it, he thought I was asleep. I can't have been for effect. He wasn't trying to get me into bed, I was already in bed with him. He must genuinely love me. In some ways it felt really nice to think that he loved her, to know that she was loveable. But it was equally heartbreaking as she had rejected him again probably one time too many now, so she might as well just forget all about him. She was doing a great job at being single, she was finally happy in her life, why would she want to jeopardise that? She got up off her bed and took a deep breath. She finally opened her blinds and let in the light. That's the thing these days she knew there was always light, no matter what, she just had to look for it in the right places. Today her light would be her friends, their friendship, their love, their support and the fun she was going to have making even more fabulous memories with them.

CHAPTER 19.

WHEN EVERYTHING CHANGES

She was doing so well; she was so proud of herself about how happy and independent she had become. But she felt like she had taken a backward step in how she was feeling this last week. She wasn't necessarily propelling backwards though, she wasn't apologising for everything again, she wasn't constantly drinking and smoking just to get through the days and nights, she wasn't trying blend in again reverting back to her tracksuit days, she was still visible and still being heard, she just felt a bit low and there was a stubborn sadness that she couldn't shift.

She got changed after work and headed out of her bedroom door so she could get something to eat she bumped into Ash on the landing. It looked like she had been crying.

"Hey, you ok?" Melissa asked as she put her arm around her.

"Yes, I'm fine."

Melissa knew she wasn't ok, in fact she'd never seen her look so upset before.

"That's my line, so now I know for definite that you're not fine, but I knew that anyway as I can tell you've been crying."

Ashlyn looked at her knowingly, she didn't deny crying but she didn't expand on anything either.

"Come on Ash, when have you ever let me be upset and not make me talk to you, a problem shared is a problem halved, remember."

After a slight pause, Ash finally opened up, "It's him, my Father, he's been released from prison."

"Oh shit! Oh Ash, I'm so sorry. When did you find out?"

"Last night, my brother called me."

"Why didn't you say anything last night? Are you ok? Stupid question, I mean how do you feel about it?"

"Honestly, my head is all over the show, and it's making it worse that my brother has told me that he's asked to see me."

Melissa's eyes widened. "Are you going to...see him? Do you want to see him?"

"NO! No way! I hate him, I'll never forgive him. He killed my mum! He ruined my life, I'll never forgive, never ever! My brother might fall for his so-called remorse but I won't. He just won't leave it though, he's driving me insane. "

"Does Giorgio know?"

"No. He knows something is wrong though. I nearly fainted at work today and they sent me home. See! He's fucking everything up already. I just want him out of my life. How can I continue having a relationship with my brother now if he's letting him back in? I'm going to lose him and then I'll have no family at all!"

"Ash you've got us, we're your family. I know it will be hard, but do you not think it's time to tell Giorgio?"

"I know, thanks I do love you guys but you this is just a bit of head fuck and I just don't know how to deal with it."

"What do you wanna do? How can I help? Do you want to go out, do you want to stay in? We can sit and talk, or I can just sit next to you in silence if you like. Whatever you need I'm here."

"Thanks hun, I really appreciate that but I think I just need to be on my own for a while."

"Can you tell G for me please?"

"Of course, but do you not want to tell him yourself? I don't know exactly what you want me to say. I don't want to let you down."

"You can tell him whatever Liss, I trust Giorgio with my life, I just couldn't bring myself to ever go though it with him. You won't let me down, don't worry. I just need some space, you understand, don't you."

"Of course I do, I'll go talk to Giorgio now. I won't keep bothering you, but please text if you need me or want anything won't you?

"I will, I'm just going to try and sleep, I hardly slept a wink last night!"

"Aww, Ash you should have woken me."

"It's fine, you know sometimes you just need to be alone, that's just what I need right now, just until I get my head a bit straighter."

"Ok, well I'll leave you alone. But don't forget I'm here if you want me. Love you Ash."

"Love you too hun."

With that Ash disappeared into her bedroom. Melissa sighed. She really felt for Ashlyn. She could see the pain in her eyes and she felt helpless not being able to make her feel better. She headed downstairs to find Giorgio, she didn't want any food anymore, she just needed to let him know what was happening with Ash, so that they could both be there for her when she was ready.

Before she went to bed that night, Melissa text Ash to double check that she still wanted to be alone.

TO ASH – HOW ARE YOU HUN? DO YOU WANT ANYTHING? I'M RIGHT HERE, SO'S G. SO JUST SHOUT IF YOU NEED US AND WE'LL BE THERE XXX.

FROM ASH – I'M FINE, I'M JUST GOING TO TRY AND SLEEP. LOVE YOU XX

TO ASH – OK, LOVE YOU TOO XX

Once Melissa felt assured Ash was ok and didn't need anything, she could go to sleep.

***

Melissa turned her head and blinked as she attempted to come round, disturbed by frantic knocking at her bedroom door.

"Who is it?" She shouted groggerly, as she was still half asleep.

"It's Giorgio, babe. I need you."

"I don't feel like an adventure G, I'm so tired." She turned back over and snuggled under her duvet, her eyes closing again. Then she heard her door open and felt a hand gently shake her shoulder.

"Babe, please come downstairs. I really need you." Giorgio sounded desperate and almost upset. It pricked at Melissa's conscience and she started to open her eyes again.

"Ok, I'm coming. What time is it?" Melissa tried reaching for her alarm clock, before Giorgio grabbed her hand and held it tightly.

"It doesn't matter what time it is hun, just come on, please."

Melissa rolled out of bed and rubbed at her eyes. She felt completely disoriented as she was still half asleep. Giorgio was still holding her hand and was frantically rubbing it with his thumb, he seemed nervous or scared. "What's wrong Giorgio? Is everything ok?"

He looked down and didn't answer her, he just continued to lead her downstairs, squeezing her hand as tight as he could.

"G, you're scaring me now? If this is a joke and you just want to party, it's not funny!"

"It's not a joke hun, I wish it was."

Now she felt really worried, she had never seen Giorgio solum before. Why couldn't he look at her? As they reached the last flight of stairs, she could see the light beaming through the open door into Giorgio's room. Her heart sank. She could see two policemen standing there. All sorts of thoughts started racing round her mind. It must be Chris, had he tried breaking in, or had he threatened her to someone? Had he done something stupid? She followed Giorgio into his room and sat down on his couch next to him. It was at this point he grabbed hold of her other hand too and held it as tightly as he could.

"Can you tell her please, I just, I just can't get the words out." Giorgio burst into tears.

Melissa braced herself, she had no idea what was coming but she knew it must be bad.

"Are you Melissa Morgan?"

"Yes"

"And you live here?"

"Yes. Please can you just tell me what's wrong?! You're all frightening me, please just tell me what's going on?"

"I'm sorry to inform you that your housemate, Ashlyn Doyle, died earlier tonight…"

The policeman continued talking, she could see his lips moving, but she couldn't hear the words. She turned to Giorgio who was sobbing uncontrollably. Her whole body started shaking, her face drained of colour.

"NO! NO! NO! She can't! She isn't! NO!" Her mind was still absorbing the words, but her body was already grieving, her tears started to fall now too. She felt like someone had just slashed her heart wide open, and the pain was bleeding right out of her. It was a completely different pain than any she had ever felt before, it ripped through her body and numbed every part of her that it touched. Just as her whole body felt void of anything, it suddenly hit her.

"No, nooooooo!" her deafening screams would have caused anyone's heart to ache, and her shocked widened eyes collapsed into floods of tears.

"She can't be, she just can't be?!" But she was and the pain was unbearable. It hurt in places that she had never felt before. She couldn't run from this pain. She knew it was here to stay forever, right from the moment she felt it consume her body. A piece of her heart had been torn away and would be lost forever, not a new town, nor a new country would help her gain it back.

Giorgio and Melissa embraced each other tightly.

"We're so very sorry for your loss, I hope you understand we just have a few questions."

Melissa wiped away her tears, and looked up at the concerned policeman's face.

"Er yes, of course, we'll help if we can. I mean this just doesn't make any sense, she wanted an early night… yes, she had an early night Giorgio, remember they must have the wrong person, because she's here, she's upstairs remember, she's in bed." Melissa jumped off the couch and raced to the door.

"No hun, she's not. I've checked, I thought the same. I woke you straight after I had checked."

It hit her all over again and she dropped to the floor, her legs buckled like they couldn't hold the newfound weight in her heart.

Giorgio rushed to her side, she clung to him tightly.

"I'm so sorry, I know this is incredibly difficult, but we have to try and establish what has happened. Can we ask, how was Ashlyn in herself when you last saw her?"

"Well, she was upset, she'd just found out her father was being released from prison...oh no! Did he do this? Did he kill her! Oh god, no!"

"It doesn't appear to us that anyone else was involved at this point."

"What do you mean? She did it too herself? I know she was upset, but no, no she wouldn't, she wasn't that upset. She would have told us? She always said, didn't she G, she said a problem shared is a problem halved and that we're a family, and we are! We're a family!" The sorrow overwhelmed Melissa again, her whole body was shaking .

The policeman continued to ask a few questions, and how to contact her family etc, but it was all a blur. As Giorgio saw the policeman out, Melissa just sat on the floor staring into space. She heard the front door close and Giorgio walked back in the room. He sat down next to her and they both remained silent for at least 15 minutes.

"I need a drink, and a cigarette. Do you want one?" Giorgio broke the silence and stood up to head towards the kitchen.

"Er, yes, I think so, I don't really know what I want." She stood up anyway and followed him into the kitchen.

Giorgio headed to the cupboard and pulled out a bottle of brandy, he poured it into two glasses and handed one to Melissa. "It's meant to be good for shock isn't it, Brandy?"

"Yes, I think so... I don't know. I just can't believe it, I don't even know what to say or do? I don't understand what happened? She was at home, she said she was going to sleep!"

The tears had stopped for a moment and they were both completely stunned.

"We should probably wake the others."

"Yes, we should." Melissa agreed but neither one of them moved.

"Let's go outside first. I can't face it yet." Giorgio suggested as he headed to the patio doors and attempted to open them. They stuck and Giorgio rattled them frantically. "Stupid fucking doors!" He banged on them repeatedly before Melissa threw her arms around him and they sobbed together.

"For Fuck's sake guys can you not kept it down? It's 4am! I don't mind you having a laugh but what's with all the screaming and banging!"

They turned to see Kieran standing in the kitchen doorway. As soon as he saw their blotchy, tear stained faces he knew something was wrong. "What is it? What's going on guys? Are you ok?" Kieran looked really concerned, he thought he was disturbing another drunken night in the kitchen but the subdued atmosphere quickly told him otherwise.

"I can't." Giorgio broke down and fell onto the sofa, crying hysterically. Melissa knew that she had to dig deep and find the strength to say the words that would sear through her heart once again, the minute she said them aloud. "It's Ash, Kieran, she's...oh god, I can't...she's died."

"WHAT?! HOW?!"

"We don't really know. We thought she was at home in bed, she wanted to be left alone, she said she wanted an early night. But the police came. She collapsed in a club and she was gone before the ambulance got there."

Kieran went white and his face was emotionless. Melissa went over to the table to pull out a chair for him. "Sit down, I'll get you a brandy." At that moment, as Giorgio was crumbling and Kieran let the news sink in, she felt that she could just find enough strength to be the strong one, that's what Ashlyn would have done and she wanted to make her proud. They sat for around an hour before waking Maddy and Charlie to break the news. Then at around 6am, completely drained, they decided to go and try and get some sleep.

She was sure she hadn't slept, she felt more like she had gone into a trance for the last few hours, in disbelief at what had happened. She felt completely hollow, like someone had carved all of her insides out and she was now just a shell. Her heart had been shattered into so many pieces that it dispersed into the void inside her too.

How could she be gone? Just like that, gone forever. She just couldn't compute it. She knew she should be crying, but she was numb. She didn't move, she didn't try to move, she just lay still, with no thoughts, no feeling, just emptiness.

All of a sudden it felt as if her throat was closing up, she reached for her throat opening her mouth to inhale a large breath, but she couldn't take it in. Her head started spinning. She ran towards the window for fresh air but she still couldn't breath. Her legs were getting tingly and she needed to get out, to get help. She was dying too, she knew, she could feel it. She fumbled her way downstairs and raced towards the front door, she left it wide open as she fled before she stumbled down the stone steps and landed in a heap on the paved path. Finally the tears came, finally she could breath again and she lay there as she wailed uncontrollably. Giorgio appeared at the door, he didn't have make-up on, he wasn't in his usual fabulous attire, he looked broken too but he couldn't have got to Melissa fast enough.

"Oh babe!" He held her tight as she cried into his chest.

"Why did she have to go G! Why! I loved her so much!"

"I know babe, I know! Me too! I loved her so much too! I'm so angry she's left us and don't know how we'll get through it but we will babe, we will!" Giorgio's tears fell rapidly and he squeezed Melissa. They both sobbed uncontrollably on the path,

"I just can't believe she's not coming home. She can't be gone, she just can't be. They've got it wrong, they must have. Oh god, please, please let her come home, please!" Her whole body was hurting, yearning for Ash to come home, it was excruciating. She felt she wanted to rip her heart out to stop it hurting.

"I know babe, I know." Giorgio could barely talk. There was nothing that he or anyone could say that would make any of this any better or any less painful ever.

She had to make so many phone calls this week. Each one either made it feel more painful or made her more numb. It was just hard talking to anyone at the moment.

"I just can't believe it, lovey. It's just so sad. Daft question but how are you? How are you feeling?"

"Honestly, I'm aching all over, my eyes are heavy and stinging all the time. I just can't believe she'ss gone, my mind won't let me. It keeps telling me that she's at work or asleep in her bedroom, tricking me because without that lie every breath is too hard to take. The realisation hits a little harder each time and it's like I can feel my heart cracking every time I think of her. I can feel my mind desperately searching for somewhere to dig a hole and hide these feelings away, but there's nowhere to hide from this and it's unbearable."

"Oh honey, why don't you come home for a bit. Let us look after you?"

"Thanks Colette, but I can't leave Giorgio. They have been best friends for 11 years. She had him listed as her next of kin, so we need to sort out her...you know, send off and everything. I just can't even bear to think about that day yet, and somehow it's all I'm having to think about. Although it helps to keep busy."

Denny had been an amazing support and said for her to take as much time off as she needed. Her dad and sisters were checking in every day to make sure she was ok. Of course she wasn't, but getting everyones messages of support gave her some slight comfort. There was one message in particular that she kept re-reading and every time she did, she could hear it in his 'prince charming' voice.

FROM JAMES – I HAVE NO WORDS THAT CAN POSSIBLY MAKE THIS ANY EASIER FOR YOU. I KNOW HOW MUCH ASH MEANT TO YOU AND YOU TO HER. SENDING SO MUCH LOVE YOUR WAY. J XXXX

No matter how she communicated to James, he always seemed genuine and managed to make her feel better.

CHAPTER 20.

FAREWELL

As soon the light started to break through cracks in her blinds, she knew the day that she had been dreading had finally arrived. She lay in a ball sobbing. She knew she had to get up, she knew she had to say goodbye, but she just couldn't bear the thought of it. It took her a while but she finally started moving. She knew she had to just take the whole day step by step.

She reached for her phone and it was filled with messages of love from her family and friends back in Manchester. She cried again, every message, every phone call made it all the more real.

The morning seemed to be going so fast. Giorgio and Melissa were keeping themselves busy making sure that everything was perfect for Ash's final party. They both desperately wanted to make her proud and to give her the send off that she deserved. Both of them kept having moments where they felt like they were sinking into the depths of despair, but they we're helping each other through it. The others had been a great support too.

She still kept waiting for Ash to walk in. It crushed her everytime she remembered that she wouldn't. As she covered the last plate of sandwiches Kieran walked in.

"The cars are here and... Ash."

Her heart sank. She didn't want to walk outside. She couldn't bear the thought of seeing the coffin, knowing Ash was in there all alone when she should have been here with them. Giorgio held out his hand to Melissa, she gripped it tightly. They walked towards the front door slowly.

As they stepped outside there were people gathered on the street, ready to pay there respects and follow them to the cemetery.

Both her and Giorgio burst into tears as soon as they saw the coffin. It was adorned with white flowers and the reality of the situation hit hard. She wanted to run back inside and hide under her bed covers but she kept walking towards the car, tears falling endlessly from her eyes.

She spotted Denny and smiled. Thenher breath was taken away as she caught sight of James, he'd made it. She couldn't believe he was there. Amongst the coldness that consumed her, a warmth in her heart soared. It was the first time she had felt anything since Ash had passed.

The funeral was painful and beautiful at the same time. Giorgio had bravely read the most amazing eulogy that captured Ashlyn's personality and spirit perfectly. Before she knew it the service was over and they were all heading back to their house to celebrate Ashlyn's life.

Ashlyn's brother didn't make it to the funeral. He told Giorgio he couldn't face coming as he felt responsible for her death. It turned out that Ashlyn had gone to the club alone that night. She had taken a lethal cocktail of drugs and alcohol and the coroner had ruled an accidental overdose as the cause of her death. Melissa had never known Ash to take drugs before and it had come as a huge shock to her. Giorgio had told her how she had struggled with addiction years ago when she first moved to London. The news of her Dad being released must have just been too much for her and obviously didn't know any other way to handle it.

As people started arriving back at the house Melissa greeted each one and thanked them for coming. The next knock at the door was James. Her heart quickened as soon as she saw him and that warmness returned. She threw her arms around him and sobbed into his chest. He squeezed her tightly and it was like she was finally able to see a way out of the hole that she had been for the month. In that moment she realised he was the one. She was in love with him and everything about him. What should she do now though? Just blurt it out 12 months too late and at Ash's wake?. What if he's moved on now, he could have already met someone over in the states, he was only back because of the funeral.

"I've missed you." James whispered, still holding her tightly as she continued to let out her grief.

"I've missed you too, I didn't realise how much." Melissa didn't want to let go, but she knew she had to. "Are you able to stay for a bit, would you like a drink?"

"Yes, I'm not going back to the states until tomorrow, so yes, let's go raise a glass for Ash."

They instinctively held hands as they walked towards the kitchen. It didn't feel awkward, it felt completely natural. She felt a renewed sense of strength to carry on and make Ash proud.

It was a lovely afternoon. Everyone was sharing their favourite stories and memories of Ash and it kind of brought her back to life a bit. Melissa felt grateful to have shared so much with Ashlyn and she would do everything she could to honour her memory always.

As the afternoon turned into the evening and people slowly started to disperse, Melissa went into the garden to get some fresh air. James followed her outside.

"Hey, you ok?"

"Surprisingly yes, I'm doing ok."

"I miss her terribly, I've just got to find a way to keep going without her. I know she wouldn't want us all to be sad all the time, it's just easier said than done."

"Would it help to have me around?"

"Well yes, of course. It's been a bigger help than you know you being here today. Thank you so much for coming back. I'll be sorry to see you go again tomorrow." she gave him a half smile and sighed. Why had it took her so long to see what everyone else could see, to see what Ash could see!

"Well it won't take me that long to pack up and get back to London."

"What? I don't understand?"

"Well I'm just going back to the states to pack up. I've decided to move back home."

"But I thought, well, I thought you were gone for good!"

"I was, but I've realised that there is something in England that I won't have in America and I don't want to be without it."

'Does he mean me?', she didn't want to get this wrong, but it seemed as though he meant her.

"Oh. I see. So you're back for good?"

"Well I'm hoping so, yes, if you want me to be?"

"Me?"

"Yes, you! You're what was missing in America. Today has taught me life is too short and you have to go for what you want and I want you Melissa!"

She had spent so long feeling lost and constantly searching for reassurance and approval from whoever was around her, that she had forgotten what it was like to make a decision based on her own feelings and what her gut was telling her. Yet now, seemingly out of nowhere there was a shift and an overwhelming sense of strength that she can do this – she can make her own decisions. She felt a sense of empowerment like no other. It was even bigger than when she took a leap of faith and moved down here. She felt awash with emotion. She stood staring at James, just trying to find the right words.

Whether the path she was about to go down was the right one or the wrong, she could never be sure. But she was certain that it was completely right for her now. How much of our lives can we really plan anyway, she thought? Things are always changing unexpectedly; people come and go in and out of your lives. Sometimes they walk out or sometimes they are taken from this earth without prior warning. Things are always changing direction and there are no maps to follow. All you have is now and what your gut is telling you to do. Maybe that's it, maybe that's been it all along. Maybe we just have to do what is right for us now and embrace the journey that it takes us on. In that moment Melissa cried tears of happiness as she realised everything that had happened had led her exactly to where she is now, which was exactly where she meant to be. It had been one hell of a long and draining storm, but despite everything, somehow she was still standing.

"I'm so worried that I have too many scars for you to be able to love me properly, or for me to be able to let you love me. I'm terrified of making the wrong decision and I can't say with 100% certainty that I know that this is the right thing to do. But I do have this overwhelming feeling that if I don't take this next step, then I will forever want to retract back to this moment and do it again differently. I'm ready to trust myself again and I'm ready to trust you too James. Are you sure you want me? "

James looked straight into her eyes, she couldn't read his face. She stood there waiting for his reply, for what was only seconds but it felt like hours. She started to brace herself for the gentle let down, when he suddenly scooped her up in his arms and started to kiss her. The passion was overwhelming and she was instantly lost in his embrace. She was in a space she hadn't found herself in before, there was no fear, no thoughts, just a blanket of warmth and security.

"I love you 'just Melissa', I always have and I always will."

Melissa felt a rush of warmth engulf her heart once again.

"I love you too, James!" She said it! She couldn't believe she had finally opened her heart again. Losing Ash had taught her that no matter how much you try to protect yourself, there are certain things in life that you can't escape from.

They kissed again and the warm rush spread throughout her body. She wanted to be as close to him as she possibly could be, she wanted to feel his skin touching hers. Today more than ever she wanted to embrace every second of happiness and make love to James.

"I hope you can stay over tonight, I don't want to be alone." Melissa held James hand and he locked his fingers in between hers.

"Of course, there is nowhere else I would rather be."

They kissed again.

"Aww, you guys! At last! Our Ash will be one happy cupid up there!"

Giorgios reaction made her realise it was ok to feel happy, that is what Ash would have wanted. They walked hand in hand up the stairs. Even though they had slept together before she felt a little nervous.

She thought it had been special the first time with James, but this was on another level. As he caressed and embraced every part of her slowly and attentively, she felt more loved and adored than she ever had by anyone. It was like a beautiful piece of music. It was so exhilarating and intense. Every touch felt orgasmic as he teased and prolonged the build up to actually touching her between her legs. Her climax was electric and the love she could feel between them added a whole other dimension to their passionate encounter.

As she lay in James arms her emotions were bitter sweet. She had just lost one of the biggest loves of her life, yet her heart felt full again somehow.

Six months had passed and her and James were stronger than ever. They were the best of friends but with an overpowering lust for one another. He held her hand as she navigated her way through her grief for Ashlyn and she often wondered how she would have got through it without him. She now knew how empowering a loving relationship could be, how the right person can help you through the bad times in life. He was understanding when she was triggered by past experiences and although they happened less and less it was an ongoing journey that would take time.

Another envelope had arrived from her Dad that was filled a number of letters for her. She recognised one had the solicitors office mark on the envelope and she hoped it would be informing her of some progress. As she opened the envelope and looked down at the solicitor's letter, she was in complete disbelief to see a cheque, she couldn't quite take it in. It had been 18 months since she had left Chris and finally he had bought her out! Something that should have only taken 6-8 weeks, had been dragged out for a year and half, just because he wanted to prolong the agony for her, for as long as he could. Finally, hopefully, she was now free.

"Are you ok?" James asked as he gently squeezed her shoulder and kissed her on her forehead.

She looked at James and felt a world away from the desperately unhappy young woman that she had been for so many years. She was finally in a relationship that consisted of friendship, trust, respect, encouragement and passion. It was everything she had ever hoped a relationship would be, filled with fun, laughter and togetherness. James had become her biggest cheerleader, he helped her to see her strengths and find the courage within her to believe in herself. So much so she had applied for one of the Assistant Event manager roles at OKORO and she had been offered the position. Her fear of losing herself if she got in another relationship was completely unfounded with James, she continually took time out for herself and still saw her friends all the time - all of whom ADORE James too. Melissa couldn't have felt more grateful for where she found herself now and she had herself, James, her friends and family to thank for that.

"Yes," she reached up to her shoulder to lay her hand on top of his, "I've never been happier!"

Not knowing what was around the corner didn't scare her anymore, it excited her. In so many ways, the worst had already happened. She was under no illusion that it would all be plain sailing from here on in, but she had her whole life infront of her and she intended to live it.

Help and support

If you feel affected by issues raised in this book, there is help and support available.

Asking for help and leaving an abusive relationship is often not easy for a number of reasons, especially if you are fearful of what your partner might do or if you feel isolated and unsure what to do. Your self-confidence may be low because of the impact of the abuse, and this can make reaching out seem overwhelming.

Domestic abuse can take many forms including emotional, sexual and financial abuse as well as physical abuse. You do not have to be hit to be abused. Power and control is at the heart of domestic abuse, and in 2015 coercive control became illegal in England and Wales, which means that it is illegal to use coercive and controlling behaviour in a relationship. Abuse can include being isolated from friends, family and other support, being cut off from support networks and having your day-to-day activities monitored and restricting your access to your money and resources. You may feel like you are never able to relax because you are worried how your partner will react.

Women's Aid is the national domestic abuse charity providing support for women and children, and there are many ways you can seek information, help and support for you, or a friend. Got to www.womensaid.org.uk for the Women's Aid Live Chat service (open daily 10am-6pm), the Survivors' Forum, The Survivor's Handbook, which includes information on safety planning, and the Domestic Abuse Directory with details for your local domestic abuse service. There are also links for national domestic abuse helplines in the UK including services for men and the LGBT community.

Women's Aid: @womens_aid

> 66
>
> It means the world to be able **support Women's Aid** through my books. I hope that Dressed up as Love will help people understand that **it's not as easy as people may think to 'just leave'**. I drew on my own experiences and those of my friends and family, to create something that so many **women can relate to**.

Lolo Stubbs
Writer & Expect Respect ambassador

women's aid
until women & children are safe

LOLO STUBBS

www.lolostubbs.com/

LOLO STUBBS

Join the conversation and
share your reviews:

 @Lolostubbs.author

 /Lolostubbs.author

 @Loloauthor

 Dressedupaslove.com

 Lolostubbs.com